HEATHER A. BUCHMAN

RET

Volume I in the
Crested Butte Cowboy Series

And Then You Fall
© 2013 Heather A. Buchman

All rights reserved. No part of this book may be used or reproduced in any manner whatsoever without written permission, except in the case of brief quotations embodied in critical articles and reviews.

This book is a work of fiction. The names, characters, places and incidents are products of the writer's imagination or have been used fictitiously and are not to be construed as real. Any resemblance to persons, living or dead, actual events, locale or organizations is entirely coincidental.

ISBN 10: 1493506617
ISBN 13: 978-1493506613

Cover and content design by Sparrow Marketing & Design

Certain song titles and lyrics in this book are by GB Leighton and are reproduced by permission.

Available from Amazon.com and other retail outlets.

All I Want Is You

Your breath and your heart
The way that you're smart
The charm of your tease
When you make me say please
Your eyes and your hair
The look of your stare

You make my soul lift higher
You set my love on fire
Baby, every word I say is true
All I want is your mouth, and your lips
And your soft fingertips,
The curve of your spine
Well it's gotta me mine
The warmth of your kiss
When we're lying like this
The heat of your touch
Well it's never too much

You make my heart beat wild
Turn me into a child
Where the hell would I be without you
The soft skin on your bones
And the smile I would own
When the blood in my veins flows
With all that remains of doom.
All I want is you.

—GB Leighton

More from author Heather A. Buchman
CRESTED BUTTE COWBOY SERIES
And Then You Dance
And Then You Kiss
And Then You Fly

COMING SOON
And Then You Dare

EAST AURORA LINGER SERIES
Linger - Book One
Linger - Book Two: Leave

For cute, guitar-playing, songwriting boys and the cowgirls who can't help but love them.

Table of Contents

Acknowledgments ix
Chapter One 1
Chapter Two 16
Chapter Three. 31
Chapter Four 53
Chapter Five. 66
Chapter Six 79
Chapter Seven. 94
Chapter Eight 112
Chapter Nine 119
Chapter Ten 133
Chapter Eleven 147
Chapter Twelve 160
Chapter Thirteen 168
Chapter Fourteen 181
Chapter Fifteen 196
Chapter Sixteen 207
Chapter Seventeen. 224
Chapter Eighteen 236
Chapter Nineteen 249
Chapter Twenty 260
Chapter Twenty-One 275
Chapter Twenty-Two 290
Chapter Twenty-Three 304
About this Book. 313

Acknowledgments

Many thanks to my sweet girl, Catie, for the hours of reading, comments, constructive criticism, and unfailing support. I'm not sure I could write a book without your help. And to Winnie, who never minds the wildly coincidental personality characteristics that the sidekick always seems to share with the author's dear friend.

Thanks to my band of readers—Angelina, Cathy, Eileen, Erlinda, Kris, Kym and Stacey. I don't know what I'd do without you.

Special thanks to a guitar-playing, songwriting boy for his willingness to lend a lyric, a song, or a particularly dead-on quote just when I needed one.

Chapter One

Liv picked up the iPad and hit replay on the song coming through the Bluetooth speakers. She intended to set the tablet back down on the ledge in the barn, but she hesitated, picked it back up, and scrolled through the Twitter feed. It took her a minute to zip through the hundred new tweets. There was nothing from the only person she hoped for. Why would there be? It was ten in the morning.

Liv had checked at least four times in as many hours. What rock star tweeted between midnight and noon? Logical, but it didn't stop her from looking. Besides, he would never define himself that way. Just a working musician, he'd say. He might even admit to being a songwriter. And a dad. Not that she'd be having a conversation with him.

A car pulled up outside the barn as she tapped the screen to check Facebook, also for the fourth time that morning.

"Oh Liv, aren't you getting tired of listening to this? Time for a new playlist." Paige Cochran planted her heels in the dirt to shift the heavy barn door open. As usual, Paige dressed more as though she was going to a high-powered meeting at the investment firm she consulted for, not to visit her best friend's barn.

"But I love this song," Liv muttered as she flicked through the playlists for something else to listen to.

"Here's the thing—"

"Don't say it. I can listen to whatever the hell I want to in my own damn barn."

"Oh, a little testy this morning?"

"I'm sick of people complaining about my music," Liv growled.

"People? What people? Who have you seen in the last few days other than Pooh and Micah?"

Pooh was a fourteen-year-old sweetheart of a mare. The quarter horse belonged to Liv's twenty-one-year-old daughter, who stood firm on the name Pooh when they'd gotten the horse when she was ten. "You don't *know* Winnie the Pooh is a boy. He might be a girl." Renie, short for Irene, informed her, not realizing the slip in her own words.

"You're right," Liv had answered, rolling her eyes. "*He* may be a she. What was I thinking?"

The other horse, Micah, was Liv's baby. The four-year-old appaloosa gelding showed promise as a barrel racer. Liv didn't want to part with him for proper training, and she couldn't train him herself. Those days were over for her. They had been since before Renie was born.

"You didn't answer me. What's going on?"

"Nothing. I'm getting tired of my own company. I'm bored, and sick of the cold weather."

"I sent you a text asking if you wanted to meet for breakfast, but you didn't answer."

"Oh sorry, I haven't checked my phone. I'm done out here, we can go into town if you still want to."

"We can stay here. I know you have coffee, and something fresh out of the oven that I shouldn't eat, but will anyway."

Liv made cinnamon scones that morning before she came out to the barn to get her chores done. With Renie away at college, she ended up adding most of what she baked to her already overloaded freezer.

"Aren't you a little overdressed to have coffee with me?"

"I have a business proposition for you. I intended to talk you into going to Denver with me later this morning."

Paige managed to get herself involved in at least one new business venture a month. For someone semi-retired, she still worked fifty or sixty hours a week. If there was a deal to be made between Denver and Colorado Springs, Paige ended up on the inside edge of making it happen. She was very different from the room mom Liv met fifteen years ago when their daughters started kindergarten together.

"I'm going to Vegas next week. Mark said he'd horse-sit so you can come with me."

When Liv met them, Mark, Paige's husband, was traveling twenty-five days each month as the lead singer of a band. Diagnosed with cancer a year later, Mark retired and never looked back. Instead, he focused on their three children, the youngest of which had remained Renie's best friend since their kindie days.

Mark still wrote music, but spent most of his time picking up odd jobs, painting houses, or other handyman projects, often for friends of theirs. He never hesitated to come and help Liv whenever she needed it, sometimes without her realizing it. Mark would come over to ride, but soon he'd be mending a fence, or heading into her house to fix something she hadn't noticed yet. Liv didn't know what she'd do without him, or Paige. The Cochrans were her lifeline, now that Renie attended college out of state.

"A trip to Vegas would help with the grouchy-bored thing. And the cold weather. Come with me. Sit in the sun. Get *ungrouchy*."

"I don't know."

"What's stopping you?"

Liv turned on her heel, grabbed her iPad and headed out of the barn in the direction of the house.

"I've come with a bribe."

"What's that?"

"CB Rice is playing at the House of Blues next Wednesday."

Paige played dirty. Liv had been listening to one of his songs when she walked in a few minutes ago.

"Yes, I know."

"And you don't want to go?"

"That's *why* I don't want to go. I'm almost forty, too old for this stalker-groupie life I've been living the last few months."

It was bad enough that the universe seemed to throw the two of them together every time she turned around. But to put herself in his line of fire on purpose? He would start to think their random encounters weren't serendipitous accidents at all, but rather her stalking him.

Six days later, Liv boarded an early morning flight, headed for a few days at Mandalay Bay, and another not-so-chance meeting with CB Rice.

* * *

Liv didn't remember when she first downloaded his music, or how she found it. But she did remember the first time she saw him in person.

And Then You Fall

Liv and Paige got tickets for a concert at Red Rocks for Renie and Blythe, Paige's youngest daughter, while they were home for summer break from college. The band headlining that night was a cross between a rock and reggae band, perfect music for a hot summer night.

Red Rocks kept the first twenty rows at most shows set aside for general admission. They arrived early and were able to sit in the center of the sixth row.

There were two opening acts that night, CB Rice took the stage first, and a band from Denver was on second.

That was the first time Liv saw him play live, and the first time she met him. After their set, he and the band came and sat in the roped off section where the sound equipment was set up. The area encompassed the center section of the rows directly behind where Liv sat.

Renie tapped her mother's shoulder and pointed behind her. When Liv turned around, she looked right at CB, who was looking at her. Their eyes met, Liv's cheeks turned pink, and she looked away. She looked back a second later. He was still looking right at her, but this time he smiled, and winked.

Liv continued to glimpse back at him throughout the show. Every so often he'd turn his head and catch her.

The main act finished their second encore, and the four turned to leave. Liv felt another tap on her shoulder. When she turned around, he was right behind her.

"I'm Ben Rice, ma'am," he said, holding out his hand.

"Hi," she answered, having a hard time looking him in the eye. No one should be that hot in person. "I'm Liv, Olivia. Fairchild. Olivia Fairchild," she eked out as she shook his hand. "Oh—and this is my friend Paige, my daughter, Renie, and Paige's daughter Blythe."

He shook each of their hands and turned back to Liv. "Thanks for coming to the show tonight."

"Um, you're welcome," Liv stumbled through a response. "Well, bye then."

Liv remembered breaking out in a near run in the opposite direction toward the parking lot, followed by an hour's worth of teasing by Paige and the girls. The entire way home they teased her about the rock star who had a crush on her.

"He called me 'ma'am,' didn't any of you catch that? I must remind him of his mother."

"Even I don't buy that," laughed Paige.

"I'm so embarrassed."

"About what? Why are you embarrassed?"

"He caught me staring at him during the concert. More than once."

"I looked back several times myself, my friend, and each time I did, his eyes were on you. I'd say the attraction was mutual."

***

They weren't in Las Vegas often, but when they were, Liv and Paige stayed at The Hotel, part of the Mandalay Bay complex. Situated near the end of the Strip, it catered to a different clientele than the other resorts. The lights weren't as bright, the casino noises not as loud, the crowd more subdued. That suited Liv and Paige fine. They didn't gamble. Paige had meetings scheduled, but otherwise they'd be camped out by one of the eleven-acre resort's pools.

"Maybe we'll bump into him in one of the elevators. Or he'll be at the bar tonight."

"Would you stop it? You're making me a nervous wreck. Didn't you say we are here to relax? Are you going to let me?"

"Oh come on, I see your eyes scanning the crowds."

"He's not here yet."

"How do you know?"

"Twitter. He has a show tonight—at home."

Liv stared off in the opposite direction. "Yep, I'm a stalker," she mumbled.

* * *

She saw him for the second time in January, a couple months ago. Renie had a few days left of Christmas break when she and Liv decided to take an impromptu ski trip. When they woke up Friday morning the sun was shining, and the weather forecast was good for the rest of the weekend.

They packed their bags and skis and got on the road, making the two-hundred mile drive from Monument, Colorado, to Crested Butte, in a little over four hours. They checked into their room at the ski area and went downtown for drink. It was the first time Liv and Renie went out for a drink together. Her daughter had just turned twenty-one.

Liv felt hideously old when they walked into "the Goat," a Crested Butte institution on Elk Avenue, the main drag of the historic downtown district. But when she grabbed her daughter's arm to tell her she wanted to go somewhere else, Renie wouldn't stand for it.

"Come on Mom," she said. "I've always wanted to hang out here, I love this place."

"But I'm a hundred years older than anyone else in here."

"You're not, and you're gorgeous, and everyone will think you're my sister, not my mom. We're staying."

They'd been there a few minutes when Liv noticed a poster promoting bands scheduled to play a show at the bar. She had to get up and walk over to it to make sure her eyes weren't deceiving her. Sure enough, CB Rice and his band were playing the following night. What were the odds?

***

"We'll get the tickets on our way to the pool," Paige suggested. She put on sunglasses and grabbed her bag.

"No, let's wait."

"Why? It'll be one less thing to worry about."

"I haven't decided whether I want to go or not."

"Isn't that why we're here?"

"No. It's not. You're here for business meetings, and I tagged along because I would've been bored at home, and I wanted to relax and sit in the sun."

"Yeah, right."

"I'm serious Paige. I don't know whether I want to go tomorrow night."

"You listen to his music almost non-stop, he's playing a show while we're here. Not going is nonsensical."

"I'm not kidding when I say he will believe I'm stalking him. I've 'run' into him twice in less than a year Paige. This will be the third."

"But, you're in Las Vegas, staying at the same complex as the House of Blues. Why wouldn't you get tickets? It makes more sense that you would go."

"I don't know. If I decide I want to, we can still get tickets tomorrow."

***

Liv walked over to the bar at the Goat, where Renie waited for her, and sat back down.

"What's up Mom?" she asked.

"CB Rice is playing here tomorrow night. Remember—"

"The guy you met at Red Rocks. Yeah, his family owns this place."

"What?"

"The Rice family. His grandfather developed the ski area. At one point, the family owned most of the businesses downtown."

"How do you know all this?"

"What are the magazines they leave in hotel rooms for? Haven't you ever read the history of Crested Butte? We've been coming here at least once a year since I learned to ski."

Liv had no idea. No, she hadn't ever read any of the magazines in the hotel rooms. As a single mom, she had her hands full unloading bags and getting skis and boots and snow clothes ready. Then figuring out where they'd go for dinner and how she'd entertain her daughter until bedtime. Not that Renie wasn't helpful, or able to entertain herself, but most of the responsibility for everything they did fell on Liv's shoulders. It had been that way since Renie was born. By the time she fell into bed each night, Liv had no energy left to read a book, or a magazine. It was true at home and worse when they traveled.

"By the way, I didn't *meet* him at Red Rocks, we saw him *play* at Red Rocks."

"But he's the guy who came up and introduced himself to you after the show, I know he is. Look." Renie pointed to the photo behind the bar that Liv hadn't noticed. "See, that's him right there."

Sure enough. There he was, right there. Liv felt the familiar ache between her legs as she looked at the photo. There was something about this man, and his music, that made her quiver. She shuddered. *I cannot think this way. I'm with my daughter. What is wrong with me?*

"And, wow! There he is," Renie pointed behind her mom.

Liv turned to see Ben stop to greet customers as he took off his red and black plaid Woolrich jacket and hung it on the coat rack inside the door. The man was a god. Well over six feet tall, he had the broad shoulders of an athlete. Ben was muscular, not body-builder muscular, but hard-as-rock muscular. He reached up to put his straw cowboy hat on the rack with his jacket, and Liv remembered he kept his head shaved.

He turned and looked straight at her, bestowing one of his charming smiles on her.

"Hey little lady," he said, reaching for her hand. "It's good to see you again."

Liv doubted he recognized her, and even if she looked familiar, she was sure he didn't remember from where.

"You were at the show at Red Rocks last summer."

Gah. Liv almost swallowed her tongue as Ben turned and gave Renie the same warm welcome.

Oh no. This was the worst thing ever. Liv was full-on imagining this guy naked, the one talking to her twenty-one-year-old daughter. What if Ben was interested in Renie?

"What's wrong?" Renie asked. Which part of that had she said out loud? Ben was looking at her too.

"Um...nothing, I realized that I left the iron on in the hotel room. Renie, can you please take me back to the hotel. You can come back here, of course, if you want to."

"Mom, I turned off the iron. You didn't even use it."

Damn. She didn't have another reason to leave. But she didn't want to watch her daughter be wooed by a man who made her heart race the way Ben did.

"Good, you can stay. What are you drinking?"

"I'll have another beer." Wait, where had that come from? She didn't want to stay and watch this, it would be as though she was watching the train wreck of her non-existent sex life. And her daughter was driving the train.

"That's my girl," she heard Ben say. Who was he talking to? Her, or Renie? Her heart beat so hard she couldn't hear herself think.

Where did Renie run off to anyway? Liv saw her a couple stools over. She was talking to a guy that came in when Ben did. She rested her hand on his forearm and leaned into him as he talked.

A wall of male blocked her line of sight as Ben maneuvered his way back to the bar stool Renie had vacated.

"Here you go. So tell me, what brings you to Crested Butte? You don't live around here. I mean, I'd know if you did."

"Skiing," she answered between drinks of her beer. "My daughter goes back to school in a few days. We thought we'd sneak a quick trip in before she did."

"I'm Ben," he said. "I'm not sure if you remember."

"And I'm Liv." Of course she remembered. He was being polite because he hadn't.

"It's nice to meet you again, Liv." He glanced at her near-empty beer, the one he had just gotten for her. She was so nervous, she practically chugged her beer.

"Be mindful of the altitude little lady. Beer goes to your head a lot quicker at 9,000 feet than it does in…"

"Monument. I'm from Monument." She felt the same way she had at Red Rocks, she couldn't look him in the eye, he was too...hot.

"Is that near Denver, or is it Colorado Springs?"

"Both, it's right between the two. And we're at 7,000 feet. But you're right, I must've been more thirsty than I thought. Listen, um, I'm going to take the shuttle back to the ski area. Please tell Renie I left her these, and I'll see her back at the hotel. Thanks."

Liv set her car keys on the bar, turned, and fled. She was little, five foot four and one hundred and twenty-five pounds. And had no problem weaving her way in and out of the crowd forming in the popular bar.

Please don't let him follow me, please don't let him follow me, she pleaded. The shuttle was a few feet from her, she jumped on right before the driver closed the door on her.

"You're my only passenger this run ma'am. Where are you headed?"

"The Grand, thanks."

Liv sat in the first row of the bus and buried her hands in her face. What was she thinking? Oh my God, she'd just left her daughter in a bar. Alone.

Her phone vibrated in her pocket. She pulled it out, and saw Renie's name on the caller id.

"Mom, where are you?"

"I'm sorry, I felt sick. It's the altitude." The driver turned around and glared at her. Maybe he thought she'd get sick in his shuttle bus. She waved her hand and mouthed, "I'm okay," which seemed to assuage him.

"What? Where are you?"

"I'm on the shuttle," she shouted into the phone.

And Then You Fall

"Why?"

"I'm a little nauseous." Shouting again into the phone. The shuttle driver was going to pull over and kick her off the bus.

"Okay, I'll meet you at the hotel. I'll leave now."

Liv hit the off button on her phone. There was no point in continuing to try to speak loud enough for Renie to hear her. And now that she'd ruined Renie's good time, she would rest easy that she was on her way back to the hotel, and at least safe. She tilted her head back and closed her eyes. That was the second time she'd raced away from him. What was it about this man that made her want to run as fast and as far in the opposite direction?

It wasn't as though all men had this effect on her. Or that she hadn't dated. She had dated plenty the last twenty years, or maybe the last ten. And, okay, not plenty, but some. Before that she had her hands full raising her daughter by herself, and never would've had the time to date.

"Ma'am, we're here," the shuttle driver said, startling her.

"Oh. I'm sorry. Thank you." She pressed a five dollar bill in the receptacle, hoping he'd consider that enough of a tip.

"Thank you ma'am and I hope you get better," he said as the doors closed behind her.

Liv saw her car in the parking lot. Renie was climbing out of it.

"What was that all about?"

"I drank my beer too fast. That and the crowd in the bar—I was very overwhelmed. I'm sorry I ruined our night out together."

"It's okay. I was worried about you. If we stayed longer, we wouldn't have wanted to ski tomorrow. Here."

Renie passed a piece of folded paper in her mother's direction. "What's this?"

"Ben's number. He wants you to call him and let him know you're okay."

Liv crumbled up the paper in her pocket. She wouldn't even consider calling him. She was sure that by now he had forgotten the crazy lady who ran out of his bar after finishing her beer in thirty seconds flat. Thank goodness she'd never have to see him again.

***

Ben recognized the petite ash blonde as soon as he saw her sitting at the bar. Liv, that was her name. The first time he saw her, after they played at Red Rocks, he couldn't keep his eyes off her. She was with friends, sitting in the row in front of him.

When her bright blue eyes met his, and she smiled, the air had left his lungs. God, she was gorgeous—one of the most beautiful women he'd ever seen.

For the next two hours, he watched her. It was obvious she loved music—and she felt it. Not everyone did. She danced, she laughed, she smiled, she lived. That was why he remembered her name when he introduced himself at the end of the show.

"I'm Liv," she'd said. And he was ready to. He'd endured too many struggles in the last few years. He'd worked so hard to keep the music, the band going. This was the year they would take it to the next level. No more local clubs. Instead, they'd tour nationally, he felt it. They had a new album, better than any other they'd released.

When he saw her again tonight, he knew fate had brought her here to him for the second time. It reminded him not to lose focus, keep his eye on the prize, to keep living. One day at a time.

Besides her beauty, which she seemed unaware of, something about her made him yearn to know her better. But, he made her skittish. Maybe she was experiencing the same magnetic pull he was, and it made her run. The draw was so strong. If he didn't know he was ready for it, it would've scared the hell out of him too.

***

"Do you want a Bloody Mary or are you ready to move onto something else?" Paige tapped her on the shoulder.

"What? Oh, yes, a Bloody Mary, please."

"Were you sleeping?"

"I must've drifted off. I'm sorry."

"You're here to relax, as you keep reminding me, so quit apologizing. I'll be right back. And put on sunscreen before you fall asleep again."

Liv hadn't been asleep; she was thinking about Ben Rice, again. She pulled out her phone and checked Twitter. Nothing. Then Facebook. Nothing. He wasn't here yet, he had a show tonight. Wait, was it tonight, or last night? She checked again. Shit. It had been last night. Now she'd never relax. He may be here already.

Chapter Two

Ben Rice started skiing and playing guitar before he learned to read, as his dad and grandfather before him. In high school, he formed a band that he named CB Rice, in honor of his hometown, Crested Butte, and his family. It confused people. They'd call him CB. That was his band, he was Ben. It didn't take long before he got used to it. If someone called him CB, they were a stranger. If they called him Ben, they were a friend.

All he'd ever wanted to do was make music. Twenty-five years, hundreds of shows, and a half dozen albums later, he was still doing it. He loved it, more than anything.

Performing, hearing the crowds, watching them get into his music—there wasn't much in life that did it for him the way being on stage did. He'd perform until the day he died. Yeah, that was attention you got addicted to. It was the only addiction he couldn't live without.

He toured as often as possible with his band. They averaged a hundred shows a year, most in Colorado. But he expected that to change. The band was solid. They'd even played Red Rocks, which had been a dream.

Ben considered himself an average guy, even if his grandfather had been one of the original developers of the Crested Butte ski area. He'd worked for his family all his life. He didn't mind hard work. When he wasn't touring he spent a lot of time at the Goat, his family's bar and restaurant.

Ben learned the importance of giving back to the community from his parents and grandparents. He and the band played at countless fundraisers for medical research, and for patients faced with life-threatening illnesses, like cancer, who didn't have insurance.

When he was thirty-seven he had been diagnosed with cancer himself. That same year, he and his wife divorced. He fought both the disease and an ugly custody battle at the same time. He'd gone through the standard treatments, and to this day, remained cancer-free. When home, his two boys lived with him half the time.

A little over a year ago his family and band mates staged an intervention. He spent a couple of weeks in rehab and quit drinking. Battling alcoholism was the hardest thing he'd ever done—harder than fighting cancer, harder than watching his marriage and family fall apart. But, he had a year of sobriety under his belt, and he'd never felt better.

It was harder to fight the urge to drink when he was on the road with the band and they'd arrive at a gig to find a case of beer and a bottle of Jack waiting for them. He didn't struggle with it as much at home, especially when he was at his family's bar. He'd get distracted by conversation, or if he was tempted to drink, he'd walk over, pick up his guitar, and start to play. Once the crowd got into the music, the adrenaline rush took the cravings away.

Singing brought him back. It reminded him not to give up, or forget how far he'd come. Performing reminded him not to give up on his kids, himself, or his life. Giving up on his marriage was hard, but he and his ex were better off apart. Ben believed, deep in his soul, there was someone out there for him, someone with whom he would spend the rest of his life. Fate would put her in his path—all he had to do was keep his eyes open and recognize when it happened.

The band was in Las Vegas to play an event. It had started out as a fundraiser for a hometown girl who relocated from Crested Butte to Vegas. They'd gone to high school together, and she was a bartender at the House of Blues. When the manager found out how hard she struggled to make ends meet, he called Ben. Sandy Smith had lost her fight with the disease, but the event continued annually. In its fourth year, it raised funds for cancer research. Mandalay Bay kicked in a hefty chunk of change as did the House of Blues. Last year they'd raised over two million dollars. This year they were hoping to double it.

It would be an all-day event, tickets were $100 a piece. CB Rice would go on right before the main headliner who Ben asked to play when they opened for them at Red Rocks. The lead singer's wife battled cancer herself, so the band was quick to agree to participate.

He didn't have much to do today, but he flew in early anyway. It wasn't his event, or even his fundraiser anymore, yet he still took responsibility for it, and wanted to make sure he was here to help if needed. It meant an extra day away from home, but it was for a good cause.

He pulled out his cell and dialed his son Jake's number as he walked through the casino in the direction of the pool.

"Hey Dad."

"Hey man, how's it going?"

"Okay."

Typical tween on the phone, he should have texted him. "I'm good. I'm headed out to the pool. This place is a giant water park. I should have brought you and your brother with me. Next year. Remind me, okay?"

"Okay Dad. Sounds good. Wanna talk to Luke?"

"Yeah I do, but Jake, wait. I miss you, and I love you."

"I love you too Dad. I'll see you in a couple days."

"Okay man. Behave."

"Dad?"

"Yeah?"

"It's not a big deal okay? You'll be home day after tomorrow."

Jeez, his kid slayed him. "It's just two days too many."

"Yeah, here's Luke."

"Hey Daddy. Where are you?"

Luke was nine, and still had a little boy's voice. At twelve, Jake's voice was starting to change. Sometimes he sounded like a little boy and sometimes he sounded like a man. And then at other times he sounded like a screeching prehistoric bird. God he missed his kids.

"I'm in Las Vegas buddy, and next year when I come to play this show, I'll bring you and your brother. You'd love this place. There are wave pools and a lazy river and all kinds of slides and other stuff. There's even a beach."

Silence.

"Luke, are you there?"

"Yeah. I'm here. I miss you Daddy."

"I miss you too. I'll be home in a couple days."

"Okay. Bye." Click.

That was quick, but at least he talked to his kids for a few minutes.

He opened up Instagram. He'd take a few shots, text them to the boys, and post a few on Twitter and Facebook about the show tomorrow. It wasn't sold out—yet. And he wanted it to be.

He stood in place and turned in a circle, taking shots as he turned. He was able to fit most of the pool-side marquee announcing the show into one.

The band had a cabana reserved, and he wasn't the first one here. He grabbed a towel and threw it on one of the lounge chairs, tossed his phone on the table, and reached around to pull his shirt off over his head. A couple hours by the pool wouldn't hurt anything at all. He didn't remember the last time he had nothing to do. Forced rest, he'd take it.

Ben sat down and picked up his phone, scrolling through the photos he took. He texted several to Jake, and then went back through them trying to decide which ones he should post. He zoomed in, and took a closer look. He deleted most of them. They weren't post worthy.

Wait. He went back to the one before and used two fingers on the screen to zoom in closer. There was a woman in the background who looked familiar. Who was she? He studied it, but it was too out of focus. He stood and looked around him. He looked at the photo again, trying to figure out where she would be sitting based on other landmarks. Damn, he didn't see her.

He wandered out of the cabana area, searching. Her familiarity tugged at him. He needed to find her.

Ben walked over to the lazy river and waited as people floated past him. He stood there for what seemed like an eternity, until he started seeing the same people floating by him, again and again. He turned to leave, and bumped straight into an inner tube.

"Oh, I'm so sorry, I can't see where I'm going," a tiny voice giggled from behind the giant pink tube. Ben lifted it out of the woman's hands and came face to face with her—Liv. Even with as out of focus as the photo was, he knew it was her. This was the third time in a year fate put her in his path. This time, he wouldn't let her go.

Liv gasped. And then got very dizzy. He asked her if she was okay. He set the inner tube down and put his hands on her shoulders.

"Liv, are you okay?"

She gazed into his devastatingly big blue eyes. She couldn't decide whether she would die, right there on the spot, or if she'd never been as okay as she was at that moment.

"Hell-o? Liv? Anybody home?"

That was a different voice. Oh, that was Paige's voice. And those were Paige's hands waving in front of her face.

"What? Yes, I'm okay. I'm so sorry, I couldn't see where I was going." Liv turned to pick up the inner tube and high-tail it out of there.

"Oh no you don't. You're not getting away so fast this time." Ben picked up the tube and held it far enough away that she wouldn't be able to reach it. He was a foot taller than she was, so he didn't have to hold it very high.

"Liv, it's me, Ben."

"Hi Ben. How are you?"

"*How am I?* Don't you think it's a little wild running into me? What are you doing here?"

"I'm here on business, and I made Liv come with me. I'm Paige. We met once before, briefly, at Red Rocks."

Paige was talking, so she didn't have to. Ben was answering her. More talking she didn't have to do. Now if she could curl up into a little ball and slink away without him noticing, she'd be fine. But wait, she wanted to listen to his voice a little longer. She loved his voice.

"Where are you going?"

Oh crap. She backed away from him. And he noticed. "Come with me. You, too, Paige."

"Where are we going? Ow. Can you ease up a bit please?"

Ben's grasp on her hand was so tight, it hurt. "I'm not letting go this time Liv. If I do, I may never see you again."

Once they were within the confines of the cabana, Ben pulled out a chair and pointed at it. "Please have a seat."

When Liv didn't sit, he took a step forward. "Liv, please." He sounded more exasperated than he wanted. Liv sat and he moved to the other side of the table, pulling a chair out for Paige.

He sat down in the chair closest to Liv. He wanted to sit and stare at her, memorize every line on her face and curve of her body. Here she was, sitting next to him, this woman who haunted his dreams; he was destined to get to know her.

She was a mystery. *Didn't she recognize him?* It sounded as though her friend did.

"Now that you may stay put…hi Liv. How are you? It's nice bumping into you here."

"Ha, ha," she answered, looking away. He touched her cheek, turning her head so she'd look at him.

"Hi Ben, it's nice bumping into you too." She took a deep breath, and added, "I'm surprised you remember me."

She looked down again. He didn't want her to look down he wanted her to look at him. He moved his hand from her cheek to her chin and lifted her gaze to his.

"Why do you run from me?" he whispered.

Paige jumped up from her chair. "I'll go get us a couple of drinks. Liv? Ben? What would you like?"

"Paige, please sit back down," he stated, without looking away from Liv. "We have cabana service. Tell me what you want, and I'll order it for you."

Paige sat back down.

"Liv, what can I order for you?"

"Lemonade?"

"Is that a question?"

"Lemonade, please."

"Paige?"

"I need something a little stronger, a Sea Breeze please."

"I'll be right back…I'm walking a couple feet away…I'm ordering drinks…do not get up from the table…" He kept his voice low and free of any inflection, like a hypnotist.

He came back and pulled his chair closer to Liv. "So—let's start over, way back at the beginning. Why don't we talk about how you bolt away from me every time I try to start a conversation with you? Is there something about me you don't like?" He rubbed his head. "I'm bald. Is that it? You don't like bald guys."

"No, I like bald guys. I mean, I like everything about you. No, that isn't what I mean. See? I can't even put two thoughts together. I 'bolt,' as you put it, because I don't want you to realize I'm an idiot."

Ben leaned back and laughed. She was so damned cute. She made him laugh. If there was one single thing he was certain of, she wouldn't be running away from him today. No way.

She started to laugh too. Then Paige did. Soon all three of them were laughing. Ben reached over and put his hand on Liv's arm. "Better now?"

"Yes," she giggled. "I'm better now."

He talked them into ordering lunch and when they finished, Paige excused herself to go to a meeting she had that afternoon.

"I should go too," Liv started to get up from her chair.

Ben put his hand on her arm. "No. Stay. Can you stay? Please?" He wasn't used to women trying so hard to get away from him. It was usually the other way.

Liv looked at Paige, as if to ask for a reason to leave. "I won't be back until dinner. Stay. *Enjoy* yourself."

"Well, I guess…"

"There, it's settled, you're staying. Before you go, what are you doing for dinner?"

"We hadn't gotten that far."

"Good, then you'll join me, and the band. We have something special planned tonight. You'll enjoy it."

* * *

She had such a nice afternoon spending time with him. She had to admit it was unexpected. They talked and hung out at the pool, sitting on the steps. He told her about his two boys and she told him more about Renie. He noticed her getting chill bumps and led her to the hot tub. "Let's get warm," he said. She was plenty warm, overheated in fact, but that wasn't something she'd admit to him.

Ben, with clothes on, made her blood boil. Without them, the sweat bubbled on the surface of her skin. Every bit of him was muscle. She longed to know what it would be like to have those powerful arms hold her, his ripped chest flat against hers, his strong legs wrapped around her.

He sat down first and pulled her to sit in front of him, as if he'd read her mind. He pulled her back closer to him. He was hard against her. She tried to move forward.

"Feel what you do to me," he whispered, pulling her closer still as he ran his lips along the place between her neck and her shoulder. Liv heard a moan and didn't know if it came from him or her. She closed her eyes and leaned back into him.

"That's my girl." He wrapped his arms around her waist and scooted her so she was sitting on his lap.

"Ben—"

"Shh...the music is starting to play. Listen." He started to hum, then sing softly.

The soft skin on your bones and the smile I would own.

He nuzzled into her hair and breathed in her scent. "You smell delicious. What is it? Lavender, or lemon?"

Liv couldn't wait a moment longer, she turned far enough that her lips touched his. His mouth devoured hers. Liv pulled back and bit her lip, her stomach lurched and her eyelids drooped. Ben's hand slid into her hair and gripped a fistful of it, gentle but firm. He tugged her head back, feasting his eyes on her lips.

She trembled at the heat between them, the steam rising off the warm water in the hot tub swirled around them. His arms moved back to her waist and tightened around her, pulling her even closer. He gave a rough groan as he lowered his head and kissed her again. His body was big and solid against hers. She sank into him, his mouth was warm and firm, yet so tender. He slid his tongue over her bottom lip and nipped at it.

"Want you," he groaned. "Want you naked, under me, around me."

Liv pulled back, gasping to get air into her straining lungs.

"Let's go somewhere we can be alone," he said, his lips parted, his eyes dark and hungry. "I want to get you out of this bikini," his finger slid under the small triangle of material covering her breast. "I want to see every inch of skin on this amazing body."

Liv shifted away from him, trying to get her wits about her. She wanted his lips back on hers, wanted him naked too, but...they needed to slow down. She moved away from him, but held his gaze as they sat staring at each other.

"Too much?" he ventured.

"Too soon," she answered.

***

Ben insisted on walking her back to her room, to her door. "This way if you run from me again, I'll know where to find you."

"But—"

"Shh...I'm sorry, I didn't mean to make you uncomfortable. I can't explain this overwhelming attraction between us. It feels as though I've known you forever, not that I'm just getting to know you. That must sound crazy. Listen, I won't push so hard."

It wasn't that. She knew he was used to getting what he wanted, and in this case she wanted the same thing he did.

She didn't know how to tell him how long it had been since she'd done this. *I hope it's like riding a bike.*

"Pretty much, but like no other bike you've ridden before baby," he said, nuzzling her neck. Oh no, did she say that out loud?

Ben leaned up against the wall outside Liv's hotel room. His body pulsed with lust, his eyes closed, his heart thundering. They opened and fixated on Liv's gaze. She had no idea how breathtakingly beautiful she was. He could spend all day studying every inch of her.

Her skin was kissed by their day in the sun, and her hair hung in waves around her face. The thin cover up that left her arms bare was so feminine, the way it wrapped around her slender body. And her eyes, the bluest he'd ever seen, were gazing at him apprehensively. He read every ounce of her insecurity in the look she gave him.

"I'm leaving now Liv, and it's not because I want to. We have reservations at Charlie Palmer at eight. Would you like me to walk down with you later, or meet me in the lobby?"

"Paige?"

"Paige is invited as well. The band has a private dining room reserved for a special dinner tonight. We'd love for the two of you to join us."

"Should you check with the band first?"

"No Liv, it's my band. Which reminds me, do you have tickets for the show tomorrow night?"

"Um, no, we hadn't gotten around to getting them yet."

"Good. You'll be my guests."

He wanted to reassure her, explain how he didn't care about anything else at that moment besides being with her.

This was new for him, having to exercise such restraint. Ben liked to reach out and take what he wanted. He doubted that would work with this woman.

He touched her face, her cheek velvety soft beneath his fingers, calloused from years of guitar playing. He pulled her back into his arms, bent his head and found her mouth again with his. He'd show her how much he wanted to be with her, when words weren't enough.

Dinner with the band was raucous, loud and fun. Liv envied the way they all embraced life with such gusto. Several members of the other bands were there too. Before she realized it, it was after one in the morning.

Paige was more of a night owl than she. And it didn't surprise Liv one bit that Paige was discussing record deals and song rights with the other guys in the band. Or that she'd gone outside to smoke a cigar with a couple of them. It would never have occurred to Paige to be unfaithful to Mark, she fit in wherever she happened to be. And if the conversation involved business, Paige was in her element.

Ben stroked his fingers down her arm, going back and forth, lulling her into a state of complete relaxation. "Tired?"

"A little," Liv answered as she stifled a yawn. "What about you? You have a big day tomorrow."

"Yeah, I do." He took the glass of wine she still held and set it on the table, his eyes focused on hers the entire time. He rose and took her hand, pulling her with him. Ben's eyes darkened, he bent down and his lips closed over hers. He ran one finger from beneath her chin, straight down and stroked the place where her dress met the top of her breasts. She breathed in, inadvertently pushing herself closer to him.

"Come with me," he murmured, walking toward the door.

"I can't."

"Oh, but you can. Let's take a walk in the moonlight."

"A walk, and then we have to say good night."

Ben started humming, then singing again.

The charm of your tease
When you make me say please
Your eyes and your hair
The look of your stare
The way that you laugh…

There was that ache again, it hadn't gone away, not since that morning. "Wooing me with your music, that's not playing fair."

He kept singing.

All I want is your mouth, and your lips
And your soft fingertips
The curve of your spine well it's gotta be mine
The warmth of your kiss when we're lying like this
The heat of your touch well it's never too much.

His lips crushed into hers. "Jesus, Liv, do you know how much I want you?" They shared a heated smile and Liv started walking in the direction of the elevators.

"But my room is this way," he tried to pull her in the opposite direction.

"And my room is this way. Would you like to say good night here?"

"No, I wouldn't like. But, if I walk you to your room, the room you're sharing with Paige, we won't be able to be alone. If you come with me, we'll be alone all night."

"Which is why I'm heading to my room. It's been a long day. Tomorrow will be too. Good night Ben."

"Not yet Liv." He brought her hand up to his lips and kissed across her knuckles.

The elevator dinged. "Walk me to my room."

They made it almost all the way down the hall to her room before he pushed her against the wall, torturing himself kissing her lips, her neck. "Let me feel you against me…"

His hands crept up to her breasts as he ravaged her mouth. He lifted her off her feet and slid her body back down his. He wanted her warm, smooth skin against his. Liv arched against him, crying out as he nipped at her neck.

"Stop, wait. Ben, stop. We have to stop." Liv put her hands on his arms and pushed him back away from her.

"No…let me stay. Let me stay with you tonight."

Liv managed to get her key card in the door, and was halfway through, "Good night Ben. Sweet dreams."

Ben turned and put his forehead against the wall as the door click behind her. He doubted the sweetness of his dreams, but he didn't, for a second, doubt how hot they'd be. He'd never wanted a woman the way he wanted her. How much of it was her resistance to him?

Chapter Three

Liv hadn't heard Paige come in last night, or this morning, but she heard her in the shower. What time was it? Eleven? She'd slept until eleven. She never slept past eight, not ever.

"Well good morning," Paige said, coming out of the bathroom door in a waft of steam with one of the hotel's big, fluffy robes wrapped around her. "I wondered if you were going to sleep all day."

"You got in after I did. Why are you so chipper first thing this morning?"

"First thing this morning? It's almost noon. I've been up since before nine. I got coffee, read for a while, and decided if you were still asleep when I finished my shower, I would blast CB Rice songs through the iPod."

Liv rolled over and buried her head in the pillow. Paige sat down on the bed across from her. "Spill. Tell me all the details. I'm dying of curiosity."

"He's so...hot."

"Yes. That part is obvious. What happened after you left the restaurant last night? Oh, before I forget, I found an envelope containing two tickets to the show slipped under our door this morning."

"Nothing happened. He walked me to the room. We said good night."

"That's it?"

"Paige, what did you expect? That I'd invite him in and have hot sex with a total stranger?"

Paige stared at her, dumbfounded.

"Paige? Is that what you thought?"

"Of course it's what I thought. I don't want to hurt your feelings honey, but for God's sake, when *is* the last time you had sex? You have had sex since you conceived Renie, haven't you?"

"Of course I have."

"Wait, I better clarify. You have had sex since Scott, haven't you?"

No response.

"Liv, that was twenty-one years ago!"

"Thank you. Thank you for reminding me. I guess it's obvious then why I didn't invite him inside."

Paige shook her head. "It's about as far from obvious as it gets." She got up and started getting dressed. "No wonder you're so grouchy."

"Hey! Be nice. Just because someone isn't having sex, doesn't make them grouchy. After a while, you get used to it. It's the idea of having sex again, and then not having it that makes a person grouchy. And to be honest, I am *very* grouchy this morning."

"Again, why didn't you do something about it last night?"

"Argh—I told you why not. He's this hot, younger guy who wants to have sex with me. How long do you think that'll last when he finds out I'm a forty-year-old re-virgin?"

"Re-virgin? Is that a thing? I haven't heard about that. Is that what it's called?"

Liv buried her head back into the pillow. This was pointless. She couldn't get through to Paige, so why bother? That was last night, she'd missed her chance. Even if she saw him tonight, he'd be busy with the show, there'd be lots of younger, hotter women at the show.

Oh God. What had she done? She'd missed her one chance to have sex, in twenty years. What if she never had sex again? She'd die a shriveled up old lady who hadn't had sex in sixty years. Maybe longer.

Liv jumped when the room phone rang. Who called anyone on hotel phones anymore? Paige answered.

"Hello, yeah, good morning. Yep, she's right here."

"It's him," she mouthed.

"Huh?"

"It's Ben," she said out loud this time, her hand covering the receiver.

"Oh."

"Here, take it," Paige shoved the phone in her direction.

"Good morning."

"Good morning yourself. I slept longer than I wanted to. Actually, I didn't sleep much at all, and it's your fault. I couldn't stop thinking about you. I drifted off around sunrise. I woke up and realized I missed my chance to have breakfast with you this morning."

"You didn't. Paige just woke me up too."

"Liv, tell me, did you dream about me?"

Silence.

"Liv? Are you there?"

"Mmm hmm."

"And? Tell me about your dreams."

"Not a chance."

"I'll try to get it out of you during breakfast. How soon can you be ready?"

"I don't know about breakfast. I should check with Paige."

Liv saw Paige waving her hands and shaking her head no. "Go. Go with him. I have a meeting."

"Oh. Paige has a meeting. I can be ready in a half hour."

"Okay, I'll be there in ten minutes."

"Wait. What? I said it would take me a half hour to get ready."

"Yeah, but I'm gonna help."

Silence. He hung up.

"What? What's happening? You're supposed to tell your best friend what's happening. I shouldn't have to force it out of you."

"He'll be here in ten minutes. He said he'd help me get ready."

Somehow Paige managed to get dressed while Liv talked to Ben. She'd even put on makeup and pulled her hair back in a sleek ponytail.

"How did you do that? Five minutes ago you got out of the shower, and now you're ready to go. And you look great. How?"

Paige picked up her bag and briefcase and went in the direction of the door. "See you later," she said as the door closed behind her.

"Wait! When? When will I see you later?" Too late. Liv would have to text her.

Oh no! Ben was on his way. She hadn't brushed her teeth, did she have time to jump in the shower? She had to try.

When she got out, he was pounding on the door. He barged in as she opened it, grabbing her and lifting her in his arms as though she didn't weigh a thing.

His hands went to the sash on her robe. Instinctively she rested her hands on his, stopping him. "Liv, I'm sorry, last night I told you I wouldn't push, but please, I can't keep my hands off of you."

"Don't. I don't want you to."

"You don't want me to what?"

"I don't want you to keep your hands off of me."

With a growl, he untied the sash and slid the robe off her shoulders. "Christ, look at you. Want you, can't think I want you so much."

He lifted her off her feet and spun her around, setting her down with the back of her knees at the foot of the bed.

Ben reached behind him and pulled his T-shirt over his head. Their hands met at his belt, both trying to loosen it.

"Hurry," she pleaded.

He slid off his jeans. They stood before each other naked. His lips started working their way down her body. She arched against him.

He was being rough, going too fast. He wanted to slow down, but couldn't bring himself to. Ben stopped and breathed her in; she was trembling. He brought his mouth back up to hers. Softer, slower this time. He wanted to savor her, not devour her.

Her fingernails dug into his shoulders as he grasped her face between his hands. "Liv, I want to be inside you."

She fell back on the bed and scooted herself toward the headboard. Ben stood, watching her as she moved.

"I need to look at you."

She started to move her hands to cover herself. He gripped her wrists, stopping her. "No, don't hide from me. Let me look at you."

He let go of her wrists and spread her legs, kneeling between them. He bent down and kissed across her pelvis then up her body. She gasped as his mouth closed on one nipple and his fingers found the other.

"I want to take this slow, but Liv, I need you. Now."

His voice broke through the haze of pleasure. "Condom," she said, as he ripped one open.

Her body arched as he slid into her. Her breath caught. He'd stopped moving.

"Open your eyes. I want you to look at me." She met his gaze, and he started to move again. "So good. It's so good." He moved faster, thrusting into her harder. Her hips rose meeting his.

"Please Ben," she said as the pleasure reached its peak, taking them both over.

Two hours later they decided to order room service since every time they tried to leave, one or the other pulled them back to the bed.

They sat as they had in the hot tub. Her back snuggled up to his front as they fed each other bites of muffin and strawberries.

"I thought you had a full day today."

"I did. I do." Ben was sure he was in a heap of crap with everyone.

Liv scooted away from him and grabbed his phone from his jean's pocket. "Here, better to face it than sit here worrying about it."

"How do you know I'm worried?"

"Worry is seeping off of you. And it's ruining my post-orgasm fog of pleasure. Figure it out so you can either leave or relax."

Ben threw his head back and started to laugh. "God, you are something else. Just when I think I've got your number, you go in a direction I never expected." He squeezed her when he said it, and started nuzzling her neck.

"Check your phone." She squirmed against him.

"You keep that up, and I won't make the show later." He checked his phone. "Huh. That's weird."

"What's that?"

"I don't have a single message, not even a text." He started to punch in a number. "Hey," he said to whoever answered. "What the hell's goin' on?"

His crew wasn't as worried about him as he thought they'd be. When he left the dinner with Liv, they assumed he spent the night with her. When he didn't come down for breakfast, and didn't show up to help set up, they figured that's where he was.

"So," he said, laying back down and pulling her with him. "I'd say we have at least another hour before I have to leave."

"What should we do with that hour?"

"The possibilities are endless," he said as he started kissing his way back down her body.

***

Paige and Liv sat near the center of the stage, in the first row of tables. They missed the first couple of opening bands, but got there in time to see the last one on the stage before CB Rice played. From the glares coming from the people seated around them, Liv guessed their reserved table sat empty for hours before they arrived.

She hadn't seen Ben since he left the room a few hours earlier. The thought of seeing him on stage, with the memory of the two of them together so fresh in her mind, brought color to her cheeks.

"Whatcha' thinking about?" Paige smirked. "Did you have a nice afternoon while I slaved away in meetings?"

"Stop it. You don't slave. You talk and everyone else listens with bated breath. And yes, I had a very nice afternoon."

"Tell me about it."

"Paige—I don't ask you to tell me about your sex life with Mark!"

"We've been married forever, no one would want to hear about our sex life. You are sleeping with Ben Rice. Everyone wants to hear about that."

"Shh, lower your voice. God, I'm so embarrassed."

"No one can hear me over the band. Why are you embarrassed? He's…"

"Hot. Very hot. Scorchingly hot."

"See?"

"And that's all you're getting out of me."

"Damn."

Liv looked in the direction of the bar, and saw one of the guys she'd met at dinner, Johnny or Jimmy, she didn't remember. He waved and motioned for her to come to the bar.

And Then You Fall

"I'll be right back."

As she walked up she saw Ben standing at the bar next to whatever his name was, with his back to her. He turned as she drew closer, and smiled, that devastatingly perfect smile that made her want to slide into his arms and never leave. His worn jeans, with holes and tears in all the right places, sat low on his hips. His Henley crept up as he reached his hand out in invitation, revealing a peak at his rock-hard abs. The True Grit plaid shirt he wore, open in the front, stretched across his broad shoulders. His cowboy hat, sitting down low on his head, almost covering his eyes, was another of Liv's weaknesses.

"Wow, look at you all sexy and hanging out at the bar. Aren't you afraid your fans will mob you?" She slid her body up against his and breathed in the scent of him.

"Nah, I've been out here forty-five minutes waiting for you. Nobody recognizes me."

"If I knew you were waiting for me, as hot as you are, I would've gotten here much sooner."

"Me? Look at you, you're fire and ice baby." Liv's sleeveless red dress clung to every curve of her body. She wore a single, solitaire diamond necklace, on a long chain that hung down, resting in the hollow between her breasts. Her four-inch nude heels made her legs look impossibly long, and her wavy hair framed her face with perfectly placed blonde highlights.

Ben sat on a bar stool, put his arm around her waist, and pulled her closer to him. "I want to kiss you so bad, right here in the bar. Would that embarrass you?"

Liv rubbed her lips across his before pulling back and away.

"That isn't a real kiss. Come here. Give me more of that."

Before he could pull her closer, she stiffened her arm, keeping him at a safe distance. "Careful, your adoring fans may not like seeing you with me."

"What's goin' on with you?" Jimmy asked after Liv walked away.

"I wish to hell I knew. God, look at her." Ben breathed in deep and let it out. "I could eat her up. Have you ever seen a more beautiful woman?"

"I'm confused, didn't you just meet her? You seem kinda' over the top."

"Yeah, I did. I mean, I met her last summer, after the show we played at Red Rocks."

"Oh yeah, now I remember, so you met her then, for five minutes, now she's coming to our shows? Hmm."

"Nah, it's not like that. I ran into her at the pool yesterday morning. And then one other time in January."

"She didn't *mean* to run into you? Come on now."

No, she was different. She hadn't meant to run into him, fate kept putting her in his path. Liv had been fighting the attraction between them. She didn't recognize it for what it was. Something special, something unique.

"I'm tellin' you, it's not that way. I like her, so back the fuck off."

Jimmy held up his hands. "Just sayin', don't get so touchy."

Liv could not wait to see Ben on stage again. She loved watching him play, up close, where she could see those big, powerful hands on the guitar, watch his eyes as he sang.

Wow, it was getting hot in here, perhaps she should go get fresh air before they started. Wait, this was Las Vegas, there wasn't much fresh air, and what there was of it wouldn't cool her off.

One by one the band members took the stage, everyone but Ben. The MC came out, "Ladies and gentlemen, please welcome…C…B…R-i-i-i-c-e." The place was packed, the crowd roared. They started to play and seconds later, Ben came out on stage, guitar in hand, already playing.

They were so close to the stage Liv saw the sweat on his brow. His eyes closed as he stepped forward and starting singing, "Twisted." It was a crowd-pleaser.

Can't blame it on the whiskey,
Can't blame it on the smoke,
Half of me's in heaven,
The other half's in hell.
I might be goin' crazy,
But I just can't tell.
She's got me twisted,
All torn up.
There's nothin' I won't do
For her sweet, sweet love.

Ben's eyes met hers as he sang the words.

Paige elbowed her. "Jeez, this is as hot as he is. He's singing to you."

Liv wanted to crawl under the table. It wasn't that she didn't like it. But anyone looking at her would know what she and Ben had been doing a few short hours ago, it was written all over her face.

By the third song Liv and Paige were dancing, along with everyone else. The band got people on their feet. Liv turned and surveyed the crowd, mesmerized by Ben. She wasn't alone in that. He pulled people to him, made them sing along, hang on every word. He was magnetic.

They slowed things down with the next song, the crowd settled back in their chairs, giving Liv an opportunity to watch Ben play. The muscles in his arms flexed, the corners of his mouth turned down, his eyes closed, and his whole body moved with every sound coming out of his guitar. He threw his head back and got into it. The way he did when they were having sex.

"Whatcha' thinking about now?" Paige elbowed her and grinned. Liv grinned back. Getting him alone again. Never letting go of him once she did. That's what. She didn't want to think about how soon they'd both get on a plane, and go back to their normal lives. Her boring, miserable, sexless life. Nope she didn't want to think about that at all.

When she looked back up at Ben, he was watching her. His brow furrowed, as though he wondered where her mind was, and why it wasn't on him. That was silly. He was playing in front of a room full of people, lost in his music, lost in his fans. She doubted very much he even remembered she was there.

They played for another hour, then came back out for three encores before the break leading to the last band taking the stage. One of the guys from CB Rice came to their table.

"Ben asked if you'd come backstage with me. Paige, will you be okay by yourself for a few minutes? Liv won't be too long."

"Of course, go! I'm fine." Liv saw Paige had already struck up a conversation with the table next to them. Liv never had to worry about Paige, she had never known a stranger, just friends she hadn't met yet.

"Hi! Come here baby," Ben reached out for her. "No, wait, I'm all sweaty."

"I don't care," she said as she rested her body next to his. "I like it when you get me sweaty."

Ben pulled her in closer, bent his head and kissed her. Liv's mouth opened beneath his. The kiss deepened, Liv put her hand on Ben's cheek, his hand went to her bottom, and pulled her in closer to him. "God, you're so sexy."

"No, I'm not. But you—" Liv couldn't finish, everything about him turned her on. His fingertips drifted down to where her dress rested against the swell of her breasts, the way they had the night before.

"You have no idea, do you? What you do to me. What you were doing to me while I was on stage? All I thought about was being inside you. Every song, every note, I'd close my eyes and see you there, writhing beneath me."

"You were thinking about me?"

"You weren't thinking about me? About us? About this? Getting horizontal with me again?" His arms wrapped around her waist, and he playfully kissed the side of her neck, under her ear, down and over her shoulder. "I wish we could go off on our own, I want to be alone with you, I don't want to share you with anyone else right now."

Liv held her breath. She'd like nothing better. But what about the rest of the show?

"But we can't, at least not for a little while. Listen, I'm gonna go talk to the guys for a minute, hang out before the next band goes on stage. They're setting up a roped off section for us. I can't come out before they start their set, but I'll be out right after that." He pulled her in again and ravaged her mouth with his. "Then later, it's you and me. Got it?"

"Mmm hmm," she nodded. She got it.

The guys in the final band were pros. Their horn section alone reverberated throughout the club. She saw them before at an amphitheater filled with ten thousand people, and even in that setting, they were bigger than life. Seeing them here, even if she hadn't planned to see CB Rice, was something she was glad she hadn't missed.

The House of Blues closed their doors after the show, but with the number of bands that participated, the place remained crowded. Everyone wanted to talk to Ben, Liv hadn't seen him for an hour. Paige was talking with a power couple that were involved with Mandalay Bay management.

She didn't want to pout, but she was bored, and tired. Exhausted. She wanted to crawl into bed. The problem was, she didn't want to crawl into it alone. Why did she surround herself with people who were more interesting than she was? Ben, Paige, Scott, even her parents were more interesting than she was.

***

Liv grew up *loving* Scott Fairchild. There wasn't a better or more handsome man alive. Her dad mentored Scott as a cadet at the Air Force Academy, and helped guide his career. He came to their house often. When Scott got his promotion to captain, her parents threw a small celebration dinner for him. Scott planned the trip to Colorado Springs so he would be promoted there, by Liv's father.

"He asks about you," her mother said to her.

"Who asks about me?"

"Scott. He asked your father if he'd mind if he took you out while he was here."

"What did Dad say?"

"Dad said it was okay with him."

Liv was stunned. She was sure Scott hadn't ever thought of her as anything other than her father's little girl, he was eleven years older than she was; she was eighteen.

They did go out, every night he was in town. She was the happiest she'd ever been in her life. When he went back to his base, they'd talk every night on the phone. Scott came the next Christmas to spend it with her family, and proposed. She said yes, and they married on Valentine's Day. Soon after Liv realized she was pregnant.

In less than a year she went from being a girl who graduated from high school a few months before, to a wife, soon to be a mother. And less than ten months after that, she was a widow. She and Scott hadn't been married a year when his plane was shot down.

Liv hadn't been with another man since Scott. She hadn't thought about it. Scott was the only man she had sex with, until last night. The truth was, she'd been too scared to let anyone else get that close to her, to share that part of herself again. The last time she opened herself up that way, her heart was broken into a million pieces.

All these years she believed if she kept her heart closed, she wouldn't ever have to experience that gut-wrenching pain again. The only person she ever loved who hadn't been taken away from her was Renie. And every day Liv prayed that God would keep her safe.

Liv didn't know whether to thank Ben for awakening these feelings in her, or curse him for it. This was different though, this wasn't about her heart, it was sex. It wasn't about forever, the way it was with Scott, it was a fling. A few days of fun. Lots of people had sex with someone they'd never see again.

***

She stood, facing the bar, trying to decide whether to get Ben's attention or head up to the room when his arms slid around her waist.

"There's my girl. Oooh you feel good."

"Hi," she whispered, turning to wrap her arms around him.

"Let's get out of here. You ready?"

"Are you sure you can leave?"

"Yep. I can't wait another minute to be alone with you. Come on, let's go."

He pulled her with him, heading to the bank of elevators in the opposite direction of hers. "You're staying with me tonight, and I'm not taking no for an answer."

Liv let out a heavy sigh. She needed to keep reminding herself, *this wasn't about her heart, it was sex*. This week, these couple days with him, would be memories she'd carry with her forever. The memories wouldn't keep her warm at night back on her ranch in Black Forest. But at least she'd be able to say she'd done this, something a little wild, a little crazy, and had a lot of good sex.

When they got on the elevator, she pushed him back up against the wall, running her hands under his shirt. His muscles tightened beneath her touch. He lifted her up and slid her down his long, hard body.

"Liv," he whispered her name, "you are so beautiful."

"So are you," she whispered back. Her hand slid down his belly toward his hip. Her heart thudded faster as she leaned into him, her body pressing as close to his.

The elevator stopped, the door opened and they twisted out, neither letting go. This time Ben pressed her against the hallway wall. "Naked," he answered.

"Room," she responded, kissing, then licking the pulse point on his neck.

He slid his hands to her breasts, trying to free them from her bra.

"Wait," she gasped. "Someone might see us."

He cupped the perfect mound of flesh and stroked her hardened nipple with his thumb. "I don't care." He moved his hands to her ass and grabbed her, pressing, grinding against her.

"Oh God, Ben, I want you so much," she groaned.

Her back was to the door of the suite and when he opened it, she almost tumbled to the floor. He pulled her back against him, and pushed the door shut behind them.

"I can't keep my hands off you," he groaned. His lips trailed down her body, "I can't keep my lips off you." He reached for the zipper on her dress and pulled it down. It slid off her shoulders to the floor. He traced the lacy edge of her bra, his gaze riveted there.

"Your turn," she murmured, tugging at his shirt. He grinned and reached behind him, pulling it off in one swoop.

"Now this." His hand moved to her back to unfasten her bra with practiced ease. He removed the pale pink lace and dropped it to the floor. "Beautiful," he murmured. "Skin on skin, this is what I've been craving."

Liv ran her hands over his firm pecs, his chiseled abs, and down to the waistband of his jeans. She reached for his belt, but he caught her hand.

"You first." His hands moved to her panties, and pulled them down and over her hips as she shimmied out of them. She pressed her lips to his shoulder blade and ran her tongue over his skin.

His breath caught and his abs tightened beneath her exploring lips. "No more waiting," she said, reaching for his belt. He unfastened it and jerked his pants off his own hips, let them fall to the floor, and stepped out of them.

He turned away from her, leading her by the hand. "Your suite is much bigger than ours," she commented. "Must be a perk of being famous."

"No talking." He turned her around, walking her backward, belly-to-belly into the large open area of the suite. She looked up at him and he caught her mouth in a deep kiss. She wrapped her arms around his neck and kissed him back. He grabbed her ass in both large hands and pressed her more securely against him.

He started moving her backward again, not stopping until her legs came in contact with the bed. Ben eased her down onto the mattress, never taking his lips from hers.

He moved her where he wanted her. "I want to look at you Liv. I need to."

He moved so he sat next to her, his hip touching hers, and touched her breasts, her belly and down across the heated flesh between her thighs.

"Ben," she arched her back and swayed her hips, trying to position herself closer to him.

"Don't rush me," he said. "I'm still looking."

"Less looking. More touching," Liv groaned.

Suddenly he was on top of her, wedging his knee between her thighs, opening her up to him.

"Can't wait."

She gasped and tried to stop him, then realized he already wore a condom. When had he put that on? Her thundering heart raced out of control, who cares?

"Ben, please."

"Oh baby, it's so good." She clenched around him, wanting to keep him there, a part of her, for as long as possible. Spasms of relief overtook her, spreading throughout her body as he moved over her, faster and faster, harder and harder, until she exploded.

"Again Liv, let's figure out what else you like," he said as he trailed gentle kisses along her jaw. "I'm not finished with you yet."

Liv wrapped her arms and legs around him. The pressure began to build again inside her. Need engulfed her senses. Ben slowed, and looked into her eyes. "Now," he growled, as he threw his head back and closed his eyes. The way he had on stage.

She kissed his temple as he murmured the sweetest sounds. Contentment.

"Be right back."

He snuggled back into her, pulling her closer so her back nestled against his front.

"I wish I wasn't so tired," he whispered. "I don't want to miss a moment of being with you, but I have to sleep."

"Mmm," her eyes closed, and she fell asleep before he did.

Ben blinked himself awake and tried to get his bearings. He lifted his head from the pillow and felt Liv's body cuddled against his. When he shifted, she woke.

"Good morning beautiful," he kissed the top of her head. He liked waking up with her in his arms.

"What time is it?" He shifted again, checking the clock on the nightstand. "Eleven."

"What? Eleven? Again. I never sleep this late." She snuggled back into him. "It's you. Your fault."

Her stomach rumbled, it made him chuckle. "Hungry?"

"Yeah, I haven't eaten since yesterday afternoon."

"Liv, are you kidding? You must be starving." He lifted her off of him and swung his legs over the side of the bed.

"No," she protested. "Don't go, come back here."

"I'm ordering food, then you'll have my undivided attention. What do you want to eat?"

"Don't care. Need nourishment."

He called room service, then he stretched his body out next to hers again.

"What time's your flight?" he asked, wishing he didn't have to.

"Tomorrow morning. When is yours?"

"Seven."

"Seven?" she gasped.

"Relax. Seven tonight."

She let out a groan that sounded more like a stifled sob.

"I can change it. What time is your flight tomorrow? I'll leave the same time you do."

"No, don't do that. You have to get home."

He sat back up, throwing his legs over the side of the bed again.

"Where are you going now? You promised your undivided attention."

"Give me a minute. Changing my flight time."

That made her pay attention. "No, Ben. I mean it. Don't change your flight. It's okay."

"It isn't a big deal, I can leave anytime I want to. Are you trying to tell me you don't want to spend another night with me?"

"No. That isn't it."

"What is it then?"

"Your boys. This…this…whatever it is, shouldn't come before your boys. I get that. I understand."

"If that's the only thing that's worrying you, if you promise that's it, I'm staying." She started to speak and he put two fingers on her lips to stop her.

"If I left tonight, they'd be in bed long before I got home. And tomorrow is the day my boys hang with Grandma and Grandpa. Dad is not allowed to interfere with grandparent time. They'll be up and gone by sunrise. By the time they get home, I will be too. And, I'll get to spend another few hours with you."

"But…"

"But what? Liv I want to spend time with you. Is that so hard to accept? If I'm pushing too hard I guess you need to say so."

"No, that isn't it." Liv got up and climbed into her panties, looking for her bra.

He walked to her, bringing his hand up to caress the side of her face. He tucked her hair behind her ear. "Talk to me," he said. "Tell me what you're thinking. Are you worried about Paige?"

"No, that isn't it. Paige travels all the time. She does her own thing. I don't need to worry about her."

"Then what is it?" He rubbed his head again. "We already determined you like the bald head. We discovered other things you like too. Come on, give me somethin' here. You ready to run away from me again Liv?"

She maneuvered out of his arms and walked to the window. She pulled the drapes back, and looked out at the Las Vegas Strip. What could she say? The more time she spent with him the harder it would be to let him go.

If she left now, her pride would stay intact. She'd walk away, thank him for a fantastic couple of days, wonderful memories, great sex, and ride off into the sunset, or at least to the elevator. If she said goodbye first, she might have more of a chance to keep her emotions in check, and not make a fool of herself.

Ben stood with his arms crossed, less than a foot from her. "Liv, tell me. I can see the wheels turning. Talk to me."

"I have to go. It's been great, a great couple of days." What else had she planned to say? She couldn't think. "It's been, you know, fun. But, it's time to get back to real life." She picked up her dress, and looked for her shoes and bag.

"Uh-uh."

"What?"

"No. This isn't going down like this. You are not, I repeat, not running out of here. Even if I was leaving tonight, which I no longer am, I wouldn't let you leave now. Who knows how long it will be before we see each other again? We haven't even talked about that yet."

Chapter Four

"Sure, that works, see you then." Liv hung up her cell.

"All set?"

She bit her lip. "I realize I said Paige is self-sufficient, but I hope she's not mad at me. As busy as she is, and as much as she has to do, she'd never do this to me."

"Do what?"

"Leave me with no one to hang out with, while we were traveling together."

"What did she say? Did she sound angry?"

"She said she wanted me to enjoy myself, more than anything, so…"

"What else did she say? So…what?"

"So I wasn't so damned grouchy when we got home."

Ben's head tilted back again, and he laughed. She loved his laugh, he did it with his whole body. His whole body experienced the joy of the moment. And it wasn't just when he laughed, he did it all the time. On stage, and when they were having sex.

He pulled her back down on the bed and shifted so she was on top of him. "Skin on skin baby, you know how much I like this." His hands worked their way up and down her back, pressing her closer to him.

"Can you sleep on the plane?"

"What did you say?"

"If I keep you up all night, can you sleep on the plane tomorrow?"

Ben hired a car to take them to McCarran. "Fly back with me. It won't be a problem for us to fly into Centennial, drop you off and then fly to Gunnison."

"I didn't realize you had your own plane when you said you were changing your flight." Liv sounded peevish.

"Well, it's not mine, it's the band's, and we share time with my folks. My dad's a pilot too."

That got her attention. "My dad was a pilot. Air Force."

"My father got his pilot's license in his twenties, to ferry my grandfather back and forth from Denver. He was never a military guy."

"Oh."

"You sound disappointed. Does it matter?"

No, it didn't matter. But Liv realized that outside of great sex and an undeniable mutual attraction, how much did they have in common?

Last night Ben insisted they talk about when they could see each other again. Liv had been evasive on purpose. He didn't think she believed him, did he? This was a fling, just sex. He didn't need to placate her by promising he'd call her. Did he think she was an idiot, or someone who wasn't sophisticated enough to recognize what this was?

"I thought we might have that in common," she shrugged.

Ben looked at Paige, who shrugged too.

"Look, it's a sweet offer, but we've got a car at DIA. Flying into Centennial will complicate things. Let's say goodbye here. It'll be easier that way."

Ben looked at Paige again. "I thought you said if I stayed another night she *wouldn't* be as grouchy."

Paige spit out her coffee as she laughed out loud.

"It isn't funny," Liv said, moving away from both of them. "I'll be back in a minute." She huffed off in the direction the ladies room.

"What...in...the...hell?" he looked to Paige. Granted, he might be used to getting his own way, maybe a little stubborn, and perhaps a tad controlling, but this woman wouldn't give *an inch*.

"Go easy on her, she's w-a-a-a-y out of her comfort zone with you. Let her be pissy, but like her anyway. She'll come around." Paige hesitated, "As long as you do."

"Is that it? She thinks I won't come around again?"

"She doesn't think it, she knows it, at least that's what she's convinced herself."

"How do you know all this? Did she get up in the middle of the night and call you?"

"No, she didn't. I know her. When I say she's out of her comfort zone, she isn't even on the same planet as her comfort zone when it comes to you. Cut her a little slack, understand what the motivation is behind her behavior. As I said, she'll come around as long as you do."

"Okay, ready Paige?" Liv touched Ben's arm, stood up on her tiptoes, and kissed his cheek. "Bye Ben, thanks for everything, I had a lot of fun. Come on Paige, let's go." Liv turned and was two feet away from him before he realized it.

Two long strides later he grabbed her around the waist and spun her back to him. "Oh no, we aren't doing *this* again. Come here baby." Ben's mouth covered hers. His hand held the back of her head close, so she couldn't break their kiss, until he was ready. His other arm came around and he squeezed her behind with his big hand. And then he released her.

"I'll talk to you later baby. Have a safe flight." With that he turned around and walked in the other direction.

Liv stood still, stunned, then looked at Paige. "Not. A. Word. Got it?"

"Got it," Paige giggled.

Twenty minutes into the flight Liv continued to behave as though nothing significant happened to her over the last couple of days. Paige was worried.

"You okay?" Paige wasn't sure whether she wanted to open the floodgates yet.

"I'm fine. Why do you ask?"

"I'm not playing this game. You know why I asked. Now start talking…tell me about Ben, about what's happened, about all of it."

"I'm not playing games Paige, when I say I'm fine, I mean it."

"Not buyin' it."

"Why not? Look, I lived out every woman's fantasy. I had a whirlwind romance with a guy completely out of my league. I had fantastic, mind-blowing sex, and then he offered to fly me home on his private plane. Why wouldn't I be fine?"

"Because you said goodbye to him."

"What does that have to do anything? I went into this with my eyes wide open. Not the first day, but you pointed out something to me that I hadn't considered. It changed my whole outlook."

"Which something?"

"That I hadn't had sex since Scott died. Do you realize how messed up that is? It's crazy abnormal in a freakishly weird way. And if it wasn't for Ben, who knows when, or if, I ever would've again. So, yeah, I repeat, I'm fine."

"No regrets, no self doubts, no wondering when you'll see him again?"

"None of the above. And as far as seeing him again, I have no intention of allowing that to happen."

Liv turned her face toward the window and closed her eyes. Every time she did, she saw Ben. Yes, she had an ache in her heart, but what good would it do to admit it, or allow herself to get absorbed by it? No good. Ben had a great big, exciting, bigger-than-life life. She had…her ranch. And there was nothing wrong with that, she was lucky to have it. But other than that, and an amazing daughter who was out creating her own life independent of her mother, there wasn't much more she brought to anyone's table.

"You don't fool me."

"Paige, please let it go."

"No I won't let it go. He wants to see you again, he said he did."

"To what end? What would be the point?" Paige made her angry. Why wouldn't she drop it?

"Why do you keep yourself on the outskirts of life? It breaks my heart. You are an amazing woman, and yet it seems as though you're done. You raised your daughter and now you're starting the descent. Your life isn't over Liv, it's just beginning. Why won't you let yourself take a chance with this guy? He seems to like you very much."

"Enough Paige! Why do you have to push me so hard? I had a great time. I had great sex. I didn't fall in love and I don't plan to, not ever again. Scott was it for me, the great love of my life. There, are you happy? You made me say it. Now leave me alone."

"Oh sweetie…" Paige tried to comfort her but Liv jerked her shoulder away.

Paige saw Liv's shoulders shaking, she'd brought her to tears. God, what kind of friend was she? Liv had been fine, but Paige had pushed her to the point where she wasn't fine anymore. Why hadn't she let it be?

Because she cared about her. Paige wanted Liv to realize what she was doing to herself. She doubted Liv would even go out if she and Mark didn't push her. They'd invite Liv somewhere, she'd refuse. Between her and Mark, they wouldn't let up on her until she gave in and went out with them.

Even this trip to Las Vegas, Liv wouldn't have gone if Paige hadn't pushed her to go. There needed to come a time when Liv decided for herself that she wanted back in the game of life. It shouldn't be up to Paige to force the issue.

Paige decided it would be best if she kept her mouth shut the rest of the flight. Liv didn't find it necessary to fill the silence. They were walking up the ramp from the plane to the terminal before Liv spoke.

"I'm sorry. I realize you mean well."

Paige sighed. She didn't want Liv to spend the rest of her life alone. It was up to Ben now. If he cared about Liv the way he said he did, Liv would hear from him.

***

Liv didn't want to tell Paige that when she turned her cell back on after the flight, there was a text from Ben, with a photo. And a voicemail from him, which she didn't intend to listen to until she got home.

He sent a picture of himself on the plane, pouting. And he wrote, *I'm not letting go of this Liv.*

She doubted their little fling amounted to much more than a blip on his radar. He probably kept a string of girls on the hook, one in every city—his hookup girls. She had no intention of being one of them. She wouldn't answer him, he'd lose interest, and go away.

Her phone beeped again, another text from him. *Hey baby, how was your flight? Miss you already.* Oh God, what was he doing? She powered down her phone and put it in her bag.

"Hear from him?"

"Nope and I don't expect to." She lied to Paige, and she didn't have any idea why.

***

She dropped her bags inside the back door and went straight to the barn. She wanted to ride as hard and fast and far as Micah would take her.

"Hey sweet boy," she said as she walked into the stall. "Let's ride, what do you say?" Micah, her lover boy, nuzzled up against her. "Did you miss me? I missed you." She scratched down his nose and led him out of the stall.

Ten minutes later she had him saddled up and out on the trail. From her hundred-acre ranch out County Line Road, she had a perfect view of Pikes Peak and the rest of the Front Range. There was nothing like the wide open spaces and blue skies of Colorado.

When her father retired he bought this ranch, knowing how much Liv wanted a horse of her own. He promised her that one day they would live in a place where she could. They were an Air Force family, and that meant they moved every two or three years. Having a horse, or even a dog, had been out of the question given the life they led. Liv's mother hadn't been keen on the idea of living so far outside of town. But the Black Forest community was a tight-knit one, and the loneliness she'd expected from their secluded location never materialized.

They made friends with other ranchers, and almost every weekend there was a social function either with them, or with other retired Air Force families.

Liv was a freshman in high school when they moved to Colorado twenty-six years ago. She left briefly when she and Scott married. Now she considered it home and never planned to leave.

Micah wound his way through the heavily-treed trail without much coaxing from Liv. Once they reached the top of the short incline, they came to a clearing and a wide-open meadow where he ran fast and hard.

"Ready boy?" she said, giving him a little kick, and Micah took off like a rocket. This was freedom. No worries, just her and her horse. She was thankful every day that her father bought this ranch.

Her parents died within a couple of years of each other. Her dad went first, ten years ago, followed by her mom. Liv still missed them. She had been an only child and very close to both her parents. Renie was the light of all their lives. Once her mom and dad passed away, the house was too quiet.

The ranch had no mortgage, and her parents left her a generous sum of money. Liv never had to worry about how she'd support herself and her daughter. But between the two of them, they decided to take in boarded horses anyway. It provided a bit of an income, but more, it provided company when the people boarding them came to ride.

One of the neighboring ranches was owned by a couple who had become a second family to Liv. The Pattersons had been leasing their ranch land for cattle since before Liv's father owned it. It added income, provided for the care and maintenance of the land, and it also gave them a little excitement. Calving season and branding gave her and Renie life experiences they wouldn't have otherwise known. Liv wasn't much of a ranch hand herself, but she would dish out a hot meal for the cowboys and wranglers at busy times of the year. Her pies became the dessert mainstay of Patterson Ranch barbecues.

She went to see if Dottie Patterson was home. She tied up Micah near the barn and walked in the back door.

"Hey-o, anybody here?" Liv never knocked first, Dottie would've been insulted if she had.

"In here, honey," Dottie called out from the kitchen.

Liv walked straight up to the woman, and let herself be surrounded by a hug like no one else gave but Dottie. Her eyes filled with tears.

"What's this?" Dottie asked, holding Liv at arms' length. "Sit down young lady and tell me why you're crying."

Liv sat, and proceeded to tell Dottie about Ben Rice, including the part about her not having sex since Scott died.

"Bill and I hoped one of the cowboys who worked our ranch would turn your head, but year after year it never happened. Not for lack of trying on their part either."

"What are you talking about? Whose part?"

"Well now…there have been a slew of 'em trying for years to get your attention."

"Who?"

"Billy Junior, but he gave up years ago, honey. You wouldn't even look in his direction. The Morehouse boy, what was his name?"

"Brandon."

"That's right, Brandon. He had a fierce crush on you. There were others."

Liv was stunned. She'd never known this.

"Are you sure you aren't talking about someone else?"

"No I'm not talking about someone else. I'm talking about you Olivia. You've never been aware of your own beauty, that's one of the things that makes you so irresistible. And from the day she was born, you've been wrapped up in being the best mama to Renie. But sweetie, we've worried about you not realizing there's more to life than that."

"Was I mean?"

Dottie laughed. "To the boys? A little. It made them want to follow you around all the more."

Liv hadn't been that interested in dating in high school, she'd already decided Scott was the only man for her. She supposed guys flirted with her, but she never paid attention.

"I didn't know."

"That was clear," Dottie chuckled again. "It's that way isn't it? The girls who do the chasin' the boys don't want. The girls who don't know boys exist, the boys can't get enough of."

And Then You Fall

Dottie put her palm on Liv's cheek. "You need to open your heart up a little. Let him in honey."

"Who? Ben? He doesn't want in Dottie. I'd be surprised if he contacted me again."

"You got your cell phone on you?"

"Yeah," she said, pulling it out of the pocket in her vest. "Is it on?"

She hadn't remembered to turn it back on since she'd gotten home. She hit the power button and set it down on the table.

It chirped. She had a new voice message, and a couple of text messages too. Liv picked up the phone to look. Her face turned red.

"That's what I thought. Ben called, didn't he?"

"Yes, but…"

"No darlin', no yes-buts. I'm gonna excuse myself for a few minutes. You listen to those messages and when I come back, you're gonna tell me what he said."

* * *

Ben didn't understand why Liv hadn't answered him. He was starting to believe she was avoiding him. Maybe she hadn't charged her phone. Her flight had landed a couple of hours ago. He figured she'd be home by now, although he had no idea how far it was from the airport to where she lived. It was somewhere between Denver and Colorado Springs, but that was all he knew.

He wished she would answer him, as it was, he couldn't think about anything else. This was uncharted territory for him, this woman was under his skin.

The door of his house flew open and Luke came running toward him followed by his brother.

"Daddy's home," Luke shouted. Ben lifted him and swung him around a couple of times before setting him down, grabbing Jake and doing the same thing.

Jake gave his dad an exasperated sigh, but Ben didn't care. You never got too old for your dad to show you he loved you. At least he hadn't. Ben's mom and dad walked in the door behind the boys.

"There he is," his mom said, giving him a squeeze and a kiss on the cheek. "We missed you around here."

Ben's dad hugged him too. They were a family who had never been shy about affection, and Ben loved it.

"Hey Dad, how are you?"

"I'm good, how were the bright lights of Las Vegas? Stayed a little longer than you thought, were you winnin' big?"

"No, I never have been a gambler."

His father looked deep into his eyes. His dad wouldn't ask, but Ben would answer anyway.

"Nothin' to report Dad. Life is good."

Ben's father put his hand on his shoulder. "Glad to hear."

They worried whenever he went on the road, and they were right to. The truth was, the time he spent with Liv, he hadn't thought about drinking at all. Even at the show. Ben wanted her, but he hadn't wanted a drink.

The boys were racing around him, each vying for his attention, telling him what they'd been doing. That morning his dad had taken them fishing, and his mom grilled up what they caught for lunch.

"There's a rodeo in Gunnison Dad. Can we go? This is the last year Luke can do mutton bustin'."

Luke was Ben's little Tasmanian devil, Jake was the more cautious of his boys. The older Luke got, the more trouble he'd get into, the same way Ben had. That worried him more than a little.

"Of course we can go. Are Grandma and Grandpa coming along?"

"You bet."

Ben pulled his cell phone out to check the time, and to see if he'd missed a call from Liv. He hadn't. "It's 2:30, what time do we have to be there?"

"Check-in's at 5:00," Jake answered. "Can we play PS3 until it's time to go?"

Ben laughed. "You can play PS3 for an hour, then you can play outside until it's time to go."

"Thanks Daddy," said Luke, climbing up Ben's leg to give him a kiss. Ben picked him up and hugged him close. "I missed you buddy."

"Me too. Put me down now Daddy, Jake's gonna pick out a game I don't want to play if you don't put me down."

"Okay, there you go pard'ner." He set Luke on his feet and turned back to his parents, who were studying him.

"What?" Ben looked behind him as if to ask what they were looking at.

"Good to see you son," his mom said, kissing his cheek for the second time.

"What's goin' on? I was away for a couple of days. You're both acting as though I away for a month."

"When you changed your flight plan, I have to admit, it made your mom and me worry."

"It's not what you think."

"What is it then?"

"I met someone."

Chapter Five

One of the new texts on her phone was from Ben. The others were from Paige and Renie. Paige wanted to make sure Liv was still speaking to her. Renie wanted to know how she enjoyed Las Vegas. Where to begin? How much did she tell her daughter?

Ben's said, *Are you okay? Answer me Liv. Please.* His voicemails said much of the same. But hearing it, rather than reading it, made it different. There was longing in his voice. He said he couldn't stop thinking about her, couldn't wait to see her again, couldn't wait to have her body next to his. Then he sang a little.

Liv put her elbows on the table and leaned her face into her hands. She didn't know what to do, or how to respond to him. Did he want her to pick up and drive to Crested Butte? He hadn't said anything specific. What did he expect?

Dottie shuffled back in and sat down next to her. "So?"

"He said he can't wait to see me again."

"And?"

"That's about it."

"What are you going to do about it?"

"I have no idea."

Liv rode Micah home, brushed him down and went into her house for the first time in several days. Mark had left the mail on the kitchen counter and watered her plants. She opened up the refrigerator, but nothing appealed to her to eat. When was the last time she ate? She thought about opening a bottle of wine, but considering she had an empty stomach, decided that wouldn't be a good idea.

Her cell phone was in her pocket. It hadn't made any new noises, but that didn't mean she'd forgotten about it, nor had she forgotten the unanswered messages it contained. She pulled it out and called Renie.

"Hey Mom, how was Vegas?"

"Good. Relaxing. We went to a CB Rice show while we were there."

"And?"

"And what?" What the heck? Had she been talking to Paige?

"Did he see you?"

Yep, he saw her. All of her.

"Mom, are you there?"

"I'm here. We, um, spent time together."

"What? You and Ben?"

"Me and Ben. We went out on a couple of, um, dates."

"Did you sleep with him?"

"Renie! That is not an appropriate question to ask me!"

"Why not Mom? Jeez. I'm not a kid anymore."

"It's complicated."

"So you did. Good."

"Renie, honey, so you realize this up front. I am not as interested in discussing your sex life as you seem to be in mine. Just because we're having this conversation, doesn't mean I'm opening the door to details. On either side."

Renie laughed, and kept laughing. "Got it Mom. I'm glad you had fun. When are you seeing him again?"

That was the million dollar question, wasn't it?

They were halfway to Gunnison when Ben's cell phone rang.

"Hey."

"Hi Ben. It's Liv. I'm sorry it took me so long to get back to you."

"It's okay. Well, it's not okay. Are you home?"

"I am. I didn't even go in the house when I got here. I went straight out to the barn and went for a ride."

"The barn? A ride? Do you have a horse?" She hadn't told him she had a horse. Had he asked her anything about herself? They'd talked about her daughter, but other than that, he knew nothing about her. Wait, her dad had been a pilot in the military, had she said Air Force?

"I have two. One belongs to Renie, but since she's away at college, I have two. Micah's mine. He's not very old, so he needs a lot of exercise. Micah likes to get out and run. I also board horses."

"As a matter of fact, I'm on my way right now to a rodeo, in Gunnison."

"Oh, I should let you go then. Take care Ben."

"Hold on, hold on, don't go hanging up yet. I told you so you realized we had something else in common. You seemed worried about it at the airport."

Ben realized the four other people in the Tahoe with him were listening to every word he said.

"Hey, it might be better if I call you back, since I'm driving and all. When I do, will you answer?"

Liv was quiet, so quiet he thought the call had dropped. "Liv, are you there?"

"I'm here." She went quiet again. "Um, it might be best if you didn't. I have a lot to get caught up on with the ranch, and I'm tired. It'll be an early night for me and a busy few days."

Ranch? She had a ranch? What an asshole. No wonder she didn't want to talk to him, he hadn't bothered to find out anything about her, he'd been too busy getting into her panties.

"Give me a half an hour. You'll still be awake then, won't you?"

"Ben..."

"A half an hour Liv and I'll call you back."

He parked the truck after letting his parents and boys off at the main entrance. "You go get checked in and I'll meet you," he said. The truth was he was so anxious to call Liv back, he wanted them out of the truck, a fact not lost on his mom and dad.

The phone rang three times before she answered. Ben was almost beside himself by the time she did.

"It is so good to hear your voice."

"Yours too."

"I'm sorry I couldn't talk earlier. My parents and the boys were in the truck. Every word I said was the most interesting thing they'd ever heard," he chuckled.

"It's okay. I bet they missed you."

"They did. But Liv, I miss *you*."

"Ben, I'm not sure what to say. I had a nice time, but now we're back to our own lives. We shouldn't get into the habit of talking to each other."

"What? We shouldn't get into the habit of talking to each other?" Getting angry would push her away, but he couldn't help it. She pissed him off. "I'm sorry I raised my voice Liv, but Jesus. Are you serious?"

She didn't respond.

"Liv, come on, don't do this."

"I'm not doing anything. We had fun."

"Did you want to say, 'but now it's over'?"

"How could something that didn't start be over? It's not over. It's…I don't know what. It just isn't."

"It isn't? It's not anything to you? It's something to me."

"Ben, go be with your kids. Enjoy your night at the rodeo. Enjoy your life."

Regardless of what he said next, she'd say goodbye. And then if he called again, would she even pick up?

"I can't let go of this Liv. You think you want me to, but I can't. More than that, I won't. So I may hang up now, but tomorrow, I'll call you again, and if you don't answer, I'll keep calling until you do."

"And what if I don't ever answer?"

"You will." He hung up, if he hadn't he might have resorted to begging to come see her. Ben's boys were with him until Monday morning. He'd give her a couple of days, and call her then. If he was able to last that long. For the first time in several days, he wanted a drink.

Liv locked the back door and went into the bedroom. It was too early to try to go to sleep, if she did, she'd be wide awake at 3:00 am. But there wasn't anything she wanted to do. She turned on the television, but nothing interested her. She picked up her iPad to read. She wasn't interested in reading either. She swiped the music icon with her finger, and Ben's voice sang to her.

You've had a rough day,
Why don't I turn out the light.
Let down your hair,
It's gonna be alright.
If you need me to dry your tears,
Baby I'll be right here.
Good night blue eyes,
May your dreams come true.
Good night blue eyes,
I love you.

Oh God, what had she done? Why did she have sex with him? Why had she let herself get involved with him? Her ache of loneliness had been manageable before, she'd gotten to the point where she hardly noticed it. Now it was all she noticed.

She was alone, by choice. She could not let herself risk falling in love again. When she loved people, they left her. Ben might say he wanted to see her again, but he didn't realize that it would matter more to her than it would to him.

* * *

Liv had what sounded like country music playing when Paige walked into the barn Monday morning. It wasn't a CB Rice song.

"Hell-o, Liv, are you in here?"

Liv came out of the stall at the end of the barn. She was filthy. "Hey Paige, how are you? I'd hug you but..."

"Not necessary. What in the world are you doing?"

"Cleaning the stall, I have a new horse coming in at the end of the week. Might as well get ready now."

"You didn't call me back this weekend."

"I'm sorry. I should have answered you."

"Are we okay?"

"We're fine." Liv walked closer to Paige and sat down on one of the barn stools. "I needed time to myself."

"You have too much time to yourself. That's the problem."

Liv gave Paige a look.

"I'm not intimidated by you, other people are, but I'm not. I have things to say, and you need to listen."

"When, tell me, when have I ever *not* listened to you? Jeez Paige, you're one of the few people I do listen to."

"Have you talked to Ben?"

"We talked on Friday."

"Did you make plans?"

"Paige, we just got home! It hasn't been a week. No, we didn't make plans."

"Did he say he'd call again?"

"No. I mean, I thought he'd call again over the weekend. But he didn't. You know how the saying goes, 'be careful what you wish for.'"

"And what did you wish for?"

"To never see him again."

Paige sat down on one of the other stools. "Oh, honey, why not?"

Liv looked as though she was about to cry. Paige walked over to hug her.

"I'm a mess, you don't want to hug me."

"I'm sure you have something I can change into after I decide I no longer want to smell like a horse. Come here."

"This is stupid. I expected it. I shouldn't be this upset. What would a man like him want with a woman like me?"

"Isn't it a little early in the game to call it?"

Liv pulled back. Paige sat back down on her stool.

"I pushed him away hard Paige."

"And has that worked before?"

"Before? What before? We don't have a before."

"You tried to push him away in Vegas, and from what I remember, it didn't work."

"That was different."

"All I'm saying is give it a few days."

"And then what? What will be different? I'm still somebody he slept with while he was 'on tour,' or whatever he calls it. I'm sure he's forgotten my name by now."

Ben picked up the phone to call Liv at least a hundred times over the weekend, and each time he set it back down. He missed her so much his chest ached. He'd never missed anyone this much, besides his boys when they weren't with him. When he dropped them off this morning, the ache multiplied.

He hated that he was divorced, and that his boys didn't have the same family life he had. Ben and his brothers had been given the gift of a home in which his parents loved each other, and them, more than anything. There had never been a doubt in his mind that his parents would love each other and be together until the day one of them died. He had failed in creating that for his boys.

Ben supposed he'd loved Christine at one point. If it had been up to him, they'd still be married. They'd be miserable, but they'd still be married. He was thankful she still lived in Crested Butte, that way the boys didn't get shuffled back and forth too awful much.

Christine had remarried, not long after their divorce was final. Her new husband was a good guy. Joe wasn't from Colorado, they'd met skiing, and soon after, he moved to Crested Butte. Ben didn't even know what the guy did for a living. It didn't matter what the courts said, Ben would continue to provide for her and his boys, whether she remarried or not. He wanted his sons to have a nice place to live, the same sense of security, whether they were at their mother's house or his.

Christine made sure the boys spent time with him when he was in town. When they were married, he played clubs every weekend of the month. Now that they were divorced, he wanted to spend as much time at home with his boys as he could. It was a tough balance to maintain.

They wouldn't be back for a week. Christine and Joe were taking them to the Grand Canyon for Spring Break, the trip had been planned for six months. He didn't want them to go. He'd be lonely without them.

Ben had seven days with nowhere he needed to be and nothing he needed to do, and all he thought about was Liv. He liked her, a lot. He wanted to get to know her, spend time with her. The fact that she didn't seem to want to see him, made the urge to win her over even stronger. It was crazy, more than a little rash, but he was doing it anyway.

An hour later he was on the road. He wasn't sure where she lived, but he'd find out. If she didn't want to see him—well, he wouldn't accept that. He had no intention of giving up that easily.

***

Micah jumped the fence into the main pasture with little effort. They'd had a good ride, much more fun than her ride on Pooh had been. Pooh was getting older, and Liv didn't ride her enough. She planned to give one of the neighbors a call this afternoon to ask if one of her grand kids would consider riding the horse for her. She'd even pay them. That way, Pooh would get the exercise she needed, with the kind of rider she was used to, someone more like Renie.

Two more months and Renie would be home for the summer. Liv couldn't wait. This was Renie's last summer before graduation. Liv planned to talk to her about an extended vacation this weekend, but they'd kept missing each other's calls. She hoped they'd be able to catch up soon.

Liv took Micah's saddle and other tack off. She'd let him relax in the pasture for a while and brush him later. She opened the gate, walked around the corner, and slammed the saddle right into Ben's stomach.

"Ow! Shit, that hurt."

"Oh! You scared me. I'm so sorry." Liv dropped the saddle to the ground and was about to make sure Ben was okay when her tummy did a little flip. "Wait. What are you doing here?"

Ben grabbed her and crushed his lips to hers. He didn't try to hold back. He wanted her, and she wanted him. He'd planned to be sensible, to be civilized, to have a rational conversation with her. But now that she was in his arms he wanted to mark her, possess her, consume her.

Liv's hands fisted in his shirt, pulling him closer to her. Ben pulled back abruptly. Her eyes were wide, he couldn't tell if it was from arousal, or from fear. His hand lifted and caressed her cheek. Her lips were red and full from his assault. "I couldn't wait."

"I'm so glad you didn't." She took his hand, leading him away from the barn and pasture.

"What about…" he pointed to the saddle and out toward the horse in the pasture.

"They'll be fine."

Liv's house wasn't exactly modest. But any thoughts of nervousness about his seeing where she lived were squashed by her desire to get him inside and naked as quickly as possible. She'd been crazy to think she'd last even another day without seeing him. She wanted to rip his clothes from his body before they reached the back door.

Once inside he kissed her again, deep, open-mouthed kisses. His fingers trailed down the side of her neck, over her collarbone. He reached up and unfastened the top buttons on her shirt, rubbing the curve of her breast.

Without words, she led him into her bedroom. His eyes took in the openness of it. Big windows looked out at the prairie, and a massive two-sided stone fireplace separated the bedroom from the master bath. An enormous king-size bed looked too high for Liv to be able to climb into. He put his arm around the back of her knees and back lifting her, laying her down on the fluffy cream-colored duvet. It puffed up around her.

He toed off his boots and lay next to her, drawing back to look into her eyes. She unfastened her buttons, finishing what he had started. He pushed the open shirt over her shoulders, and she took her arms out of it.

"So beautiful. You're so beautiful for me, aren't you?" He kissed her mouth softly, reverently.

She stared up at him, at his big blue eyes, his long thick eyelashes, the stubble of darkness on his strong chin. She ran her hand along it. He smiled and the corners of his eyes crinkled. He smiled often, he had laugh lines. Her body tingled all the way from where his lips met hers to her toes. Ben's powerful leg stretched over the top of hers, his hardness pressing into her hip. Her other hand reached for him.

His kisses grew stronger, in a frenzied hunger. Every nerve ending in her body hummed, throbbing, heat rushed through her veins. "Ben," she breathed.

They broke apart, each removing their own clothes. His hand came back to her hair, tipping her head back, he kissed his way over her lips, to her chin, then throat, then to her breasts. His breath was warm on her stomach as he continued working his way down her body.

Sensation sizzled across her skin, an inferno built inside her. She gave a whimper and in a flash he was inside her, once again she had no idea when he had donned a condom.

"Don't move," he whispered. "Shh, be still, let me feel you."

Liv ached to move against him. Slowly he started to move again. Too slowly. She arched to him and he moved faster, harder, slamming himself into her. Pleasure began to flow from the center of her out to her fingertips and toes. A coiling tension rose inside her. He took her higher and higher until she burst with a sweet sensation flooding her, she cried out.

"That's it, oh Liv," Ben groaned as he came apart with her.

They stayed that way, both stopped moving, slumped together in the softness of the duvet. Her head was spinning as his lips begin to work their way back up the side of her neck. They continued beneath her ear, across her chin, and up to brush back over her lips. "Liv," he breathed, as though it was a prayer. He kissed each of her eyelids, then back to her mouth, where he kissed each corner.

"How did you find my house?"

"It's a secret."

"Paige?"

"As long as you won't be mad, yes, Paige."

"How long can you stay?"

"All week. Or as long as you'll have me."

"We'll see how it goes," she said as she moved to stretch out on top of him, skin on skin, body on body. "I need to go take care of Micah. Can I interest you in a ride later? Around sunset?"

"Sounds like heaven." He didn't say that anything would sound like heaven as long as he was with her. He wanted her, and he planned to have her. He was into this deeper than she was. By the end of the week, he'd change that.

Chapter Six

When they rode that night, they saw Dottie and Bill over the crest, sitting by the campfire. Bill stood up and waved at them.

"You don't mind do you? They're family to me."

"Don't mind at all. If they mean something to you, there isn't anybody I'd rather meet."

It took them ten minutes to make their way down the rocky terrain. It was almost dark. Liv decided if they stayed for any length of time, they'd leave the horses in the Patterson barn overnight. Bill would give them a lift home.

They tied the horses off, and walked over to the fire. Bill had chairs set up for them, and a bottle of wine open.

"Bill and Dottie, I'd like you to meet Ben Rice."

"Pleasure to meet you," Ben reached out and shook Bill's hand. Dottie stood up and when he tried to shake her hand she pulled him in for one of her big hugs.

"I don't shake hands, Mr. Rice. Men will judge you by your handshake. I like to see what you young fellas have in the way of a good strong hug. Tells you a lot about a man."

"Nobody hugs the way Dottie does," Liv added.

"You don't do too bad yourself sugar," Ben stooped down and kissed her forehead.

"I like him already," proclaimed Dottie.

"Glass of wine Liv? How about you Ben?"

"Sure, I'd love a glass. Especially now that I see what you're pouring."

"Dottie had me run in the house to get it when we saw you comin'. Livvie here loves Zinfandel. We keep it on hand for her. Before she taught us about wine we thought Zinfandel was the pink stuff. I thought she'd have a fit the first time we tried to serve it to her."

"That's me, always gracious," Liv turned ten shades of pink.

"We love you anyway darlin' girl." Bill pulled her close to him. "When Livvie lost her parents so close together, Dottie and I adopted her. She's one of our own. You better keep that in mind young man."

She'd lost her parents? Another thing he hadn't known about her. He should start making a list of questions, so he didn't feel like such a jerk when someone else pointed out something he should already know.

"How about you Ben, can I get you a glass?"

"No, thank you, don't touch the stuff."

"Well, can I get you a beer then?"

"No, sorry. I'm not a drinker. If you've got a coke or a bottle of water, I'll be fine."

He turned toward Liv. There was a flash of confusion on her face. She quickly masked it away. And that was something he hadn't told her. Not that she'd asked. It hadn't seemed as though it was a big deal when they were in Las Vegas. She had a drink here and there, and it hadn't been necessary to point out to her that he abstained.

"Have a seat you two, make your selves comfortable."

An hour into their campfire and several rounds of s'mores later, Bill asked Ben to help him with the horses. "They're better off sleeping in our barn tonight Livvie."

Great minds, she thought, but didn't say anything.

The Pattersons were the only people who called her Livvie. She didn't remember when it started, but she loved it. It made her feel special, as though she was really a part of their family. Liv would've been lost without Dottie and Bill. They didn't remind her of her parents necessarily, they were bigger, louder, more openly affectionate versions of her mom and dad.

"How'd you and Livvie meet?" Bill asked Ben while they were getting the horses settled.

"Fate kept throwing us together and we started paying attention." Ben told Bill about meeting her at Red Rocks, and again at his family's bar in Crested Butte. He told him about bumping into her at the pool in Las Vegas, but that's as far as he took the story.

"So did you come back with her from Las Vegas then?"

"Nope, I went home first, to Crested Butte, spent a couple days with my boys, then got here this afternoon. I surprised her."

"Boys?"

"I have two. Jake is twelve and Luke is nine. Before you ask, I'm divorced."

"I guess I'm transparent when it comes to my kids, and I consider Livvie one of 'em. She's not an easy one to get a fix on. Plenty boys 'round here would tell you that. My own son had a mad love on her for years. He gave up, not for lack of trying." Bill chuckled. "Either she's real good at playing like she doesn't notice somethin' or she was clueless all them years." He thought for a minute before he continued. "But don't go thinkin' she's not smart as a whip son, she's one of the brightest women I've ever had the pleasure to know. Sad that she lost her husband so young. Renie wasn't even born yet."

Ben wanted to ask more. How did he tell Bill that he was staying at Liv's house, but didn't know about her husband, her parents, or even where she grew up?

"Did Livvie tell you Scott was shot down in the Gulf War? They'd only been married a few months. Tragic. I gotta tell you, for a long while I thought that man held her heart for good. We thought that was why she didn't pay any attention to men trying to catch her eye. Guess we were wrong."

Tonight, tomorrow, the day after that, he planned to get to know her. As much as she would let him.

"You're awful quiet."

"She's a remarkable woman. One I want to spend as much time with as I can. I appreciate all you've told me Bill."

"You care about her then?"

"I do."

"Then you'll be all right with Dottie and me."

They walked back down to the campfire. Dottie and Liv were snuggled up under a blanket. Liv had her head rested on Dottie's shoulder.

Ben stroked her cheek with his finger. "Tired?"

"Content would be a better word." Liv stood up and put her arms around his waist. "Let's head back to my house."

"You got it."

Bill handed Ben a set of keys. "You take the old Ford. I'll come get it in the mornin'."

"Thanks Dottie. Thanks Bill. I'm glad you got to meet Ben."

"We are too. Ben, how long you in town for?"

"Through the weekend. If she'll have me."

"Well if she lets you stay, I expect the two of you for dinner on Friday night. You can take her out on Saturday. That's date night after all."

"I'll do that. Good night both of you, it's been a pleasure, and thanks again."

"Can you drive a stick shift?" Liv asked him as they walked up to the driveway.

"You're kidding right?"

"Does that mean yes?"

"That means *of course*. I have to get you back to Crested Butte. You don't seem to have any idea how much of a good ol' boy you've gotten yourself mixed up with."

"I noticed you didn't have any trouble finding your seat on a horse."

"Did I pass a test tonight?"

"You did. With flying colors."

"Will there be more?"

"Lots more cowboy."

The next day Ben followed Liv around like a combination between a newspaper reporter and a lost puppy. He wanted to know everything about her, and didn't want to let her out of his sight.

By dinner time, she was exhausted. They ate, cleaned up, and sat in the family room. "This house is spectacular," Ben said, looking up at the cathedral ceilings and the rafters that looked as though they'd come from an old barn. "Did your father build it?"

"No more talking Ben," she pulled him to the couch, and pushed him down. She put her hands on either side of his head and sat down, straddling his lap. He pulled her in and kissed her deeply. His arms went around her and pushed her over so her back was up against the arm of the sofa. "You're trying to distract me."

"Are you writing a book Ben? Is this a 'This is Your Life,' interview?"

"I want to know everything about you. He pushed the bottom of her shirt up, and put his hand on her breast. "I want to memorize every curve of your body, and every nuance of your soul baby."

"Let's focus on the body for the rest of the night, okay?"

"You got it." He nuzzled under her ear and breathed in the scent of her. "You smell so good I want to bottle you and keep you with me all the time."

"Ben." That one word, his name and the way she said it, and he wanted to devour her. He kissed her hard, pushing her into the sofa. His hands roamed wherever they reached, his body strained to get closer to hers.

Fingers fumbled with buttons and zippers. Ben reared back from her. "Bedroom." He pulled himself up, he reached under her back and knees, picking her up as if she was no more than a pillow in his powerful arms. He carried her in and stood her by the bed. He broke their heart-stopping kiss to finish undressing her. When she stood before him naked he said, "Now me."

Liv's hands pulled at his shirt, trying to get it off over his head. "Lean down," she breathed. Her hands were on his belt, pulling it loose, grabbing at the button on his jeans and pulling down the zipper.

He threw his head back. She leaned forward and licked across his throat, down over his nipples to his sternum. Ben groaned, "Need you now baby, so bad."

Her mouth slammed into his, cutting short his demands. His rough hands cupped her bottom and lifted her. Her legs automatically circled his waist. "Wait," he said, lowering her to the bed. He reached for a condom.

"I wondered about that, how you got them on so quickly, I thought you had a magic trick."

His mouth was hard on hers again, picking her back up, putting his hands on the back of her thighs helping her circle his waist again. "Shh, no talking, remember?"

With a quick snap of his hips, he was inside her. "Hold on to me," he demanded. Liv wrapped her arms around his neck. He thrust hard again and again, holding her firmly against him with both hands. He started humming, the deep vibration of his voice spread through her and she trembled.

"Come fly with me baby. Fly apart for me." Liv gasped at his words and cried out, her body spasming around his. "Take me with you Liv." He groaned deeply, then held her very still and lowered her to the bed.

As soon as her head stopped spinning she opened her eyes, and he was gone. The bed shifted as he lay back down beside her.

"Wow."

"Liv, can I ask you something?"

She rolled to her stomach and groaned. "I thought we agreed, no more talking."

"This is different. I don't want anything to come between us. I don't want to use a condom when we're together."

Liv hesitated. "I'm not on birth control Ben."

He put his arm across her back and kissed her shoulder. "Do you want to be?"

"By the time I do…"

"Finish the sentence Liv."

"We might not be together any longer."

Ben rolled to his back and looked up at the ceiling, taking a deep breath and trying to gather his thoughts before he spoke. Liv hadn't moved. "Have I given you the impression I wasn't in this all the way?"

"No, I guess not."

"Then why are you so hell bent on ending this thing between us?"

Liv had to answer him, Ben would keep at her until she did. "I'm very independent Ben."

"Oh baby," he pulled her until she was stretched out on top of him, her head resting on his chest. "I'm not letting go of this Liv. I haven't felt this way for a very long time. I'm not sure I've ever felt this way. I want to be with you every chance I get. Can you please accept that and quit fighting me on it?"

"I can try."

"That's all I can ask of you. But Liv?"

"Yeah?"

"I want you to try a whole heck of a lot harder, okay? I want you to let go, let yourself fall for me."

"I'll give it my best shot."

"Repeat after me, 'Ben, I will let myself fall for you."

Silence. "Come on Liv, do it. Repeat after me."

"Ben, I will let myself fall for you."

"There, that wasn't so hard. Now keep repeating it in that beautiful head of yours."

"I'll try Ben. I promise I will."

He waited until her breathing got more even. She fell asleep splayed out on top of him. His heart surged with joy. No more sleepin' alone, that's what he was after with her. He sensed the road to it wouldn't be an easy one, but she was worth whatever it took to get them there.

He closed his eyes and let himself drift to sleep.

***

Ben wanted to make time stand still, the week sped by too quickly. Wednesday night they went out for dinner in town with Paige and Mark, and then back to their house. Ben had an acoustic guitar with him, and he and Mark went off on their own to jam for a while.

"Was he on his way when we were in the barn Monday morning?"

"No, he called after I left your place. I wouldn't have lied to you about it. He wanted to surprise you, so you wouldn't tell him not to come, and so he got an honest reaction out of you when you did see him." Paige poured Liv another glass of wine.

"He doesn't drink."

"I noticed that when we were in Las Vegas."

"I didn't."

"You were too busy paying attention to what the rest of his body was doing."

Liv blushed. "Don't get me wrong, it doesn't bother me, but he hasn't talked about it. He doesn't talk much about himself at all. He asks me plenty of questions though."

"He wants to get to know you better."

"But it's as though he wants to know everything right this minute. Why is he in such a hurry? It's not natural…he's forcing it."

"Have you told him that's the way you feel."

Liv shook her head. "And that's the other thing, I'm not used to having to tell somebody 'how I feel,' all the time. I'm used to being alone Paige. All this togetherness…"

"How long is he staying?"

"Through the weekend, he says. His boys are on vacation with their mom and step-dad."

"That's a lot of together time for you, isn't it?"

Liv didn't answer. Her problem was that she liked it, the togetherness. Even after just a couple of days, she liked waking up with him, spending the day together, being a couple.

"What's he say?"

"About being together? That he wants us to do it as much as we can. I don't know how that looks, or how it feels, or what his expectations are."

"You should try asking a few questions of your own."

Liv woke up before Ben did the next morning, got a pot of coffee going, and went out to the barn to feed the horses. Yesterday he had helped her, today she wanted time alone with her routine.

She stroked Micah's nose as she led him out of the stall. "Let's get you outside this morning. We'll take a ride a little later." She threw the lead up and over Micah's withers. "What do you think of him? Seems okay, right? And when he leaves, you'll still be here for me, won't ya boy?"

Ben stood right outside the barn door, listening to Liv confide in her horse. It sounded more as though she expected him to leave permanently, not just leave at the end of the week. He wasn't sure how to convince her he wanted more.

Only time would show her that. A week ago they were in Las Vegas, and he was trying to convince her he wanted to see her again. It was hard to imagine it had only been a week ago.

He was so impatient when it came to her. The more she resisted, the harder he pushed. He didn't understand it himself, how could he explain it to her?

He came around the corner and cleared his throat. "Mornin'," he said as he wrapped his arms around her waist and kissed her cheek. "I was lonely when I woke up and you were gone."

"You used to having a woman next to you every morning when you wake up Ben?"

Ouch. He hadn't expected that from her. "No, can't say as I am. I can say though, that these last couple of mornings I liked waking up next to you. Not any woman Liv, you."

Liv pulled away from him, leading Micah toward the panel door at the back of the barn. "Be back in a minute."

Ben guessed that meant she didn't want him to follow her. He went in the opposite direction, got his guitar out of the back of his Tahoe, and sat on the deck.

The view was spectacular from the deck that wrapped all the way around the back of the house. In one direction were the big trees that made up the Black Forest, in the other direction, prairie. On a clear day, Ben would bet you could see all the way to Kansas, and most days in Colorado were clear.

He sat down and started strumming his guitar. This is what he wanted to do when he was alone. Liv was probably used to quiet mornings taking care of her horses. He'd give her space, he understood her need for it.

Besides her daughter, Liv had lived alone since her mother died. Ben hadn't found out how long ago that had been yet, but he decided that today he'd stop asking her questions and start telling her more about himself. For now, he'd play his guitar. There was a song inside him, itching to get out.

A while later, maybe as long as an hour, he heard her moving around in the kitchen. As tempted as he was to go in and wrap himself around her, he stayed put. He'd let her come to him when she was ready. His yellow pad was full of lyrics and notes, the song he was working on was coming together.

"Whatcha' doin'?" Liv sat down on the arm of the Adirondack chair next to him.

"There's my girl." Ben put his hand around the back of her neck, and pulled her closer. His lips covered hers. What he intended to be a chaste and simple kiss, turned into something much hotter.

He pulled back. "I'm sorry, I do that a lot, don't I?"

"Do what? Kiss me? Don't be sorry, I like it."

"I'm an affectionate guy. My mom and dad were. Still are. They never held back showin' each other how much they cared. They never held back with me or my brothers either. Not everybody is used to that I guess."

"It's okay. I like it."

"But you're not used to it."

"Ben I've been alone a long, long time. I've been alone a lot more than I've been with somebody. My husband died before I had a chance to learn how to live with somebody that way. My mom and dad loved each other, and me. But you're right, they weren't as openly affectionate as even Dottie and Bill are."

"I like being here with you Liv."

"I like having you here."

Ben raised his eyebrows at her, set his guitar down, and patted his lap. "Come here." He pulled her down on this lap and snuggled her into him.

"This isn't a normal way of going about courtin' you, I admit that. I should be callin' you up, askin' you out on a date, givin' you a few days in between to decide whether you like me or not. But it hasn't been that way between us, has it? And now here I am, invadin' your space, not givin' you much choice about it."

Liv didn't say anything. She ran her finger up and down the back of his hand, lost in thought.

"Do you want me to leave?" He hated to ask, he was afraid she'd say she did. He got here on Monday and dug his heels in, telling her he was staying rather than waiting for her to ask him to stay. He held his breath, waiting for her to answer.

"No, I want you to stay."

He let the breath out, so relieved he started to laugh. "God—what you do to me girl."

"I don't know how to do this. I've never done anything like this. I've never had a man come and stay with me. Ben—wow, this is harder to say than I thought it would be. I should tell you…" She wanted to jump up, run into the house, lock the door, and never have to look at him again. Once the words were out of her mouth, he'd look at her in a whole new light, and not a favorable one. "I haven't been with another man since Renie's father, and that was a long, long time ago."

Ben tightened his arm around her shoulder, keeping her next to him. Her muscles strained, but he wouldn't let her go. How did he say this? He was as torn. "I know."

"You do?" She tried to pull away from him again, and he held her tighter.

"It wasn't anything you did, or didn't do. Don't go getting all insecure on me. It was a feeling. I can't explain it."

"It's the re-virgin thing."

"The what?" He saw her smile, he hadn't hurt her.

"I told Paige it had been so long since I had sex I was a re-virgin."

His leaned his head back and laughed, one of his big Ben laughs. It warmed her soul and she started to relax. "Hungry?"

"Starving. Guess what I want to do?"

"What?"

"I want to cook in that *fan-spacular* kitchen you've got in there. I've been *jonesin'* for it since I saw it." Ben nudged her off his lap, and they went inside.

"You're on cowboy. I'm going to give Paige a call and invite her to join us, if that's okay with you. Paige usually has breakfast here with me a couple times a week. She's staying away on purpose."

"Please Liv, it's your house, you don't need to check with me before you invite somebody to breakfast. Does Mark usually come along?

"Sometimes. Would you like me to invite him too?"

"Yeah, I would." Ben started to chuckle. "Mark's one of the funniest guys I've ever met. I had a good time last night at their place."

"Most people say that. And you're right. I spend most of the time I'm with him laughing so hard that my stomach aches by the end of the night." Liv hugged him.

"What's that for? Although, you never need a reason to wrap yourself around me."

"You like my friends."

"Baby, I like a lot more than your friends."

Chapter Seven

"We should go out and do something today since it's going to be warm and sunny. Away from the ranch I mean," Liv said as Ben and Mark were clearing the dishes. "I have a new horse coming in tomorrow to board. I should be here most of the day, to make sure he's settled."

"And tomorrow night we're having dinner with Bill and Dottie. Is that still on?"

"Yep, Dottie left a message on my cell asking us to be there at six."

"Whatever you want to do is fine with me baby."

Paige got up from the table and motioned for Liv to follow her. They walked out on the deck, and Paige closed the door behind her.

"What? What's going on Paige?"

"I had to get out of there before I opened my big mouth and stuck my foot in it."

"Why? What's wrong?"

"Nothing's wrong. You are such a…couple."

Liv swatted at her. "Oh, stop it. We are not."

"But you are. Making plans, figuring out your day. 'Whatever you want do is fine with me baby.'" Paige mimicked him.

"He's being polite. Stop it." Liv got up to go back in the kitchen.

"Wait. It's nice to see you this way."

"It's nice to feel this way." Liv turned and closed back the door. "I won't like it when he leaves."

"You'll cross that bridge when you get to it. Enjoy your time with him, and then make plans for the next time you'll be together."

"But what if—"

"Really? You're going to go there?"

"No, I guess I better not."

Since it was unseasonably dry and warm for late-March, Ben and Mark made a plan to take Mark's Jeep up Mount Herman Road. They were like two little boys when they talked about it.

"What do you say? Liv? Paige?"

"Liv will be in, I will not," announced Paige. "I have too much to do anyway. Go enjoy yourselves."

"Liv, you're sure you want to go?" Ben asked.

"Liv loves to ride in the back of an open Jeep and get all dirty, don't ya?" Paige answered for her.

"Nothing I like more than getting dirty," she answered with a wink.

After a late lunch, they decided to take another road back into Rampart Reservoir and survey the fire damage from the wildfires the summer before. They toured Eagle Lake, the camp Renie had gone to every year. Signs of the fire's devastation surrounded the camp, yet the cabins, outbuildings and main lodge were spared. Even the trees surrounding the buildings and the lake showed no signs of fire. Liv was astounded.

The road they planned to take back was closed. Mark pulled over and put the cloth top back on the Jeep, so they'd have a more comfortable ride home. Before they got on the road again, Mark popped a CD into the player. A CB Rice CD.

"One of my favorite people gave me this CD," Mark told Ben. "I like it, but she *lurves* it, so I'm humoring her."

Mark turned toward her. "Been on their Facebook page? How about Twitter?"

Liv wanted to throttle him. Mark was the world's biggest tease. Sometimes he went too far, not realizing how much he was embarrassing the target of his playful joking. Liv wanted to pull her hat over her head, and crawl onto the floor.

No one spoke. Mark laughed nervously. Ben didn't know what to say. It was cute that she liked his Facebook page. It wasn't a surprise, he'd seen her name, and her picture. He didn't want to freak her out then by friending her, but he'd thought about it. That was after he met her again in Crested Butte, but before Vegas. He'd noticed her on Twitter too. He wondered if she read his posts.

"W-e-e-l-l, I guess I said the wrong thing," Mark tried to joke it away.

"Have you Liv?" Ben figured the best way to make her more comfortable was to talk about it.

"I haven't." She hadn't even thought about it. Why would she? He was *with* her. Ben reached over from the back seat and rubbed her shoulders. She remained silent the rest of the way home.

"It's nothing to be embarrassed about," Ben said after Mark dropped them off at her house.

"You must think I'm a stalker."

"Why? Were you?" Ben tickled her. "Were you stalking me baby? Did you run into me with your inner tube on purpose, just to get me into bed?"

She rolled her eyes at him and scooted away. "No, I didn't. But, we planned to go to the show."

"What show? The fundraiser?"

"Yeah. Paige and I were planning to go. I mean before she talked me into going to Vegas with her, we talked about getting tickets to your show."

"Nothin' wrong with that, is there?"

"I did check out your Facebook page. And Twitter. Instagram too."

"That's how I knew you were there."

"Where?"

"At the pool that day. I saw you in one of the photos."

"What are you talking about?"

"I took a few photos that day at the pool. First I sent them to Jake. Then I posted a couple on Instagram. As I went through them, trying to decide which ones to use, I saw you. When you ran into me, I was trying to find you."

"You were? You're not saying that to make me feel like less of a dork?"

"Who's the stalker now baby? Sounds as though I am."

She loved him for teasing her. Wait. She *loved* him? Oh God, where had that come from? She stopped laughing and turned away from him. There was no way she would let herself fall in love with him. Nope, wasn't happening. She needed time away from him, for at least a few minutes.

"Whoa, what happened?" Ben tried to get her to turn back to him.

"Nothing."

"No, it isn't nothing. Your face went from laughing to full-on thundercloud. What did I say?"

"It's nothing. I'm fine. You didn't say anything." What could she say? Oh, no big deal, *I realized I'm falling in love with you.*

"Come on Liv, don't do this. We've had such a great day. We've had such a great week. You've had fun, haven't you?"

"I've had a great time Ben. Everything is fine. I remembered something I have to do. I'll be right back."

Liv went out the back door and into the barn as fast as her feet would carry her. She checked on the horses, put a few things away, made sure the stall was ready for the new horse arriving tomorrow. She ran out of things to do, she had no choice but to go back and hope Ben had let it go.

When she came back inside, Ben was still in the kitchen, where she'd left him. He hadn't let it go.

"Liv, please sit. We need to talk."

"Ben, we've done nothing but talk."

"Liv, sit. Please."

She sat.

"This is hard for you. I've invaded your space, I follow you around. Won't let you alone for five minutes without wanting to touch you, or kiss you, or get so close to you that we're one, not two. I like being with you. A lot. I like you a lot. When you do that thing you do, what you just did, it makes me crazy. You close yourself off from me and then you bolt."

"It was *nothing.*"

"It wasn't. Don't *lie* to me about it. Talk to me." As much as his instincts told him to hide his anger from her, if he did, he'd be doing the same thing that made him angry with her.

"Maybe you should—"

"Don't," he shouted. "Don't tell me I should leave." He rubbed his face with his hands and continued to pace the kitchen.

"That wasn't what I was going to say."

"What then? What were you going to say?" He was still shouting at her.

"I was going to say you should sit down."

Shit. What was wrong with him? He hardly recognized himself. She had him so tied up in knots he was acting like somebody he didn't recognize. He wanted a drink. *Fuck no.* Where had that come from? He needed to leave. He stormed out of the back door in the direction of his truck.

"Ben, wait!"

Oh, thank God, she was following him. What he would have done if she hadn't? He stopped and turned back to her.

She threw her arms around him and crushed herself against him. "I'm sorry, please don't leave."

"Liv, I'm an alcoholic."

She held onto him.

"And right then, for one of the first times since I've been with you, including in Vegas, I wanted to take a drink."

"Oh Ben, I'm sorry."

He took her hands from around his waist and moved away from her. There were tears in her eyes.

"It happens, it's not you. I think about drinking. But when I'm with you, I don't. That's why it freaked me out. All week, even when Bill asked if I wanted a beer, or when we were at Paige and Mark's and you had wine. Not once did I have that horrible craving to join you."

"I'm so sorry." She kept saying the same thing over again.

"No Liv, listen. It's not you. You need to understand that. It's not you, and it has nothing to do with you. No, that's not right. It does, but in the opposite way. I love being with you. There, I said it. *I love being with you.* And this will make you bolt for sure. I think I'm falling in love with you. How's that for putting pressure on you?" He let go of her hands and walked toward his truck.

"Where are you going?" Liv asked.

"I'm not going anywhere. That's the thing. I can't."

"What do you mean?"

"If I got in my truck right now and left, I wouldn't even make it to the highway before I turned around and came back."

"Then come inside with me." She put her arm around his waist and led him in the direction of the house.

He slung his arm around her shoulder and brought her head closer to him. "I'm sorry, baby."

"Nothing to be sorry for."

"After dinner I need to call Renie. She and I have been playing phone tag since Saturday, and I need to talk to her."

"Where does she go to school?"

"Dartmouth."

"Holy crap."

"What?"

"It's a long way away, and damn, it's a hard school to get into."

"You're right. It's both of those. And I miss her. This is one of her last summer vacations before she graduates. I want to see if she'd like to travel."

Ben did his best not to react. He prayed the expression on his face didn't change. They'd known each other a little over a week, longer than that, but a week. Her making plans that didn't involve him was the most natural thing in the world. His pang of jealousy was the most unnatural thing in the world.

"Where are you going?" He hoped his voice sounded interested, not interrogatory.

"I want to take her to Europe, but anywhere she wants to go would be fine with me. All I care about is getting to spend time with her."

That's what I want with you, he wanted to say, but didn't. "Tell you what, why don't you give her a call now, and I'll make dinner."

She smiled. "You wouldn't mind?"

"I told you, I love your kitchen, I might even apply to be your full-time cook."

"How good at it are you?"

"Oh baby, you wait and see."

Ben liked his kitchen at home, but Liv's was out of a magazine. A large cedar beam, similar to those in the family room, was the focal point of the kitchen. Lighting fixtures hung down from it over the island, where there was a seven burner Wolf cook top. Even more impressive were the bells and whistles hidden away. Electrical outlets and an exhaust panel hid within the rough-edged granite, and popped up at the push of a button. He'd seen her do it when they made breakfast.

On the other side of the kitchen, a cutting board was built into the surface of the granite. A wine storage refrigerator sat next to the double-wide Sub-zero. Double-stacked Wolf convection ovens were in the wall to left of the old farm-house style sink, which was made of stone. And from there, three big windows looked out over the deck and a view of the prairie. Farther on the other side, in the opposite direction of the ovens, was another double-sided stone fireplace, similar to the one in the master bedroom. This faced the family room on the opposite side.

If Ben had been given the chance to redesign his house, he'd design it similar to hers. He was like a kid in a candy store.

He pulled out a chicken and decided to make a twist on *coq au vin*, except he'd make the stew without wine. His mother came up with the alternative recipe that used Balsamic vinegar in its place. He found a cold storage bin, similar to an in-kitchen root cellar where Liv kept potatoes, carrots and onions.

It would take him at least an hour to prepare dinner, she could talk to Renie as long as she wanted.

"Hey Mom, whatcha' doin'?"
"Well…I have a lot to tell you."
"Yeah, what's up?"
"Ben's here."

She heard her daughter's phone drop followed by a lot of hooting and hollering. "You better not be joking," Renie said when she picked up the phone.

"Nope. I'm not joking."
"When? Why? For how long?"

"He got here on Monday—"

"Which is why I haven't been able to get a hold of you. Okay, keep talking."

"And he's staying through the weekend."

The phone dropped again, followed by more loud celebratory noises.

"Oh for goodness sake Renie," she said when her daughter came back again. "It isn't that big of a deal."

"No Mom, it is a big deal. Do you have any idea how happy this makes me?"

"Nowhere near as happy it makes me."

"I'll refrain from dancing around my room again until we've finished our phone call, but Mom, this is great. I'm so happy for you, I mean that with all my heart."

"We didn't get married. This may be just…a fling."

"If it's a fling, and it makes you happy, I'm all for it. This is so cool."

"It is. But listen, I called to talk to you about more than that."

"Okay, I'm all ears."

"I was wondering if you want to take a trip with me with me this summer."

"Of course I would, I love to travel with you. Where should we go?"

"How about Europe? Two or three weeks in Tuscany, and then take side trips from there. Then go to France for a couple more weeks, then end up in England for the same amount of time. Unless you want to try to fit Spain or Germany in too."

"That's a big trip."

"It is, but I figured once you graduate we won't have the opportunity to take a trip of this nature. You'll either start working or go to graduate school. Either way, you wouldn't be able take a couple of months off to travel."

"I love it. It sounds wonderful."

"But?"

"But what about Ben?"

"What about him? I'm not planning my life around him."

"Why not?"

"Why would I? Renie, stop this. This thing between Ben and me is very new. Your summer break starts in less than two months. If we're going to do this, I need to start planning now. I'll have to hire someone to take care of the horses. I'm sure Bill and Dottie would be happy to recommend someone."

"You've given this a lot of thought."

"I have. It'll be our last big mother-daughter trip for quite a while sweetie. I want to do it up big."

"Then I'd love to go with you. As long as you're sure."

"Of course I am. Oh Renie, I'm so excited! I can't wait to start planning, I'll email you websites. There's a place I have in mind in Tuscany, which is why I want to go there first."

"This is exciting…we'll have so much fun. And Mom?"

"Yes sweet girl?"

"It thrills me that you sound so happy, and so excited."

"You make it sound as though it's unusual."

"It is Mom. I don't want to hurt your feelings, but it's not as though you're miserable or anything, but…you're not happy either."

"That hurt a little, but I'll take it in the spirit you mean it. Let's focus on the positive, not the negative."

"That's right. I love you Mom."

"I love you too. I'll call you in a few days, and we can talk more about our plans."

Liv danced her way back to the kitchen.

"Good conversation?" Ben asked, opening the oven to stir the stew.

"The best. I worried Renie might say she didn't want to hang out with me this summer, and it would've crushed me. I wouldn't have said so, but it relieves me to say she wants to go with me."

Then it wouldn't be a good idea to tell her he was crushed. "So, tell me what you're planning."

"We'll leave at the end of May, a few days after she gets home." Liv continued to tell Ben all she had suggested to her daughter. "We should be back early to mid-August, plenty of time for her to get ready for her final year in college."

Ben's mind raced. Liv would be gone all summer. He couldn't wrap his head around the idea. "What about the horses?"

"Oh, that's not too hard to work out. Bill and Dottie have so many people working their ranch, a few who are part-time. There will be one or two interested in picking up extra cash who are qualified to man my little operation. I may even let them board here themselves, if we can work out the arrangements."

"In your house?"

"No, in the barn. Of course, in the house silly."

"You'd let a stranger come and stay in your house?"

Liv raised an eyebrow at him.

"This is different."

"You're right," she said. "It's different. I won't be here when the other stranger comes to stay."

She was happy, he wouldn't spoil it. Maybe he should leave earlier than planned. He needed to get his head back on straight. Stop trying to figure out what came next for them. He'd even considered asking her to come back to Crested Butte with him on Sunday. What an idiot.

"When will dinner be ready *mon chef*?"

"*En quinze minutes mon amour.*"

"Wow, I should take you with me, do you speak Italian too? You'll be my translator as well as my chef."

"Is that all you'd have me for? Not your lover too?"

"*Mais, oui, mon amoureux d'abord.*"

"Your lover *first*, until what? You grow weary of me?"

"I will never grow weary of you Ben."

She wouldn't? He was relieved to hear it. Liv had him wrapped around her finger so tight, he didn't recognize himself. Never had a woman affected him this way. He controlled the situation, got what he wanted, pulled away when he wanted. He'd never had a woman turn the tables on him, and he didn't like it, not one bit.

Liv walked over to the wine rack, pulled out a bottle and put it back. Then she walked to the refrigerator and pulled out a bottle of water.

"You can have a glass of wine. Do what you would usually do. If you'd have wine with dinner, have it. I'm very comfortable in my sobriety Liv."

"Are you sure?"

"I work in my family's bar, and tour with a band. I needed to learn how to live my life being around alcohol. I just can't drink it."

"This is another thing I don't know how to do."

"Be yourself. Do what you'd normally do, and everything will be fine. If I'm having a problem, I'll say so. Deal?"

"Deal." She walked back to the wine cooler. "What's for dinner?"

"Balsamic chicken."

"Hmm..." She pulled out a bottle of Bordeaux and opened it. "You make it so easy on me. Everything. Are you this way all the time?"

He laughed. "I'm *never* this way. I have an ex-wife who would be more than happy to confirm it."

"So this won't last?" As soon as she said the words, she wanted to take them back. "That isn't what I meant, it came out wrong."

"I'll see if I can figure out a way you can make it up to me." He put his lips on hers, pulling her against him. "After dinner."

Liv was flabbergasted by the meal he prepared. "You weren't kidding, were you? You would make a great chef. It would be a tragic waste of the rest of your talents, but wow, you can cook. I'm beginning to realize you're extraordinarily good at everything."

"Like this? Am I good at this?" Ben pulled her up from the table, and set her on top of the wide, cold, granite island. His hands went straight to the button on her jeans and pulled them off in one fell swoop. He grabbed the hem of her shirt, pushed it up, and then pulled it over her head. Next he reached behind her and unfastened her bra. All she had left on were her panties and they were the next thing to go. "Lift up," he said as he pulled them from under her bottom, tossing them into the pile of clothes that now scattered her kitchen floor.

"I'm ready for dessert," he said as he lowered her until her back and head rested on the granite. He stood in front of her and spread her legs.

"Ben."

"Shh, the no talking rule is back in effect." He kissed down her stomach, then moved to the inside of her thighs. First one and then the other. She breathed in deeply, arching her back away from the coldness of the counter, bending into his warmth as he buried his mouth inside her.

His gazed at her, the smooth curve of her shoulders, the jut of her collarbone as she arched her back. Her ribs were faintly visible beneath her satiny skin. She had a shadowy hollow between her breasts. He pulled her toward him, so her bottom rested at the edge of the granite.

"You're so beautiful," he murmured. His hand came up and fisted in her hair, pulling her up so his lips met hers. It was the softest, gentlest kiss, a brush of his mouth on hers, then again. Then he deepened the pressure, opened his mouth against hers and tilted his head for a better angle. Their tongues touched, tentative, questioning, but warm. They kissed again and again, long, delicious kisses, lush licks, clinging lips. Small whimpers came from Liv's throat.

Ben lifted his mouth from hers and muttered her name. His hands slid back into her hair and held her head. "I want to kiss you for hours, sweet Liv."

Her hands slid up his chest and held onto his shoulders; her fingertips stroked his neck. Ben was lost. Her mouth destroyed him, soft, warm and eager, kissing him back as though she was starving for him. Her desire for him ignited something inside him, a spark turning into a blazing fire, heating him from the inside out, burning him.

Ben's clothes landed in the same pile on the kitchen floor right before he lifted her hips, and slid inside her. "Oh God," she muttered. She leaned her head back until it touched the surface of the granite, her back arched with pleasure. God this man was good at this. She cried out, her skin tingled, her body shivered. She tucked her fist against her mouth and squeezed her eyes shut.

"That's it baby, let go." Her hands flew to his shoulders, and she clung to him. He moved away from her, no longer inside her.

"What?"

"Condom." He lifted her up and put his hands under her thighs. "Put your legs around me." He carried her into the bedroom and gently laid her across the bed. "Are you still with me?"

She practically purred in answer. He lay down next to her and pulled her on top of him. "You know what I like baby, skin on skin." She gazed down at him. Words of love came to her lips, but she held them back. She didn't love him yet, did she?

"It's such a beautiful night, should we go for a walk in the moonlight?"

"Let's stay right here...and talk." Ben laughed to himself. When had he become such a big talker?

"What do you want to talk about?" Liv stopped herself from adding the world "now" to the end of her question.

"I should head home tomorrow."

"Okay."

"Okay. That's it?"

"What do you want me to say?"

"Ask me to stay. Tell me you want me here with you."

"Please stay. And Ben, I do want you here with me." *More than I should.*

Friday and Saturday were a blur. They had dinner with Dottie and Bill but otherwise spent most of the two days in bed.

Ben stopped asking her questions and started telling her more about himself. He told her that while she was in Europe with Renie, he and the band would be on the road touring the majority of the time. Their album was ready to release, and the record company had been pushing them to get out and promote it.

He hadn't said anything about when they might see each other again. When he jokingly told her to check the CB Rice Facebook page for the tour dates, dread settled in the pit of her stomach.

Sunday morning when she woke up, for the first time since he'd arrived, Ben wasn't in bed next to her. She got out of bed and went into the bathroom. There was no sign of him, his toiletry kit no longer sat on her counter. She walked back out into the bedroom, his clothes and his duffel bag were gone too.

She threw on jeans and a sweatshirt, put her hair in a ponytail, pulled on her socks, and went in search of her boots. There was no sign of him in the living room or the kitchen either.

She went out the back door, holding her breath, willing his truck to be in her driveway. It was not.

She wrapped her arms around her waist, putting one foot in front of the other, making herself walk in the direction of the barn. Halfway there she started to cry. By the time she reached Micah's stall, she let it all out. All the pent up emotion she'd been holding in the last few days worked its way to the surface, and she cried.

Ben was gone, and he'd left without saying goodbye.

Chapter Eight

She cried so hard she didn't hear the truck pull in the driveway, or the barn door open.

"Liv! What's wrong? Did something happen to Renie?"

"Ben? I thought you were gone."

He held her close, and stroked the back of her hair. "I'm right here. Shh now." He leaned back and kissed each of her eyelids. "I wouldn't just leave."

She hiccupped trying to stop crying. "But your stuff. I woke up and you were gone, and your stuff was gone, and your truck was gone."

Ben held her tight, stroking her hair, telling her again and again everything was okay. He tried to stop himself from... smiling. What kind of asshole did it make him that he wanted to smile? And not a little smile, he wanted to grin from ear to ear. She thought he'd left, and it wrecked her. And that made him *happy*. God he was a sadistic bastard.

"Liv, I wouldn't have left without saying goodbye. When I woke up, you were sound asleep sunshine. Your body took the rest it needed. So instead of waking you up, I came out and fed the horses. When I finished, you still hadn't woken up, so I put gas in the truck."

"But the last couple of days..."

"What? I haven't pushed as much? Haven't made you as crazy hanging on you, asking you to promise me your heart, and begging you to let me stay forever?"

"Are you trying to be funny?"

"Half-funny. Listen, it's been what? A couple of weeks? Yeah, I realize I've been pushin' you real hard, real fast. And no matter what I say, you won't believe that I'm not usually this way, 'cause for whatever reason, with you *I am* this way." He laughed, but then got serious. "I'm not gonna lie to you Liv, leaving today won't be easy. Every part of me wants to figure out a reason to stay or beg you to come with me. And before you say anything, I know how crazy that sounds."

Liv's head rested against his chest, but he wanted to see her face. "Look at me baby."

She did.

"I'm not letting go of this. Not at all. But I am going home to give us both time to breathe, time to figure out what this means. And it definitely means something to me. Does it mean something to you Liv? I want you to be honest with me. If it doesn't, I need to hear it."

"It does. Ben, I was *sobbing* because I thought you left." She turned her head so her cheek rested on his chest. "I feel more than a little foolish," she whispered.

Ben put his hands on each side of her face, turning her to him again. "Don't. Don't be afraid to show me you care."

Liv closed her eyes and listened to his heartbeat. She was stunned by her reaction to thinking he was gone. This had been such a whirlwind between them, and even from the beginning, she was sure it wasn't a fling, but so much more. She'd miss him. A lot. And instead of trying to play it off as if it didn't matter, she should tell him that it did.

"I'd rather have waited to rest after you left."

"I have a little time before I have to get on the road if you want me to wear you out again."

"I guess you're packed, would the condoms be hard to find?"

"Not at all little lady, I left 'em in the drawer of your nightstand. And I counted 'em, there better be the same number left in there when I get back," he laughed.

"You're coming back?"

"Soon as I can baby. Soon as you'll let me."

Before they were through the bedroom door, Liv pulled at Ben's clothes. She tore at them until he stood before her, naked. "What now Liv?" he asked.

She pushed him onto the bed, on his back, climbed up and straddled him. "My way this time," she said and kissed him—seductively and wantonly; passionately and relentlessly. She bit his lower lip, and it destroyed him. She ran her fingertips over his skin, each stroke a flame. Liv touched his body, everywhere, trying to memorize his body with her hands. Then she sighed and let herself cover him.

"I need you naked too baby." Ben rolled her over and began to tear at her clothes, the same as she had done with his. "Need you now. Right now. Can't wait."

Ben wanted to go slow. He wanted every inch of her skin against his, savor being with her. In the days to come, he'd remember this, every moment of it. But he couldn't stop himself, his desire for her was all-consuming. His need to possess her overtook him and he buried himself inside of her. He went still, his hands in her hair, his face inches from hers. "Liv—." The words wouldn't come, he longed to tell her that he loved her, but he didn't. She'd never believe him. But he did, as he'd never loved before.

"I need you," he said.

"I'm right here," she answered, her eyes burning into his, questioning.

"Come with me. Come home with me." *Give in to me, give yourself over to me, he wanted to demand.*

"I can't," the words came out almost as a sob.

He brought his head closer, his lips hovering right above hers, her hair still twisted in his hands. He started to move slowly inside her.

"Come home with me, Liv." He demanded again. She wanted to, but she wouldn't give in to him.

"I can't," she said again, crying out as she did.

"I need you," he breathed. He'd never had such an overwhelming need for a woman. He wanted to worship her body, treat her tenderly. He brought his lips to hers again, kissing her gently but deeply. He broke the kiss, needing to take another moment, again, to look at her. When he closed his eyes he wanted to be able to see her face. He wanted the image seared in his memory.

Her long hair fanned out around her, and she gripped the back of his head, pulling him closer as their lips met again. Ben started to move faster, harder, Liv arched into him and cried out.

"I'll never stop needing you," he gasped as he exploded into her.

"Ben." The way she said his name, every time, as though she reached in and squeezed his heart.

***

They'd gotten dressed, and Ben was out on the deck, the door between them closed, on his cell phone. He paced as he spoke, his hand rubbing over the top of his head.

She trusted Ben handled the horses fine earlier, but she needed something to do with herself. The nervous energy was eating her alive. She longed to saddle Micah and take him out for a long, hard run, but she'd wait until Ben was gone. The thought filled her with an ache.

She walked to the fence where Micah stood, expecting she'd have a treat for him. She reached in her jacket pocket and pulled out a strand of red licorice. She didn't like it herself, red or black, but for her horses, there seemed to be no better treat. He nuzzled up against her, as though he realized she needed his affection.

She heard the back door close. Ben walked toward her. The way he looked at her, with such passion in his eyes, and when he smiled—Lord help her, her knees went weak. Did all women react to him this way? And was he aware of it?

"Time to go?" She wanted to be the one who said it first.

"Yeah, as much as I don't want to. I'm already getting a late start. If I don't get on the road, I'll want to stay another night." He pulled her hard against him, so hard it almost hurt. But even then the hurt inside overpowered it.

"Come home with me."

"I'm already home Ben. This is my home."

"Come for a few days. I'll fly you back when you're ready."

"Ben, I'm not going with you." She stroked the side of his face and reached up to brush her lips over his.

"Next time?"

"Maybe."

He held her so tight she couldn't breathe. When he kissed her again, he took the rest of the air out of her lungs. She was dizzy, but it didn't have anything to do with breathing. It was him.

And Then You Fall

* * *

Liv didn't watch his truck leave the driveway. It might have been nicer of her to turn and wave him off, but she didn't. Instead, she walked in the opposite direction.

She brought Micah into the barn and saddled him. They headed east, away from the sunset and rode and rode and rode.

When they got back to the barn, she was ridden out. She got Micah settled and brought the other horses into the barn, swept it out, and walked around. Liv needed to keep busy. She pulled up a barn stool and read through the week-old newspaper someone had left behind.

She ran out of things to occupy herself, she had to go inside the house. It was the last place she wanted to be.

* * *

Ben pulled up to his house a few minutes before ten. He thought about stopping at his parents' place, but when he drove by all the lights were off, so he didn't. He considered going back into town and swinging by the Goat, but it would be slow on a Sunday night this late in the ski season. Without a big crowd to distract him, being there would make him think of Liv. Everything did.

He went inside and slung his bag on the floor of the laundry room. He walked into his kitchen, and was disappointed, in it and the loneliness of his house.

Tomorrow his boys would be home, and he hoped their antics were enough to distract him. He was present with them, the same way his father had been with him. His boys were his world, the two most important humans on the planet to him. But now there was another human, a person, and he thought about her all the time.

His arms were empty; he longed to hold her. He'd gotten used to being able to hold her whenever he wanted.

He went back into the laundry room and picked up his bag. He took it into his bedroom, threw it on the bed and sat down next to it. He opened the zipper, pulling out the last thing he had packed. One of her scarves. He meant to tell her he took it before he left, but it slipped his mind. He wondered if she'd found his shirt, the one he left hanging on the knob on the back of her closet door. He'd left it for her on purpose.

He brought the scarf up to his nose and inhaled deeply. He loved her smell, he closed his eyes and imagined her with him. Scent was the most powerful of the senses when it came to remembering. He rested his head back on the pillow, holding her scarf close to him, and drifted off to sleep.

***

Liv climbed into bed and slid under the sheets. They smelled of them, him and her together. She nestled into the pillow, breathing in the scent he left there.

She rolled to where her cell phone sat on the nightstand, and for the first time in almost a week, she checked Facebook. Nothing. Twitter. Nothing there either. She scrolled through photos he'd posted before, many from months ago. There were several of him playing the guitar. In some, he smiled straight at the camera. She loved his smile.

She wondered if he made it home yet, or if he was still out on the road. She hadn't heard from him since he left, but she hadn't expected to. And she had no idea when she would again.

Chapter Nine

It had been three weeks since Ben left Liv's house. They had now been apart longer than they had been together. In his first few days home, he thought about calling her or texting her at least once an hour. She answered when he sent her a text. But never sent one on her own, one that wasn't in response to something he'd said. He called and she'd answer. And they'd talk. Sometimes when he called he got her voicemail. She'd call him back. But she never called him otherwise.

He kept her scarf tucked under his pillow, and now it smelled more of him than it did of her. He still missed her as much as he had the first day he'd been home.

The first week he kept busy with his boys. His mornings became about making breakfast, dropping them off, and coming home to try to get his work done in the hours until he picked them up from school. At night, they worked on homework, ate dinner and wrestled with bedtimes.

A week later, it came time to take the boys to their mom's. He wanted nothing more than to pack a bag, and head over the mountain to Liv's. But he didn't.

The next few days he thought hard about whether his feelings for her were as strong as he believed them to be. Was it because she held herself back from him, did that only make him want her more? Was she a conquest he didn't want to give up on until he won?

Or was his need for her loneliness? He'd been so lonely after he'd gotten divorced that often he sought the comfort of any warm, feminine body. He hated to think that Liv was nothing more than someone to soothe the ache of loneliness. He didn't think she was, he believed it was more than that. But if she wasn't feeling what he was, how hard could he push? He needed to back off and give himself as much time to think as he was giving her.

In six weeks, he and the band would leave on tour. Next week all hell would break loose when the dates were announced. He had so much work to do between now and then. Even if he wanted to go and see her, he wouldn't be able to. She could come to him, but she wouldn't.

The band was scheduled to play the Paramount in Denver at the beginning of June, and she'd be in Europe with Renie by then. He couldn't imagine not seeing her before she left, but he wasn't sure it was as important to her as it was to him.

He wished she'd give him something, a sign that it was, but she didn't. And if she did, he wasn't seeing it, or hearing it.

One of the other guys in the band took over their social media. The record company told them it should be less about Ben and more about CB Rice, so he'd stopped posting anything at all. He wondered if she had noticed. He hadn't asked.

**

When Liv saw the black bear walking across the meadow below her back deck the day after Ben left, she took it as a sign. Dottie told her that if a bear crossed her path it meant she should *hibernate*. Symbolically it meant you should be introspective, bask in silence and solitude, focusing on rebirth and self-understanding.

For the last three weeks, she'd hibernated. She avoided everyone. Even Paige had stopped dropping by. She still called and texted, but Liv didn't respond. Mark came out to see if she needed anything and begged her to, please, tell them if she did.

"Liv, there's no music playing. I've never been here when you are, that there wasn't music playing," said Mark.

"Silence is my music these days," she answered.

When Liv reached the one month mark *AB* "after Ben," Paige showed up at the barn.

She walked in, took Liv by the shoulders and said, "Enough! You either need to go and see him, or let him come here, or figure something else out. But this has to stop. You're behaving as though you're in mourning, and Liv—he isn't dead. This isn't you. You need to snap out of it."

"That's where you're wrong, this *is* me. I am a very solitary person Paige, I have been for years. I don't have any experience with this kind of relationship."

"Listen to me. Go and see him. Call him, right now, and go and see him."

"I…can't…"

"Why in the world not? Nothing is stopping you, other than your own stubbornness. He wants to see you."

Liv got up and walked to the front of the barn.

"Liv, are you listening to me?"

"Have you talked to him?"

"No, I haven't. It's not my place to. But I don't need to, I know you well enough to know what's happening."

"And what is that Paige, what do you think is going on?"

"You're living in limbo. You're waiting for Renie to come home so the two of you can leave for Europe. In the meantime, you're waking up, and you're sleeping, without much else in between. Remember when we came back from

Las Vegas and I told you I thought you kept yourself on the outskirts of life?"

Liv nodded.

"It's gotten *worse,* if that's even possible. Call him Liv. I'll sit right here until you do. Call him and tell him you want to come and see him."

"The horses."

"The horses will be fine. Mark will come out and take care of the damn horses. Call him Liv. Call him right now."

"What if—"

"Don't. No 'what ifs.' Call him."

"Okay. I'll call him."

"Now. I'm not leaving until you do."

Liv took her cell phone out of her back pocket and called.

***

Ben jotted lyrics down and absentmindedly hit the talk button when his phone rang.

"Yeah," he answered.

"Ben?"

"Liv? Is that you? Sorry, I'm in the middle of something. I didn't mean to be so abrupt."

"Oh, do you need to get back to it?"

"No, no, of course I don't. I'm so glad you called. How are you? What's up?"

"I wondered…" Ben heard another voice in the background, but couldn't catch what they were saying.

"I was thinking…"

Oh my God, she was killing him. What was she trying to say? "Liv? What is it?"

"I wondered if you want company."

Ben was in shock. Every day for the first two weeks he asked her to come and visit him. Each time he did, she said no. He stopped asking. And never once, did she invite him to come back and see her.

"I would like company, very much, as long as you were the company."

"I wouldn't be intruding?"

"Liv, you are welcome here anytime."

"Your boys?"

"They're with their mom this week, but they would love to meet you."

"You're sure about this?"

"Never more sure of anything. When?"

"I hadn't gotten that far."

He laughed. "Sounds as though Paige is there."

"Your first clue?" She laughed too.

"Today?"

"Tomorrow."

"It's a long drive, Liv, especially by yourself. Say the word and I'll be there in less than hour by plane."

"I'm not sure."

"I wouldn't keep you prisoner here Liv. I'd fly you back when you wanted to leave. I promise."

"It isn't that."

"Then what is it?"

Liv walked out of the barn, where Paige couldn't hear her. "I'm scared," she whispered.

"I'm a little scared too baby." He wasn't about to let her change her mind though. "Four o'clock. Ask Paige if she can give you a ride up to the airport."

"When?"

"Today. And if she can't, I'll rent a car and come down and get you."

"No, not today. Tomorrow."

"Liv, I'm flying over this afternoon. If you don't want to leave today, I'll come and help you pack."

Ben hung up and called his mom. "I need to talk to you and dad."

"Anytime, you know that."

"Okay, I'll be right there."

***

Ben's parents, Bud and Ginny Rice, owned the Flying R Ranch on the south side of Mount Crested Butte near East River Valley. It had been in their family since 1853. He and his brothers, one older and one younger, grew up on the ranch, and it remained their home. When Ben's oldest brother, Matt, turned twenty-five, their father gave him a fifty-acre parcel where Matt built his house. When Ben and his younger brother, Will, turned twenty-five, their father gave them each fifty acres. The parcels were situated in such a way that when their parents passed away, the ranch would be split into three large parcels, four hundred acres each. The boys would be able to keep it one working ranch or divide it, and work each parcel on their own.

An aerial view of the ranch would show the boys' houses sat at the furthest points from the center of the ranch. Which was where their parents' house and the ranch's outbuildings were located.

Ben and his brothers were very close, they had decided long ago that the ranch would never be divided, they would always run it as a single entity.

The drive to his parents' house took a few minutes. Both his mom and dad were out front waiting for him. Ben joined them on the porch, and told them about Liv.

"And what about the boys?"

"I don't have the boys this week, but if she stays through the weekend, they'll be fine with it."

His father raised his eyebrows, but didn't say anything.

"Dad, I told the boys about her."

"What did you tell them?"

"When they came back from the Grand Canyon, I told them that I had been on vacation while they were gone. I told them I visited someone very important to me, and I told them about her."

"Do you think you jumped the gun a bit?"

"It sounds crazy, but I care about this woman. There's something about her…I believe fate has put us together for a reason. I love her Dad. I needed to tell them about her."

Ben turned to his mother who hadn't said a word. "You're awful quiet over there."

"Hmm? I'm thinking."

"What about?"

"That the apple never falls as far from the tree as we think, does it Bud?"

"What are you talking about Mom?"

"Do you want to tell him or should I?" she asked her husband.

"You'll tell it better than I would."

"When we went on our very first date, your father told me we were meant to be together. He said it was fate. It took me a year to believe him. He was right all those years ago. He's my soulmate and no other man would've been right for me."

Liv was his soulmate. He was sure he loved Christine, but he never felt this way about her. He was meant to be with Liv. Now he had to convince her of it.

***

Paige delivered Liv to the airport in Centennial at four in the afternoon. Ben waited, with his dad, in the small terminal. When she walked in the double-doors, he was struck again by her beauty, and how she seemed unaware of it. In all the time they'd spent together, Liv never primped or preened. She was comfortable in her own skin, confident, and he found it irresistibly sexy.

Ben walked forward, savoring the sight of her, drinking her in. When she stepped into his arms, her body melding against his, he remembered how well they fit together. Their bodies and their souls were meant to be together.

He closed his eyes and held her close. There was no awkwardness between them. It was as though they were coming home, to the place they were supposed to be. Ben's lips brushed across hers. He longed to kiss her deeply, ravish her, but they'd have plenty of time for that later.

"I missed this," she said.

"Me too. I've been…empty, not being able to hold you in my arms." Ben's hand came to her cheek, his fingers stroking it. "There's someone I want you to meet."

They walked to where his dad was waiting. "Dad, this is Liv." She needed no more introduction than that. "And Liv, this is my father, Bud Rice."

"It's a pleasure to meet you Liv," his father said. "My son speaks very highly of you.

Liv's cheeks turned pink as she shook his father's hand. "It's a pleasure to meet you, sir."

Ben remembered then that Liv's father had been a military man. Of course she would address his father as "sir." He had been raised to treat his elders with the same level of respect. He thought he'd burst with pride as he watched his father make conversation with her. It struck him then, and he was surprised it hadn't before, Liv reminded him of his mother. Beautiful, gracious, and refined, yet so down-to-earth that she made those around her immediately feel more comfortable. He was in awe of her.

Ben gave Paige a hug hello, whispering thanks in her ear and introducing her to his father. He doubted Liv would've agreed to this trip without Paige's prompting. She was a good friend.

"Shall we get back in the air?" his father asked.

Liv hugged Paige goodbye and told her she'd be in touch. They hadn't talked about how long she'd stay with him, and he didn't want to yet. The last thing he wanted to think about was her leaving and them being apart again.

The fifty-minute flight went quickly. The skies were clear and the scenery spectacular. Liv was no stranger to Gunnison or Crested Butte. When Renie was growing up, it had been their favorite place to ski. The ski area had plenty of beginner and intermediate slopes. When Renie got better, there was enough challenging terrain that they never got bored.

The valley at the base of Mount Crested Butte was surrounded by the most spectacular scenery in the Rocky Mountains. Roads led to remote canyons where groves of aspens splattered the hillsides. Driving in from Gunnison, the butte rose majestically to the east.

"I love Crested Butte," she murmured as they drove into town.

"My grandfather played an important role in the town's development," answered Ben.

"I have to admit, my daughter filled me in on the Rice family's role in the history of the town." Liv chuckled. "She gave me a lecture about not ever reading the magazines left in our hotel rooms." She sighed and grinned. "That was the night I met you for the second time, at the Goat." Her cheeks turned pink again.

"Nice memory?" his father asked.

"An embarrassing one," she laughed.

"Liv feigned illness to get away from me that night," Ben added. "What was it that made you run from me?" he whispered in her ear.

She didn't answer him.

They turned onto a remote road before they got all the way into town.

"Where are we going?" Liv asked.

"This is the Rice family ranch little lady," Ben answered. She heard the pride in his voice.

"We'll stop in at my parents' place and drop my dad. My mom will want us to stay for a bit, but I told them we'd be having dinner at my house tonight."

"Okay," she answered softly.

He watched her as she studied the scenery of the ranch. He thought back to one of their first telephone conversations, when she told him she'd gone riding, and that she had a ranch. He remembered beating himself up for not asking her about herself. Now he realized that he'd never told her much about where he lived. Or that he came from a ranching family. All he told her was she'd gotten herself hooked up with a good ol' boy.

The butte was visible from the ranch, the south side of it, if you looked north through the valley of tall grasses. A river ran through the center of the valley; the Rices kept cattle to the south of the river, and horses to the north. Even in the winter the ranch was beautiful, but in the spring, wildflowers bloomed as though it was a painter's palette. The deep blue sky, touched with billowing white clouds looked like a pastel. The land, as far as the eye could see, belonged to his family.

"It's so beautiful here."

Ben heard the awe in her voice. He experienced it too, every time he drove these roads.

"Oh wow," she said as they pulled up in front of his parents' house. "It's wonderful."

Ben had to admit the ranch house was idyllic. Built of dark wood, it was as though it had been there forever, part of the surrounding land. The wraparound porch offered views of the valley in three directions and the peak of Mount Crested Butte in the fourth.

Ben's mom came out to the porch to greet them.

"Mom, this is Liv."

She realized that was the second time he introduced her in such a simple way.

"It's nice to meet you ma'am," Liv said as she extended her hand in greeting.

"Oh please, call me Ginny, and come here, give me a hug sweet girl, I don't shake hands."

Liv looked at Ben and they both laughed. "Dottie," Ben said and Liv nodded yes.

"Who is Dottie?" Ginny asked.

"Someone who reminded me very much of you, Mom" Ben answered.

"She doesn't shake hands either," added Liv.

Ben was antsy. There would be time for his parents to get to know Liv better tomorrow, or the day after that. Right now all he wanted to do was whisk her away and be alone with her. He longed to hold her close, sink his body into hers, skin on skin.

As it was, he couldn't take his hands off her. He stroked her arm, then pulled her in closer, kissing the soft skin right along her hairline. She smelled so good, like lavender and something else, he couldn't place it, but it was Liv.

"These kids would like to be on their way Ginny," his father interjected, sensing his son's impatience.

"What's your hurry?" Ginny winked at Liv.

Ben stood and held his hand out to Liv, who wrapped her fingers through his. "We'll see you soon Mom," he winked back.

"It was so nice to meet you both," Liv said, walking over to hug his father.

"And you too. We hope to see more of you during your visit." Ginny hugged her. "We're so happy you're here."

"Where do you live?" she asked as they got in the truck.

"Over this hill a little ways," he pointed in the direction of his house.

"On the ranch?"

"Yep. I guess I didn't tell you that, did I?"

"No, you didn't mention it."

He told her about his brothers and pointed in the direction of their places, and explained how his dad had divided up the parcels for each of his three sons.

"No sisters?"

"Sisters-in-law, but no, no sisters." Ben realized again how little he'd told her about himself.

"Oh Ben," was all she said as they approached his house. It was a more modern version of his parents' place. Built from the same dark wood, with weathered corrugated steel roofing and accents. He loved his house, but he had to admit, he loved hers more.

"I'm warning you, my kitchen isn't half as nice as yours. And I have one fireplace, not one in every room."

"I don't have a fireplace in every room Ben."

"Just about," he teased.

They made it through the front door, but giving her a tour now was out of the question. He'd waited long enough to hold her, and bury himself deep inside her.

Ben cupped the back of her neck, touching his mouth to hers, warm, barely there at first, then firmer. He parted her lips, angling his head, trying to get closer to her. His hands pulled her jacket away from her shoulders and tossed it on the floor. "Need you naked and need it now baby," he groaned.

A flush warmed her skin as he nipped at her earlobe. "You taste so good."

A groan escaped her lips as she ran her hands over his shoulders, down, caressing his solid chest, moving lower, to unfasten his belt.

Before she did, Ben picked her up and carried her up the stairs. "Once you are in my bed, it will be a long, long time before I let you out of it."

He took her mouth again, hungrily. His hands traveled over her back, lingering as they slowly moved down the length of her spine, over her bottom, pressing her closer into him. She made him burn from the inside out at the mere touch of her body.

Liv's piercing blue eyes bore into his as he slid his hand into her long hair, holding her still and feasting himself on her lips.

"Talk to me Liv. Tell me. Did you miss me? Did you miss this?"

"I missed you so much," she whispered. She got up and started taking off the rest of her clothes. Ben watched, the vision of her caused him to growl. He cupped her chin and kissed her mouth lightly. He trailed his lips down her body, over the swell of her breast, softly kissing the curve of her stomach, then her hip.

Ben lifted her back onto the bed and pushed her softly so she was on her back, spread out in front of him. He reached behind his back and pulled his shirt over his head, then quickly took off his jeans. He reached for the drawer in the nightstand and Liv sat up, stopping his hand with hers.

"No, it's okay, nothing between us tonight Ben."

"I need you Liv. All of you. I want your eyes on me, watching what I do to you."

Liv didn't say a word, nor did she move from where she was. Her eyes stayed locked on his, never wavering as Ben's slow rhythm took them both over the edge.

Chapter Ten

"Are you feeling as though you're a hostage yet?" Ben asked her two days later. They hadn't seen another person since they'd left Ben's parents house the night she got there, but they hadn't spent the entire time in bed either.

Ben drove her around the ranch, somewhat stupefied that they didn't run into one of his brothers, or even the other ranch hands. He wondered if his dad and warned everyone to be scarce.

"Not at all. Although…"

"Will you tell me, or do you want me to guess? Wait, don't tell me. You want to go riding today."

Liv stared at him. "How did you know?"

"When you're nervous, you like to ride."

"Am I nervous?"

"We won't be able to avoid seeing other humans much longer, which means you may meet more of my family. And that makes you nervous."

"What about your boys Ben?"

"Is that what you're most nervous about?"

"I understand if you don't want me to meet them."

Another thing he needed to talk to her about. He'd told his boys about her, that she was someone special to him.

"I want you to meet them more than anything. They won't be back here with me until Monday, but I thought it would be nice to have dinner with them Saturday or Sunday. So it's not too overwhelming."

"For me or for them?" She laughed.

"You have a charming daughter. I have two rough and tumble boys. One is at the beginning stages of puberty, so he'll be as awkward as humanly possible around anyone of the opposite sex. The other is still a little boy. He will crawl into your lap, and never want to leave." Luke was his rascal, but also his cuddler. The one who never wanted to sleep in his own bed, wanted five more minutes of talk time, or another story at bedtime.

"And will I meet their mother?"

Ah, the truth about what bothered her, meeting his ex-wife. Scott died, but if they were divorced instead, he would've been nervous about meeting someone important enough to father her child.

"We should talk about them."

"Who them?"

"Your husband, my ex-wife. I want you to tell me about him. What made you fall in love with him, your life then."

"Scott and I weren't married very long before he died."

"It's still part of who you are. In a way, it's harder. With my ex, we decided we didn't want to be together anymore, she didn't die. I worry sometimes about living up to his memory. Particularly given how he died."

Ben wanted to talk about Scott. She hadn't seen this one coming. Liv never talked to anyone about him. She painted a picture for Renie, but it wasn't based on reality. Most of what she told her daughter was how she imagined Scott would've been as a father. He wasn't a father yet when he died.

And as much as he wasn't sure about living up to Scott's memory, at least Scott wasn't a living, breathing, human being. He still saw his ex-wife at least once a week. How could she compete with that?

"Liv?"

"I heard you. I don't want to talk about him. And I don't want to hear about her."

Why did he want to talk about everything all the time? She didn't remember her father ever being so *talkative*.

"Tell me about him. How did you meet him?"

* * *

Scott was what her mom referred to as a "fly boy," an F15 fighter pilot. He was the most handsome man she had ever seen. She worshiped him, from the day she met him. He worshiped her father, and he was a gentleman. The happiest day of her life was the day she found out Scott looked at her as a woman.

The first time he took her out, he opened doors, and pulled out her chair for her. He asked her what she wanted for dinner and ordered for her. She remembered thinking he was a prince. In fact, he'd called her his princess. And rather than Liv, he called her Olivia.

They started seeing each other in June, two months after she turned eighteen, when he was in town for his promotion to captain. They saw each other every night for a week. When he went back to his base, he called her every night at eight o'clock. Funny she remembered it so well, waiting for him to call, and that he was so punctual.

They kissed, but Scott never pushed her to go any further. Liv wondered why not. She had been so innocent then she hadn't thought about it. Then again, she hadn't dated anyone in high school, no one measured up to Scott. He asked her one night, during one of their phone calls, if she was a virgin. She remembered being aghast, and embarrassed, that he would ask. She hadn't told him she'd been saving herself for him, but she had been.

He came back at Christmas to spend it with her family, and he proposed, on Christmas Eve, in front of the Christmas tree, with her parents watching. She hadn't questioned it then. It was odd how happy her mother and father had been. She wondered now if they'd been happy for her, or happy that she landed such a "catch."

She visited his base soon after. He took her around, introducing her to his friends, most already married, with families. In particular, she remembered him never failing to ask if they thought she was the most beautiful woman they'd ever seen. Her appearance, and her innocence, were important to him.

One evening during her visit they went out for dinner with several other couples. One of the wives asked Liv what she liked to do, about her hobbies. Liv told her she had a horse, and that she dreamed of being a barrel racer. She'd been training and exploring rodeos to enter.

Later, when he dropped her off at her hotel, Scott sat her down and told her he didn't want to hear any more talk of rodeos. She would be too busy as an Air Force wife for such foolishness. He also told her that he wanted to start a family as soon as they were married. She loved him more than anything, giving up her dream to be with him, didn't seem a sacrifice.

When she got home, she talked to her mother about it. Her mom assured her that life with Scott would be an unimaginable series of adventures. She'd travel the world and have opportunities as the wife of a pilot, few dreamed about.

Rodeos and barrel racing were for women of a different caliber than Liv. And not a better caliber.

The next month was a flurry of activity as they rushed to plan the wedding. They held the ceremony at the Air Force Academy chapel, and the reception at their ranch. Liv knew so few people at her own wedding, most were Scott's friends, or friends of her parents. Again, it seemed odd to her now.

Scott took her to Hawaii for their honeymoon and treated her like a queen. He was romantic and charming. He made her feel as though she was the most special woman who ever lived. He was gentle when they made love, and patient as he taught her how to please him. She never dreamed sex could be so spectacular.

While they were in Hawaii, he made sure they did everything she wanted to do. They went sailing and whale-watching, hiking and snorkeling. He took her to each of the islands and when they were in Kauai, they made love on a beach, under the stars.

As a captain, and a fighter pilot, Scott arranged for a very nice home for the two of them, off base. Not nearly as nice as her parents' home, but Liv hadn't expected it to be. She missed her horse more than anything, but being with Scott meant everything to her.

Liv was accustomed to the life of an Air Force officer. She understood what the expectations would be of her, there would be wives' clubs to join, dinner parties to host, and functions to attend. She had seen and learned it all from her mother.

In early April, Liv found out she was pregnant. Scott was beside himself with happiness. If she'd felt like a princess before, now she felt doubly so. He was attentive and caring, making sure she had everything she wanted or needed.

Each month, on the fourteenth, he brought her a gift, to celebrate their anniversary. In March, he brought her an emerald four-leaf clover necklace; in April a pair of diamond earrings, in honor of her birthday, April 17. In May, he gave her tickets for the two of them to go and visit her parents for Memorial Day. And in June, he gave her a bracelet that belonged to his grandmother. Scott never failed to tell her his sun rose and set with her. God, she loved him so much, heart and soul.

In August he was deployed, and by November, he was gone. Those had been such dark days for Liv. Her world ended when they told her Scott died.

Her parents flew in right away. She wondered now if her father knew Scott was shot down before she did. They took care of everything. She moved home to live with them. She remembered Scott's funeral, the day they buried him at the academy cemetery. Everyone told her she should be so proud, her husband was a hero.

Irene Louise Fairchild was born a few weeks later. Her world went from revolving around Scott to revolving around her daughter.

***

Ben watched the expressions on Liv's face change as she told him the story of her life with Scott. She had been so young, so innocent, but it sounded as though he had been a decent man, and good to her. And she loved him, completely. Which made it easier to understand why she hadn't found someone else, hadn't ever remarried.

"When Renie was little, I had no desire to do anything but be her mom. My parents would've been happy to watch her if I had ever wanted to go out, but I never did. I believed that Scott was it for me. I shut off that part me.

"The day Renie started school, I met Paige. Her daughter Blythe was in the same kindergarten class."

Soon Liv became busy with mother-daughter play dates, helping in Renie's classroom, and on field trips. When that happened, her parents started traveling more. Liv never realized how much they put their lives on hold to help her.

When Renie turned ten, Liv's father had a heart attack. He died the next day without ever regaining consciousness. Liv got Pooh, Renie's horse, as a way to distract her daughter from the pain of losing her grandfather. Two years later her mother passed away from breast cancer. The time between her diagnosis and her passing had been brief.

Between then and now, Liv had her hands full raising her daughter. Paige and Mark tried to fix her up with different guys, but there had never been anyone who held a candle to Scott. She enjoyed the time she spent with her daughter. They were as much friends as they were parent and child.

"I guess you didn't ask me to tell you my life story, but it's hard to tell you about Scott, without doing so. The truth is, we were together such a short amount of time. Even so, he was my life, and he impacted the rest of my life in a profound way. It's hard to separate one from the other."

Wow—her life story, she thought. Liv had been a daughter, then a wife, then a mother. She liked Ben, but the idea of adding "Ben's girl," as the fourth title on her life's resume, didn't resonate so well. Liv needed to do something for herself, be something for herself, before she woke up twenty years from now and resented the fact that she never had.

***

Liv believed no one measured up to her long-dead husband. That wasn't what bothered Ben the most. Hearing that her birthday had been a little over a week ago, bothered him more than anything. Had she celebrated it alone? He hoped Paige and Mark had done something nice for her.

"Are you getting hungry?" They were sitting out on Ben's deck, the sun was going down, and he turned on one of the outdoor heat lamps.

"I am. What should we make?"

Ben decided he wanted to take her into town. He'd surprise her and they'd celebrate her birthday. "Let's go out tonight. How does sushi sound?"

"Oh fabulous. I love sushi, I would eat it every day if I didn't have to drive so far. Um, what should I wear?"

"Something comfortable. I'd be happy if you wore nothin' at all baby, but then I wouldn't want to leave the house." Ben snuggled her closer to him. "Thanks for telling me about Scott."

"I'm still not sure I want to hear about your ex-wife Ben."

He needed to tell her about Christine. But more, he needed to tell her about himself. That included the things that led to the demise of their marriage. He didn't want to keep any secrets from Liv. While he wasn't proud of the way he lived his life back then, but living through it, getting beyond it, made him a better man, a better person, now. At least he hoped so.

"Tell you what, let's leave that story for another day. I want to take you out on a date tonight. And show you off a bit."

The thought filled Liv with a new sense of dread. Was she another one of Ben's conquests? Did he date much? How many other women would they be running into that he'd slept with? This was all so new to her.

The dates she'd gone on had never been with anyone she cared about. When she had dinner with Ben and the band in Las Vegas, she hadn't given any thought to other women, it hadn't mattered then. At that point, Liv considered the thing between them a fling, something that would last a day or two. She no longer saw it that way.

She wished she brought something nicer to wear, but she made do with a sleek black cashmere sweater and black wool pants. She took a little more care with her makeup than she did at home, where she never wore it. She remembered to throw in her black boots at the last minute, the ones with the four-inch heels. Ben was so much taller than she was, she wouldn't feel as short wearing them.

He waited on the deck, leaning on the railing with his back to her while she changed. God he looked hot, even from behind. His jeans, slung effortlessly low, hugged his tight behind in all the right places. The sweater he wore taut over his broad shoulders, made her heart beat a little faster. Maybe she should rethink the cashmere, she was overly warm already.

Ben turned as Liv walked by the fireplace, the light from it cast a warm glow around her. He had never seen anyone more beautiful in his life.

"Look at you," he took her hands in his but stood back, his eyes gazing over her. "Remember when I said I wouldn't want to leave the house if you wore nothing at all? This counts too. Baby you are so hot, I want to keep you all to myself."

"Uh-uh," she said. "You promised me sushi and I'm holding you to it."

They stopped first at the Dogwood Cocktail Cabin. It was dimly lit and very romantic. Liv studied the menu.

"Where to begin," she said. "These are the swankiest cocktails I've ever seen." She decided on the Bee Sting, a mix of tequila, honey, mint and lemon, with a splash of habanero. Ben ordered a Latin Lover, hot cocoa, habanero, and whipped cream. He asked them to hold the tequila on his.

"I thought you might enjoy this place," he said. "It seems as though it would be a good place to start a date."

"Is this where you start all your dates?"

Ben pulled her close and nibbled on her earlobe. "You're the first woman I've brought here Liv, and you'll be the last. It's you and me baby, I thought you knew that by now."

She turned her head and brushed her mouth across his. Ben cupped the back of her head, holding her close, nibbling her bottom lip. "Do you know what you do to me?" he whispered. "You make me crazy with wanting you."

Liv brought her hand up and stroked the side of his face. "I've never wanted anyone the way I want you," she whispered in his ear as she kissed his neck below it.

"Ben? What are you doing here?" Ben didn't have to look to know that Christine, his ex, stood next to their table.

Every muscle in Liv's body tightened in an instant. She tried to pull her hands, caught in his, away, but he tightened his grip. Before he spoke, he brushed his lips against hers one more time. "Shh," he whispered.

He kept his eyes fixed on hers, not even blinking. "Liv, this is my ex-wife, Christine." She tried to wiggle her hands free from his, but he wouldn't let go.

"Christine," he said, eyes not leaving Liv's, "what brings you out tonight?"

"Drinks with the girls. I didn't expect to run into you here. Who's your friend?"

Ben's gaze still hadn't left Liv's and he had no intention of letting it. Every instinct told him Liv was trying to pull away from him. He wouldn't let her. "This is Liv," he said.

"Oh, uh, nice to meet you. I'll let you get back to it, I guess."

Ben wanted to breathe a sigh of relief when Christine walked away. But Liv's body remained so taut, he was afraid to let a single breath out of his lungs. "Liv, honey, what's going on?"

That seemed to snap her out of it. Her hands relaxed and she took her eyes from his.

"She's stunning," Liv murmured.

"She doesn't hold a candle to you," he answered, keeping his voice soft, hoping to soothe her.

"Don't be ridiculous, she's gorgeous Ben."

"You don't have any idea how beautiful *you* are, do you?"

"For an older woman, who spends more of her time with horses than humans."

He dropped her hands and sat back. "Liv, how much younger than you do you think I am?"

She shrugged, trying to be nonchalant. "Ten years?"

"How old are you?"

"Forty."

Ben shook his head. "I'm three years older than you are baby," he chuckled. "Not that it makes any difference. I thought you should know, since it seemed to bother you."

"You are not."

"I am, and I'll prove it." He dug out his wallet and handed her his driver's license.

"I don't need to see that," she said, while at the same time taking it out of his hand. "Wow. You look damn good for your age, Benjamin Caldwell Rice."

"Let's see yours, Olivia."

"Not on your life, your picture is way better than mine."

There, he could breathe that sigh of relief he'd been holding in. She was fine, the awkward moment running into his ex-wife passed, thank God.

He brushed his lips across her knuckles. "Wanna get out of here?"

"More than anything."

Ben threw a fifty on the table and they walked out, before their drinks were even delivered.

They walked, hand in hand, around the corner and downstairs to LoBar, the sushi restaurant. It was crowded as usual, but there were four open seats at the sushi bar. Ben led Liv over to them and pulled a stool out for her.

"Shouldn't we check in with someone? We might be taking someone else's seat."

"Well there he is," she heard a deep male voice say. "And this must be Liv."

Ben hugged the man and slapped him on the back. "Good to see you big brother. Liv, I'd like you to meet Matt. Matt, this is Liv."

Matt took her hand in his and brought it to his lips. "The magnificent Liv, I've heard so much about you." He turned to Ben, "she's even more beautiful than you said."

"Back off brother," Ben said, taking Liv's hand from Matt's and tucking it in his.

Matt threw his head back and laughed, the same hearty, whole-body, soulful laugh as Ben's.

"This is Matt's place," Ben explained. He waved his hand over the corner section where they were seated. "Reserved for family, no matter how crowded it gets."

Matt stayed and chatted with them for a few minutes and then excused himself to seat open tables. Less than ten minutes later, Will, Ben's youngest brother, joined them.

"Is this a coincidence?" Ben asked as Will pulled out the stool on the other side of Liv and sat down. "Or did Matthew give you the word we were here?"

"I had to come and meet Liv," Will answered. "Who knows if you'll leave your house again while she's here. Liv," he turned to her, "I'm Will, Ben's younger, handsomer, more romantic brother."

"Will it's nice to meet you," Liv responded. "Ben, didn't you say you had 'sisters-in-law,' plural sisters? Do you have more brothers?"

"Damn," said Will. "You already told her I'm married?"

They both laughed. "Seriously Liv, I'm Will, and I am all the things I said before, as well as happily married."

"It's nice to meet you Will."

"Speaking of which, Maeve wanted me to invite you to dinner while Liv's here."

A few minutes later, two women approached them, both gorgeous. Liv stiffened again, but relaxed when Will stood.

"And here she is now. Hey darlin', fancy running into you at LoBar."

"Will Rice," said the woman with coal black hair, and the palest, but most beautiful skin Liv had ever seen. "Don't pretend you didn't call me to come and meet her. Hi," she turned in Liv's direction, "I'm Maeve, Will's wife, and this is Allison, Matt's wife."

Will and Ben pulled more stools over to the bar. When the couple around the corner from them left, the group took over the whole far end of the crowded bar.

Ben watched as Liv as she interacted with his family. She fit, he thought as she talked and laughed with them. She fit perfectly.

They never ordered, the guys behind the bar kept the sushi and other house specialties coming without them needing to. Matt was showing off, thought Ben with a smile.

"Oh, I'm so full," Liv said, putting her hand on her stomach. Moments later the lights around the bar dimmed as the group broke into a rousing version of "Happy Birthday." Liv tried to figure out who they were signing for, and then they set the candle-filled mochi ice cream in front of her.

"Happy birthday baby," Ben said, brushing his lips against hers. "Make a wish."

Chapter Eleven

When Ben woke, the heat of Liv's body next to his flooded him with a sense of calm. He loved having her here with him, he loved being with her at her place too, he loved being with her. As long as she was next to him, he was at peace.

Ben needed to talk to her today about running into Christine last night, about her reaction. He wanted her to meet his boys, but he didn't want to run into them with his ex-wife or her husband.

He'd call her today, pick them up, have them stay here with them for a couple of days. There wouldn't be a problem with it on Christine's end. Ben would be traveling so much once their tour started, she would be glad to have the boys spend time with him before he got back out on the road. He hoped that Liv wouldn't have a problem with it.

Before any of that, he needed to tell Liv more about himself, not all good. He'd overcome a lot of his demons, made significant changes in his life, but living life on tour and living life at home were two different things. Life on the road was crazy—a different city every night, sometimes several nights in a row. They'd have a day off here and there, but never enough time to come home and regroup.

A part of him wanted to take her on the road with him, but that wouldn't be fair to her. He didn't need or want a babysitter, he wanted a lover, a mate...someday a wife.

Liv shifted so her back faced his front, and he wrapped his arms around her, nestling her close. For someone who slept alone as many years as she had, he wondered if his constant need to touch her bothered her. Even in his sleep he clung to her. Awake he wanted to bury himself in her every chance he had.

"Sweet Liv," he whispered in her ear, hoping to wake her gently.

"Hmm, is it morning? What time is it?"

"It's almost nine. You can sleep longer if you want to."

"No, I'm awake."

Now or never. "I need to tell you the not-so-nice stories," he said, kissing across her back from one shoulder to the other. Her muscles tightened. He hoped he could get through it and be honest with her. He'd never be free with her unless he told her all of it.

"Okay," she said. "You can tell me."

***

"A little over a year ago, I hit rock bottom. Will, Matt and I had been snowboarding all day and I'd been drinking, a lot. They took away my keys and drove me home, where they figured I'd pass out and sleep it off. Unfortunately, I didn't. I got my hands on a set of keys to one of the ranch trucks. I drove to Will's, prepared to give him shit I guess. I don't remember anything about that night.

"When I got there I must've passed out in one of the bedrooms. Something must've woken me up, and I went out into the living room. Maeve, Will's wife, sat on the couch, I don't know where Will was. Anyway, I sat down and started a conversation with her.

"Will came out and started screaming at me, asking what the fuck was wrong with me. Then he apologized to Maeve and he got her out of there fast. I don't remember much of this, but I do remember the last thing he said to me. 'You need to straighten your shit out dude or get the fuck out of my life.'"

Ben took a big deep breath. He punched the pillow behind his head a little higher. He wanted to see at least part of Liv's face. If he went too far, he hoped he'd be able to tell.

"The reason Will was so done with me that day, was because I came out, sat down and started talking to his wife, naked. On top of that, I must've fallen, or I ran into something before I got there. By the time Maeve saw me, I looked as though I had been in a fight. I scared the hell out of her."

Ben tightened the hold he had around Liv's arms. He hoped that if he held her as close to him as possible, he'd be able tell her everything he needed to.

"Before that night, there was a long, ugly road of random acts of misery I left in a trail behind me."

Ben told her that he'd started drinking as a teenager hanging out at the ski area. It got worse when he started the band, worse still when he got married, and almost killed him when he got divorced.

"That night, Will took Maeve to my parents' place. He called Matt, who rounded up Jimmy and Phil, guys from the band I've been friends with since we were in first grade. They all came back to Will's, with my mom and dad, and told me that they were taking me to rehab. I mean, there was a lot more to it, but Liv, the sad part is, there isn't much I remember about it. The only reason I can tell you what happened with Maeve is because I've been told the story so many times."

"Keep talking." Liv said, almost a whisper.

"When I met Christine the band was hot. We'd released a couple of albums and were playing all over Colorado. We had a sold out show at the Belly Up in Aspen. The crowd was crazy that night, and I saw her in the front row. I expected I'd be getting her under me sometime that night. She wanted nothin' to do with me." Ben laughed, in an uncomfortable way, and rubbed his eyes. "God this is sounding too familiar even to me." He kissed Liv's neck. "Are you all right, is it okay for me to go on?"

"Mmm hmm, keep going Ben."

"She came to a lot of our shows. Young guys, hot band, girls followed us. She never got together with any of the other guys, she never got together with me, but she was always there. We had a few days off, and I asked her to spend time with me when we weren't performing. That was the first time she said yes to anything I ask her."

Ben told her that he and Christine partied together, non-stop, for a week. She drank more than him, and did a lot of coke, which he hadn't. During their week-long bender, they had sex, and he'd been too drunk or stoned or high to remember to use condoms.

"You can guess what I'm gonna tell you next. Christine came into the Goat trying to find me a couple months later. I didn't recognize her. She'd put on weight, which I later found out was because she'd stopped doing coke. She was also pregnant, and scared out of her mind that there would be something wrong with the baby."

Both Ben and Christine saw the pregnancy as a wake-up call. She stopped partying. Ben stopped too.

He moved her into his house and rather than *asking* her to marry him, he *told* her they were.

"I realize now that my parents knew what was happening then. I tried to play it off as though I was a responsible guy who'd fallen in love, gotten my girl pregnant, and we were getting married. They were on to my shit the entire time. Part of them played along, hoping that it *was* the thing that would make me stop drinking. And maybe make me start acting like the grownup I was old enough to be."

Ben shifted again. Liv put her arm around his waist and put her head on his chest, right above his heart.

"Thankfully Jake was okay when he was born, there were never any signs that he was adversely affected by Christine's partying.

"We played house for a couple of years and did our best to find a common ground that didn't have anything to do with partying. I had to hand it to her then, she changed when she got pregnant, and she's a good mother to Jake and Luke.

"Not as much changed for me as it did for her. I still played clubs almost every weekend. I stopped doing drugs, and convinced myself that as long as I only drank, I'd be fine."

He told her the benders stopped, but in between Jake's birth, and when Christine got pregnant with Luke, he'd slept with a lot of other women. Whenever they played out of town, they'd stay to the next morning. No matter where they were, Ben never slept alone. He'd learned his lesson about unprotected sex though, and he never went without a condom.

He and Christine had major problems, because he was never home. Living out on the ranch was hard because even though it wasn't as far from town as Liv's place was, Christine was isolated. His mother was nice to Christine, but they were never close.

In an effort to repair their marriage, they did the thing everyone says not to, they tried to have another baby. It didn't take long for her to get pregnant, but if she thought Ben would make changes in his life because of it, she was wrong. And that didn't make her happy.

At home, all they did was fight. Ben realized, in rehab, that most everything that went wrong between them was his doing. He hadn't been committed to the relationship, ever. He loved her, more as the mother of his kids. She was beautiful, no question. But he wasn't the man she wanted him to be, and he realized now, she wasn't the woman he wanted her to be either.

Liv shifted when he said it, but kept her arm around his waist and didn't try to move away from him. He kissed her forehead, and started to run a trail of kisses down the side of her face.

"Keep talking," she whispered.

She was right. He'd better get through it before he lost the nerve to tell her the whole story.

Two years after Luke was born, Ben made arrangements to record the band's next album in Los Angeles. Christine wanted to go and bring the boys, but Ben said no. He told her it wasn't a good environment for the boys to be in. The truth had been he didn't want her there.

When he left, she told him she wouldn't be there when he got back. Where would she go? Ben never met her family, never heard a single thing about them, even after they'd gotten married and had two kids.

They'd been in LA a week when a knock on the hotel room door early one morning woke him. Hung over, it took him a while to answer. When he did, Christine stood on the other side of it. She held Luke in one arm, and held Jake's hand with the other.

He answered the door naked, and had little choice but to let her push her way inside. When she did, she practically threw Luke in his arms before she attacked the woman still asleep in Ben's bed.

Five at the time, Ben still prayed Jake had no memory of that day.

Trying to manage a two-year-old and a five-year-old, both of them screaming, and rein Christine in was more than he was able to handle. Ben put Luke down on the floor and tried to get Jake settled, while he tried to keep their mother from pummeling the woman in his bed. Jimmy heard the commotion. He came to help, but it was still ugly.

They got the woman out of the room, and the kids settled with another member of the band. Then Christine told him she was done. She wanted a divorce, and she wanted full custody of the kids. On top of it, she wanted a hell of a lot of money.

Ben knew little about his financial situation. There was money, but how much? He also didn't know if he'd put the ranch at risk by marrying her without a pre-nup.

He flew home with Christine and the boys, dropping them off at the house, while he stayed with his parents.

He looked like hell. Between the shit with Christine, the band trying to cut a record with a detached producer, and the non-stop partying, he wanted to die. And then he learned he was sick. Very sick.

Less than a month later he was diagnosed with cancer. The record went on hold, the divorce did not. He went through a tough surgery, followed by both chemo and radiation therapy. He stayed at his parents' place through it all, while Christine and the boys remained in the house. She was adamant that she wanted full custody of their boys, and she used his illness to fuel her fight.

He learned later that his dad intervened and made a deal with her to finalize the divorce. In exchange for giving up all claims to the ranch, and other family holdings, Ben's family would take care of her for the rest of her life. It would continue provided she never tried to take Ben's boys away from him. If she ever tried, she'd lose everything.

The negotiations his father worked out on his behalf included a joint custody agreement. Christine moved into a house in town, and Ben went back to his place on the ranch as soon as he was well enough.

"You'd think with all that happened, the way Christine and I got together, the boys, the divorce, the cancer…that I would've stopped drinking. I didn't. I got worse."

Ben and the band went back to LA to finish the album, and it wasn't long before he started picking up old habits. He continued to drink, and self-destruct, for another five years.

"That brings me back to the beginning of the story. When I nakedly terrorized my sister-in-law." Ben tried to put a light-hearted spin on the words he spoke, but there was nothing light-hearted about the story he told Liv.

"What happened between now and then?"

"With Christine?"

Liv nodded.

"The years before I got sober were tough. She tried to do the best for our boys. Sometimes I was easy to get along with and other times—not."

Once he got sober, Ben asked Christine to go to counseling with him so they'd be better co-parents. They'd been able to work through a lot in those sessions, and came out of it far better than when they'd started.

Now they managed to have somewhat of a friendship. Christine met a guy not too long after they divorced and married him. Ben told Liv he didn't know a lot about Joe. He seemed to be good to his boys, his life with Christine stable.

The scene from the night before still plagued him. Christine knew, as well as he did, that casual drinking would never be an option for them. Christine had been going to AA since she got pregnant with Jake. Granted, he'd been in the same bar last night, but he wasn't drinking. Maybe she hadn't been either. Apart from how it affected Jake and Luke, what Christine did or didn't do, wasn't any of his business. Something else he needed to let go of.

"Addicts tend to be very sensitive people Liv. We have a need to be in control, which should mean control of ourselves, but sometimes it spills onto other people in our lives.

"We also talk about everything, at least most of us do. We've learned that talking things through, acknowledging how we're feeling is the key to our sobriety. As soon as I stop thinking through the decisions I make, I run the risk of making bad ones."

***

Liv tried to wrap her head around everything Ben told her. So much of it was foreign to anything she'd encountered in her life. It sounded almost absurd, but she didn't think she'd ever known another alcoholic. Never anyone close to her. Her parents drank, but in moderation. She'd never seen her mother or her father drunk.

There were occasions that Scott may have had more to drink than he should have. But never enough that it worried her. Or that she'd even noticed. And drugs had never been a part of her life, not in any way.

Liv wanted to believe this wouldn't change how she felt about him, but it did. She didn't have any way to relate to so much of what he told her. She didn't understand what drove someone to do the things he did.

His desire to talk about everything made more sense, so did his impulsiveness, and his insecurity. Above all, she understood his need for control, better than she had before.

But nothing about his life before his sobriety or since, explained his attraction to her. They had an undeniable sexual attraction, but other than that, what did they have in common?

She began to worry that Ben might see her as safe, or innocent, the same way Scott had. She wasn't anyone's savior, not Scott's, not Ben's, not even her own.

She was a normal woman who led a very safe life. She rarely took risks, of any kind, rarely even stepped out of her comfort zone.

What if Ben needed her to be someone she couldn't be, and she failed him? What would happen then, would he start drinking again? Would he blame her?

And what if it was all about her being *safe*? What was she supposed to do? Babysit him? Keep him from doing things he didn't want to do? Liv's life had been very sheltered in comparison to most, maybe he saw that as a plus.

He knew her story, she lived with her parents most of her life, except when she and Scott were married. And when her parents passed away, Liv inherited everything. Everything had been handed to her. She never had to worry about working or providing for her daughter.

Ben knew that when Scott told her to let go of her dream of being a barrel racer, she had, for him. Did he think she'd give up the life she'd created for herself for him the same way she had for Scott? Funny she was thinking about it yesterday when she told him the story of her life, that she wouldn't give herself up again for someone else.

If that's what he thought she'd do, he was very wrong. Bottom line, they had nothing to build a lasting relationship on. She and Ben *were not* meant to be, and it was best if they both realized it now, before either of them got in any deeper.

Ben knew the moment, the very instant, Liv disconnected from him. Her head remained next to his heart, but his heart hurt worse than he ever imagined.

"We can't get beyond this can we?" he ventured.

"No," she whispered.

"Is what I've told you so hard to accept? Is it so hard to think that I may have done all that, yet am still a good man?"

"That isn't it."

"What is it then?"

"You are a very good man, that I'm sure of. But I'm also sure that I am not the woman for you. As much as you think I might be, I know in my heart I'm not. I know it now more than ever."

She was rejecting him. He'd say it was unexpected, but he'd be lying. If he hadn't thought she might, it wouldn't have been so important for him to tell her the whole story. He didn't want any secrets between them, no lies, not even lies of omission. It was the risk he had to take, he'd done it, and now he had to face the consequences.

"Do you want me to take you home?"

"It would be best if you took me to Gunnison. I'll take a commercial flight from there."

"You don't even want me to fly you home." It wasn't a question.

***

The thing that Ben struggled with more than anything was that deep in his soul, he believed that he and Liv were meant to be together. He couldn't deny she shut down, shut off, shut him out. But he wouldn't let go of his belief that they belonged together.

The ride to Gunnison was one of the worst of his life. Everything about her closed to him. He had no idea how to break through the wall that went up the moment he finished his story.

She started to argue with him when he insisted on paying for her plane ticket. But arguing meant you had to show emotion. You had to care about a person to argue with them.

When the ticket agent handed her the boarding pass, Liv turned and took Ben's hand in hers. "I wish you all the best in life Ben. I wish love and happiness for you. You deserve it, more than anyone I've ever known."

He stared at her. She talked to him as though he was a total stranger. Like she was a caregiver wishing her ward the best as he took his leave.

"You can't be serious? That is what you have to say to me, after these last few weeks. That's it?"

"Please don't do this. I don't know what brought us together. I don't believe in the proper alignment of stars as you do. You and I were attracted to each other sexually, and we acted on it. And yes, it was wonderful, and spectacular. But don't make more of it than that."

He turned away from her and started to walk away, but stopped. When he turned back, she said, "You will meet the woman you are meant to be with, and she will be all that you need. She will love you for who you are, and she will be supportive of you. She'll be strong enough for you to lean on, but she will not be safe. You deserve so much more than *safe*. Go out and find it Ben. And be happy."

***

The words kept playing over in his head. *She will be strong enough for you to lean on, but she will not be safe.* What did she mean? It had to mean that she didn't see herself as that person.

Did that mean she believed she was weak? And what did she mean by *safe?* There was a key in the last words she spoke to him. Something that he should understand, and when he figured it out, he'd be able to convince her she was wrong.

Chapter Twelve

Paige knew damn well there was more to the story than Liv told. She acted as if everything was fine, *they had a wonderful time. Ben was such a great guy.* Bullshit. Something was up, but Liv would not talk about it.

"I still don't understand why you're back already?"

"Busy lives Paige."

"And he didn't fly you back. I don't understand that either."

"We weren't as compatible as he thought we were once he got me there. When the challenge wore off, his interest level dropped. It's what I expected all along Paige. It was a fling, a great one. And now it's over. I should write a book."

Paige was determined to get to the bottom of whatever was happening. Did she have any right to call Ben and ask him? Did she put her nose in where it didn't belong? What would happen if she did? Would Liv and Ben work through it and end up together? Or, would she make a complete fool out of herself if it ended up that everything Liv told her was true?

She'd have to talk to Mark about it later.

***

Liv got it. Completely. There were people who were meant to be alone. Love had come into her life once, briefly, and then it was taken away.

The reason she'd stayed alone all these years, was because that is how it was meant to be. Even the bear crossing her path, if she'd been paying attention, she would have recognized it.

Her time for silence and solitude wasn't finished, neither was her time for reflection and self-understanding, because she *hadn't gotten it.*

From the moment she'd met him, she ran from Ben, and not because she was protecting herself. Her instincts told her she wasn't right for him. She'd refused to listen.

She didn't blame Paige, but if Paige hadn't pushed, Liv never would have gone to see Ben in Crested Butte. Their fling, as she kept referring to it, would've died a very natural death, rather than being forced.

She'd gotten all caught up in the attention Ben lavished on her. She'd been seduced by it. Sure, she wanted him to find her attractive, she loved that he wanted her, that he chased her. But she'd known all along that she was nowhere near as interesting as Ben thought. What she knew, and he wouldn't admit, was that he got everything he wanted. His attraction to her was more about her not giving in to him as anything else.

The same would've been true with Scott, had he lived. She was a shell of a person. She didn't have big, bold life experiences like Ben had. She had a little, tiny risk-free life.

The only thing she'd ever wanted to do in her life, she'd never done. She'd never even tried. She hid behind the excuse that she was too busy being a mom. She wouldn't trade being Renie's mother for anything in the world, but even she recognized her mother's shortcomings. What had Renie said that night?

It's not as though you're miserable or anything, but… you're not happy either.

It wasn't as though she was miserable, but she wasn't happy either. She was a *shell*. She had no passion in her life. She'd lived her entire life without ever truly being in it. Once her daughter came into the world, everything became about Renie. Liv was a mother. And that's what she remained. Every decision she made was based on Renie and what she needed.

Paige said it too. She was doing nothing more than waiting around to die. And it might be a very long time before she did, so she'd better find something to live for, something for herself.

She knew the person to talk to. Liv saddled up Micah and took off a breakneck pace. When she got to the Pattersons' she prayed Dottie was home. She needed to talk to her now. Right now.

"Hey-o," she shouted out when she walked in the back door.

"In here," Dottie shouted back from the kitchen.

"How come you're always in the kitchen when I come over?"

"Oh there's my sweet girl! How are you Liv? I have missed you something awful."

"Dottie, I have something important to talk to you about. You may call me crazy, but there's something I want to do, and I want you to help me."

Dottie listened as Liv spelled out her plans. "I know just the person you need to go see," Dottie said. She got up from the table, and pulled out her address book.

"Her name is Jolene Berger, and she'll help with everything you need. You may have to go to Oklahoma for a spell, but it'll be worth it in the long run."

"I'll have to hire someone to work the boarding stables while I'm gone."

"I've got just the fella. Wait for a minute and I'll give you his number too before you leave."

Liv rode Micah home, and went into the house to call Renie. Her daughter would be disappointed, but Liv had to do this.

"Hey honey, how are you?" Liv said when Renie answered.

"Good Mom, how are you?"

"I'm fine. You sound tired."

"Finals. Ugh. Two more weeks, I can't wait to be finished and on my way home…"

"Listen, that's why I'm calling. I have to cancel our trip to Europe."

Silence.

"Renie? Are you there?"

"Mom, is this about Ben?"

"No, honey. I'm not seeing him any longer. And before you say anything, I'm fine. I had a great time. It was an adventure I'm happy I experienced."

"Mom, are you okay? You're not sick, are you?"

"No honey, and I'm sorry if I scared you. But there's something that I have to do. It'll mean I have to be away from home for a while, and I can't afford the time away to go to Europe and do this."

"Okay…you're being very cryptic."

"We'll talk more when you get home in a couple weeks. That is if you're still coming home."

"Where else would I go Mom? I mean, is it okay if I come home?"

"Of course it's okay, but you don't have to. If you're coming home for me, don't. If there's something you want to do, you should go and do it."

"All right crazy person. Whoever you are, can you please ask my mom to call me when you see her again?"

Liv laughed. "I miss you sweetie, and I can't wait to see you. Oh, and I hope you're not too disappointed about our vacation."

"No, but I would like to hear what happened with you and Ben. We can talk about him when I see you too."

Liv didn't answer her daughter, but they would not be talking about Ben. Not next week, not ever. That chapter of her life was closed.

***

"Can I go with you?" Renie asked when her mother sat her down and told her what she planned to do.

"Of course you can, but it won't be very exciting. I have a lot of hard work ahead of me."

"Maybe I can help. There's something else I want to talk over with you. About school."

"What's that?"

"I've been considering this for a long time, and what you're doing has influenced me a little. Not a lot, but a little."

"And? What are you going to do?"

"I'm transferring to Colorado State University's College of Veterinary Medicine. Next year."

"You are?"

"I'm not cut out to be a people doc Mom."

Renie had been on a biomedical track at Dartmouth, but seemed ambivalent about what she might do with it. She wondered for a while if her daughter would take a couple of years off, and continue with the graduate portion of her education, after she decided what she wanted to do with her life.

"Large animal vet, huh?"

"It's what I'm meant to be Mom. It's so obvious."

"Have you started the transfer process?"

"It's done. Which is one of the reasons I wanted to come home this week. I need to go to Fort Collins and complete the paperwork. I can do that tomorrow, and we can still leave for Oklahoma the day after."

* * *

More than anything Ben wanted to cancel the show in Denver, but it sold out three hours after the tickets went on sale. It was the last place he wanted to be, but he didn't have a choice.

He was sitting in the dressing room when Jimmy knocked. "There's someone here to see you. Remember that woman from Las Vegas, Paige? She's here."

Ben's heart stopped for a minute, then fell. "You can tell her she can come back."

"Hey," he said, standing to greet Paige and give her a hug. Mark was with her. "How have you been? Glad you came to the show."

He tried to sound enthusiastic, but his heart wasn't in it. He hoped they didn't notice.

Mark made small talk, but Paige was antsy. She wanted to say something to him.

"Spill Paige," he said.

Paige turned to Mark. "Go ahead, you'll tell him whether I think it's a good idea or not."

"It's about Liv."

"Is she enjoying Europe?"

"She didn't go."

"Why not?"

"She's in Oklahoma."

"Paige, no offense, but can you get to the point? You're killing me here. Liv didn't go to Europe, she's in Oklahoma, none of this makes sense. Just tell me for fuck's sake."

"Before I do, tell me what happened between the two of you."

"Oh my God," Mark groaned. "He's supposed to be on stage in less than an hour."

"She dumped me. How's that for putting it in a nutshell? I told her things about my life she didn't like, and she dumped me. That's the end of the story."

Paige walked to the other side of the small room, and walked back. "That isn't Liv."

"I didn't think so either. Guess we're both wrong."

"No, neither one of us is wrong. There's more to this, but I haven't been able to put my finger on it yet. What did she say?"

"She said a lot. The part that stuck with me was she hoped I found a woman strong enough for me to lean on. Someone who wasn't safe."

Ben would give a million bucks, on the spot, to know what Paige had on her mind. And somehow he knew she wouldn't tell him yet. And he said so. "You don't plan to tell me, do you?"

"What?"

"Where she is, what she's doing, why you think we're not wrong about her. You're gonna leave me hanging, right before a show. Aren't you?"

Ben looked at Mark. "She is, isn't she?"

Mark nodded his head.

"Come on Mark, there's something we need to do."

"Are we staying for the show at least? And if you're not, can I please stay and get a ride home with someone else? I'll even take a cab home."

"No, I need your help. You have to go with me. Sorry Ben. I'll be in touch."

"Nooo," he heard Mark pleading as she dragged him away.

***

Racing legend Mary Beth Wagner agreed to train Micah, while Jolene Berger trained Liv. No one Liv had spoken to thought forty too old to start barrel racing. Jolene in particular, who'd won nine world title championships in her career, the last at fifty-eight. And barrel racing did not have age classifications. Jolene competed against eighteen-year-olds, twenty-six-year-olds, fifty-year-olds and everything in between.

"There's a lot more to barrel racing than people think," Jolene told her. "It's all about making sure your horse picks up his shoulder around the turn. Making sure you have control of the horse's poll, neck, shoulder, barrel, and hind end. You're a good solid rider. What you need to do now is be a sponge. Squeeze every bit of knowledge you can out of the horse you're gonna train on. Then shower it on Micah when he's ready."

Liv and Micah started training and when they did, Liv tried her hardest to put everything and everyone else, out of her head.

Chapter Thirteen

"No, no, no," Jolene yelled at her. "You're not focusing. You need to *blast* home. Micah knows it. Where is your self-confidence today? Come on, do it again."

"Whaddaya think?" Mary Beth asked Jolene.

"She's got it in her. There are days she doesn't believe in herself. She knows that horse, no question about it. They have a strong connection. It's her head that's giving her trouble."

"Let's get her in the game."

"Is she ready?"

"She's ready. This'll show her. That's the only piece she's missing, enough confidence in herself. She's almost all the way there, and then somethin' makes her get back in her head."

"I'll get her into Woodward. The people are friendly and it has real good ground condition."

"Yep, that'll be the perfect start for our Livvie." Bill Patterson drove down the day before with Dottie to check on Liv's progress. He was astounded by what he saw. He'd wager anyone who would take the bet that she'd finish in the top three at this rodeo, and she'd be in the money.

He'd known Jolene Berger almost all his life. Dottie had been a bridesmaid in Jolene's wedding to Larry. And Larry was the best farrier Bill knew. Dottie did good getting their girl set up with these folks. He was as proud of Dottie as he was of Livvie.

***

"What's goin' on in that sweet head of yours darlin' girl?" Dottie asked her as she walked Micah.

"I dunno. Not on my game today I guess. I'm missin' Renie. Paige texted. Too many distractions."

"I hope you aren't countin' Bill and me as a distraction. I'd hate for us to be the reason you can't get your focus."

Liv let Dottie enfold her in one of her big hugs. "No, not you and Bill, not ever. I don't know how to thank you for this Dottie. It's because of you that I'm doin' this."

"No, it's not. It's because of you that you're doin' this and don't you ever forget it."

"A little bird told me that Livvie is competin' in her first rodeo this weekend," said Bill, joining them.

"Bill Patterson, are you tellin' the truth? Our Livvie is gonna be barrel racin' in a rodeo this weekend?"

Liv bent over with her hands on her knees, and took in a deep breath. When she stood up her hat flew into the air. She let out the loudest "Woohoo," Dottie had ever heard out of a girl.

"Micah, did you hear that?" She nuzzled up against him. "We're ready boy."

She wished Renie would come this weekend to see her mom in her first barrel race, but she'd be too busy with school. *Oh the hell with that,* thought Liv. Her first barrel race—Renie damn well better come down for it.

There were a couple other people she'd love to invite. One, in particular, but he was the reason she lost her focus today. She dreamt about Ben last night, and this morning she couldn't get him off her mind.

It wasn't unusual for her to dream about him. She did almost every night. Sometimes, he'd be talking to her. Or she'd dream she was walking Micah out of the barn, and he'd be standing there waiting for her.

Last night had been a different dream. She and Ben were having sex, and the dream was so vivid, she swore he was in the room with her when she woke up, sweating.

She missed him. Every day. She missed him more than she thought possible.

It had been two months and twenty-eight days since she walked out of his life. She counted the hours too. He was on tour now. She knew because she still checked CB Rice's Facebook page. And Twitter. And Instagram. He wasn't writing the posts, they didn't sound anything like him. Every once in a while she'd be able to tell when he answered someone's question on Facebook, or retweeted with a comment on Twitter. Those were the posts she longed for, when she felt a connection to him.

The photos from the tour were amazing. He looked good, and healthy. Sexy as ever, with that smile that made her knees weak. As much as she tried to tell herself she didn't love him, she did. She'd always love him.

She wondered if he'd met someone yet, someone who fit him better than she did. Liv shook her head, hard. She needed to stop this. If she didn't, she might as well not even go to Woodward this weekend. Her focus would be shot to hell.

***

Ben wanted to kill Paige Cochran. He'd been texting her for two days and the last he heard from her, she said she had news about Liv. He'd give her another hour and then he'd call her.

Fifty-three minutes later, he got an answer. *Woodward, Oklahoma is 9 hours and 48 minutes from Crested Butte.* That's what it said. What in the world was Paige talking about? And had that text been meant for him?

Huh?

Get in your truck and DRIVE cowboy. Mark and I will meet you there.

Ben had no idea what Paige meant. But what the hell, he had five days off between now and the band's next show. He might as well get in his truck and drive.

There were at least ten different times during the 570 mile drive that Ben thought about turning his truck around and heading home. But something in his gut told him to keep driving. Paige was a live wire, no question about it. But if she wanted him to come to Woodward, Oklahoma, home of exactly *nothing*, it must have something to do with Liv.

His palms were sweaty. When was the last time his palms were sweaty?

***

The day Liv left, Ben went and talked to his mom. He hoped she'd help him figure out what Liv's words meant.

She sat quietly for a long time before she answered him. "Liv needs time to figure out who she is Ben. And she needs to do it on her own."

"Do you think she might come back to me after she does?" He'd wait forever for her, but he hoped it didn't take that long.

"It all depends on what her journey leads her to," his mother answered.

That hadn't helped at all. What if Liv's journey led her to another man? A better man, not an alcoholic?

"Then that's the road she'll take," his mother responded.

He didn't like her answer. But what could he do? He could either accept that Liv would never come back, or live with the hope she would. Since he had no intention of pursuing any other woman ever again, he might as well live with hope.

***

He was fiddling with the radio, trying to find a station when the road sign caught his attention. "Hope, next exit," it said. As with everything, he convinced himself it meant something. Something about Liv.

Where are you? Another text from Paige.

Filling up the gas tank in a place called Hope, he answered.

You're close. Hurry.

Ben swore Paige would be the death of him one day. But she connected him to Liv. He'd put up with her until he took his last breath if he had to.

Ben got back on the highway and drove to Woodward. As his Google search had predicted, there was nothing in Woodward, except a rodeo, taking place tonight. He parked the truck and texted Paige.

At the rodeo, is this where I'm supposed to be?
Ticket waiting at will call for you.

Yep, she was a laugh a minute, that Paige.

Ben saw Paige and Mark sitting in the center section of the stands, halfway up. Renie was sitting with them. He turned toward the arena. Why was he here?

He gave Paige a kiss on the cheek when he got to his seat and whispered, "This better be good."

"Oh, it will be," she answered. "I guarantee it."

Mark shook his hand and shook his head. Renie waved at him. He supposed there'd be time for talking later.

"Ladies and gentlemen, our next event tonight is barrel racing," the announcement came through the loud speaker. "We've got a line-up of a few of the finest barrel racers in the state of Oklahoma. Y'all are in for a real treat. And, I'm told two of the grand dames of the sport are with us tonight, with one of their protégé riders. Everybody give a big round of applause for Ms. Mary Beth Wagner and Ms. Jolene Berger."

The two women rode the arena loop as the announcer listed their impressive achievements in barrel racing. The crowd stood and cheered for them.

"First up tonight is a little lady out of Monument, Colorado. Ms. Mary Beth and Ms. Jolene have been workin' this girl hard, and they tell us they expect her in Las Vegas come the end of the year. Everybody give a big welcome to Olivia Fairchild, ridin' Micah."

Every bit of air left Ben's lungs as he saw Liv and Micah come out of the alley. They took off. Micah went left around the barrel, then right. Both barrels were standing as Liv guided him to the third and final barrel. He rounded it perfectly and she headed home. The horse and rider flew.

"Ladies and gentlemen, coming in with a time of sixteen-eight is the little lady from Colorado. That is an unbelievable time for a first-time racer. Let's give her and Micah a big round of applause. Wow! I'd say Mary Beth and Jolene have trained a champion, wouldn't you folks?"

The crowd stood again. Everyone except Ben, who was still trying to find the air he needed to breathe. He looked up at Renie who met his gaze. They both had tears in their eyes.

"She's amazing, isn't she?" Renie came and sat next to him.

"So amazing." He wiped his eyes, but it didn't seem to do any good. There were so many reasons he wanted to cry. He was so proud of Liv he couldn't contain his emotions.

"You must think I'm…"

"I don't think you're anything, except in love with my mom." Renie put her hand on Ben's. "I don't know what happened, but this change in her is because of you."

"I wish I saw it as a good thing," he laughed.

"It will be, eventually. I've never seen my mom so determined about anything. And passionate. I never knew she had it in her, is that terrible for me to say?"

"Your mom is one of the most passionate people I've ever known. And I don't mean that in the way you're assuming I do."

Renie laughed out loud. "I'm not assuming anything Ben." The smile it brought to her face stayed there.

"I better get going."

"What do you mean?"

"Are saying your mom knows I'm here?"

"No. She doesn't." The smile faded.

"This is her night. Not mine. She was very clear the last time we saw each other that we were through. If she changes her mind, she knows how to get in touch with me."

"She doesn't know Paige and Mark are here either."

"Yeah, and I'm sure she didn't kick them out of her life either."

Renie shook her head. "Nope, she didn't."

Ben squeezed Paige's hand and winked at her, there weren't tears in her eyes until their eyes met. "Thank you," he mouthed before he stood, shook Mark's hand and left the stands, hands in his pockets.

He only hoped he could get out of there, and into his truck without completely breaking down. It would be so humiliating if he cried all the way to the parking lot.

Something by the barn caught his eye. Liv. He watched her run into the arms of a cowboy who picked her up and spun her around in a circle. The look on her face was pure joy. The cowboy's too. Joy. He forgot about trying not to cry, now he worried he wouldn't make it to the truck before his chest cracked open with the pain burning in it.

"Olivia Fairchild, am I ever proud of you," Billy Patterson hooted at her before he swept her off her feet and spun her in a circle.

"Can you believe it? I got a sixteen-eight? I thought there was something wrong with the clock and I would be disqualified. Shit Billy, sixteen point eight!"

"My mom and dad said you worked hard for it girl. They're damn proud of you. And I hope you don't mind me sayin' I am too."

"Thanks Billy, that means a lot to me."

"Whaddaya say we go do a little celebratin' tonight, just you and me?"

"Billy—"

"Shit I'm messin' around, but it was worth a try. Maybe you're so delirious with happiness that you forgot I don't do it for ya. God Livvie, I've loved you most of my life."

"There are plenty of girls you do it for Billy Patterson. Plenty. And you never loved me. I'm somebody safe you flirted with."

There was that word again. Safe. She was sick and tired of being safe. "Come out with us later. I'm meeting up with your folks and some friends. I'm awfully happy right now," she winked at him.

"Whoo-wee, you keep that up girl and I'll be flirtin' with you all night long."

Liv turned to walk Micah back to the barns. There was another round tomorrow night, and if she did well, she might be in the money on Sunday. At her first rodeo.

She walked back out after Micah was settled and looked up at the stars. "Ben, are you seeing the same night sky I am?" She put her arms around her waist, as though she held him close to her. "What I would've given to have you here tonight. I wonder what you would've thought about all this?"

She knew damn well Ben would be proud of her. If she'd told him she wanted to do this, he would've done everything in his power to help her. He never would've tried to talk her out of it. She could say all this *now*. Three months ago she didn't know whether she would ever qualify for a rodeo, let alone do so well her first time out.

For the hundredth time today, the millionth time this week, Liv wondered if she'd made a horrible mistake saying goodbye to Ben Rice.

Don't go home, the text from Paige said. What the hell? If heartbreak didn't kill him the heart attack Paige gave him would. Was there a more infuriating woman alive?

Ben pulled off the road. Where he was going? He couldn't drive home, at least not tonight. He needed to find a place to stay, sleep, and leave in the morning.

Don't go home, the text came through again.

I'm not, he wrote back.

Where are you?

Couple blocks away.

Meet us at Blue Water on Main.

Shit. What was Paige up to now? Enough with the texts, he called her.

"Hey," she answered.

"Paige, I gotta tell you, I haven't been this close to havin' a drink in a year. You have to let up on me a bit. You mean well, but..."

"She knows you're here."

"What are you talking about?"

"Renie decided she needed to know."

Fuck. Now what? Ben laid his head against the steering wheel. He never should have come. Liv would not be happy about this. No matter what he did next it would be the wrong thing.

"Does she want to see me?" What did he just say? Of course she didn't. He hit the steering wheel, hard, and answered before she had a chance to. "Fuck Paige, why are you doing this to me?"

He hit the off button on the phone and threw it against the passenger window, hoping it would break. Why had he come?

* * *

"Hey sweet mama," Renie said, meeting her mother outside the barn. "Do you have any idea how proud I am of you? How happy I am for you?"

Liv hugged Renie with all her might. Thank God she was here. If she hadn't been, tonight would've meant so much less.

"There were people in the stands tonight cheering you on that you didn't expect to be here."

Liv's eyes flew open, she tried to breathe in, and almost choked. She tried to catch her breath.

"Mom, are you okay?" Renie started slapping Liv on the back.

"Stop! Stop it. I'm okay, it went down the wrong pipe." Liv coughed a couple times trying to get her breath back. "Who?"

"Well, Paige and Mark came down, you probably figured they would. And you already knew that Dottie and Bill were here. There was another person you didn't expect."

Liv wanted to strangle her daughter. "Who Renie? Quit playing games and tell me."

"Ben."

Liv turned and walked back toward the barn. Ben was here. Where? Why? A million questions ran through her head.

"Mom, come back. Don't run away."

Liv looked back at her daughter but kept her feet firmly planted where they were. "You shouldn't have interfered in this." She went into the barn.

"Mom, wait a minute. Stop, quit walking away from me dammit!" Renie had never once, in twenty-one years raised her voice to her mother, she'd never had any reason to. Until tonight.

"Irene, you had no right," Liv said through her tears.

"First of all, I didn't interfere, Paige did." That made Liv laugh at least. "And secondly, that man loves you so much, you should have seen his face. He had tears in his eyes he was so proud of you."

"He did?" Liv whispered.

"Yes, he did. And if you don't talk to him, at least thank him for being here, be gracious to him, then I will be very, very disappointed in you."

Renie sounded like her. Whenever her daughter did something wrong, Liv's typical tactic was the one Renie was using. She didn't yell, or even a shout. She'd simply tell her that she'd be very disappointed in her if she didn't improve her behavior. Renie handed it back to her.

"I expect better from you Mom."

Yep, Liv had used that line too, plenty of times.

"Where is he?"

"Paige is trying to keep him from leaving."

What should she do? Liv had no idea. Should she call him and thank him for coming? Should she let Paige handle it? Should she run as fast and as far away from all this as she could?

"Renie?"

"What Mom?"

"I don't know what to do." It came out somewhere between a gasp and a whisper. She grabbed her daughter's arm, as if it had become her lifeline. "Help me."

"Call him."

Liv walked in a circle. Why was somebody always trying to get her to call him? First Dottie, then Paige, now Renie. Should she call him?

***

Ben picked his phone up off the floor of his truck and hit the "on" button. Nothing. He'd done it. He broke it. Wasn't that his intention? That way Paige wouldn't be able to reach him. He wouldn't know if Liv wanted to see him. What the hell was he thinking?

"Straight to voicemail. Shit." Paige said to Mark, furious at how she had handled it.

***

"It went straight to voicemail." Liv said to Renie, not knowing what to do next.

Chapter Fourteen

Ben got out of the truck and paced along the side of the road. He didn't know what the hell to do. Paige told him to come to Blue Water on Main. He assumed that was a restaurant, or a bar. He could find Main Street, since there were only two roads in the whole town, and he was on the other one.

He had two choices. To go, and see Liv. Or? He only had one choice.

Ben walked into the restaurant and didn't see Paige or Mark. He didn't see Renie or Liv either. Or even Dottie or Bill.

"Is there another Blue Water in town?" he asked the bartender, who laughed at him.

He ordered a coke and rubbed his hands over his face. He sat with his back to the door, he couldn't bear watching for her. If Liv walked into this bar and wanted to see him, she'd know he was there.

"I told him where we'd be." Paige said to Renie. "I don't know whether he'll come or not."

"Have you tried calling him again?"

"Only once a minute, keeps going to voicemail."

"She's gonna be wrecked if he doesn't show. We handled this wrong."

"Thanks Renie. I appreciate you saying 'we,' but this is all on me. I handled this wrong."

"Nope, you're not taking all the blame. It was my idea to tell her he was here. If I hadn't, he would've left. My mom never would've known he was here. Instead of looking as though she's gonna throw up any minute, she'd still be celebrating."

"Where is she?"

"She's walking toward me, she was freshening up in the ladies' room. Gotta go."

"Ready?" Renie said to her mom.

"Where are we going?"

"We're going to Blue Water on Main. Paige, Mark, the Pattersons, Jolene and Mary Beth are coming. And Mom, we're celebrating tonight, one way or another. I screwed this up, and I hope you can forgive me."

Liv went into mom-mode. "It's okay baby girl. This thing between Ben and me is complicated. I realize everyone wants to help, but some things can't be. Come on, let's go celebrate. Your mama is a barrel racer after all."

Everyone, except Ben, was waiting under the bright light near the front door when Renie and Liv pulled into the parking lot.

There were so many shouts and cheers, people picking her up and hugging her, Liv almost, for a second or two, forgot about Ben. Not a whole second, but part of one.

"Let's go eat," Bill said. "Dottie's treat."

Dottie slugged him, "That's right big spender, make your wife buy your dinner, and everybody else's too."

"I'm just kiddin' sweetie," Bill said as he nuzzled up to Dottie. Liv would give anything to have a love like the Pattersons did. She'd had a chance to, but she'd pushed him away.

Bill went in to get a table, followed by the rest of the group. Paige grabbed Liv's arm and held her back. "Walk in with me," Paige said to her and hooked her arm through Liv's. Renie was right in front of them, and Mark was right behind them. Liv wondered if they thought she would back out, so they had her surrounded.

It took a minute for her eyes to adjust to the darkness, but she saw him. His back was to her, but he was there. She stopped where she was, taking her arm from Paige's.

"Go ahead," she said. "I'll meet you in there."

Ben turned around. He felt her. The only thing he could do was smile, he was so damn happy to see her.

She loved his smile. She could look at him for hours. Ben smiled with his whole face, his eyes, his mouth…God, his mouth.

He stood, held out his arms, and she walked into him. Her mouth sought his, she couldn't wait.

Neither could he. His lips crushed into hers. His arms were around her waist. He lifted her and brought her mouth to his, her body against his.

The noisy restaurant went silent in his ears. It became a dull hum, he heard his own heart pounding. And he heard Liv, her soft, quiet whimpers as she kissed him, as her lips tore at his, as she ravaged him. *She ravaged him.* Not the other way.

"Ben."

It was the only word he wanted to hear.

"There's my girl."

"I'm so happy you're here. I heard you watched me chase the cans."

"You were magnificent."

She looked down and even as dark as it was in the bar, he knew her cheeks were pink. He put his finger on her chin and tilted her head so her eyes met his. "Magnificent."

Her smile left her face and her eyes bored into his. "I missed you so much."

"I know baby, me too."

"I'm so sorry."

"Shh. Nothin' to be sorry for."

"But—"

"Uh-uh. No buts." He smiled at her and kissed her again. "Let's go join your party darlin'."

***

Ben stood back and watched Liv as she circled the table, greeting each person there to celebrate her phenomenal success. He pulled out a chair at the end of the table and sat next to Mark.

"You didn't go home."

"I sat next to you because I thought you were the only person at the table who wouldn't talk to me about Liv. Can't we talk about guitar strings, or baseball, or another random topic you're so good at pullin' out of thin air? Please, let's not talk about me and Liv."

"You got it buddy." Mark pulled out his cell phone and started to show Ben videos on YouTube. The guy had the sense of humor of a fourteen-year-old and sometimes that was a very good thing.

"Tomorrow's another day of training, as it would be back home. Don't go gettin' all full of yourself tonight, thinkin' you have this in the bag," Jolene said to Liv.

"Oh Jolene, can't you give the girl a break? Give Cinderella a midnight curfew if you have to, but let her enjoy the ball while she's here." Dottie stood up in Liv's defense.

"You don't win world titles enjoying the balls," the gruff sixty-five year old spit out, which Mark picked up and ran with.

"What did she say, Liv isn't allowed to enjoy the balls? Is that what she said? Bummer for you dude."

"Yep. You're fourteen, a fourteen-year-old with gray hair."

***

Liv moved from person to person at the table, and between the end of one conversation and the beginning of the next, she'd look at him, fleetingly. Was she checking to make sure he was still there, or that he was okay, or was she wondering if he was watching her?

All three, he'd guess. And he moved from okay to well beyond it if in that moment, she smiled at him.

Too soon and yet not soon enough, Liv came and sat in the open chair next to him. What came next for them? Did they act as though they hadn't spent the last three months apart on purpose? Did he act as though he was another of her friends celebrating her big night? He had no idea.

"This is so much...more." She said to him. "More than I ever imagined, more than I expected, more than I dreamed of."

"Which part, the barrels, the friends, the celebration?"

"All of it. I'm not used to being the center of attention. I'm not used to having a reason to be."

So humble. Liv was completely unaware of her significance in the lives of the people sitting at this table. And with him? She saw herself as a soft place for him to land. It was the reason she worried they had nothing in common, why she told him he should find a woman strong enough for him. She saw herself as nothing more than a pretty pillow where he rested his head.

More than she dreamed of, that's what she said. But in her eyes, nothing she'd achieved in the last three months, or she would achieve in the next year, or two, or five with her barrel racing would make her more to him. Liv would still believe she wasn't enough for him.

They hadn't even come close to moving beyond square one. He was here, she was happy he was, but as far as something *more* between them? Nothing had changed. His mom suggested Liv needed time to figure out who she was, and she seemed to be doing that. But how did he make sure that while she learned who she was for herself, she also learned who she was for him, with him, why he wanted to be with her? He had no idea.

"You're quiet cowboy."

"I'm thinkin' about how much more you are than you realize."

"The things you say, sweet talker. Sometimes they sound as though they should be in a song."

He laughed. "And sometimes they are, or they work their way into one."

Liv rested her head against him. Her breath warmed the curve between his neck and shoulder. When she shifted far enough that her lips were where her breath had been, he thought he'd come apart. "Liv—"

"Will you stay with me tonight cowboy?"

Oh man, he *liked* confident Liv. But at this rate, he wouldn't last another five minutes before he took her out and plundered her in the parking lot. He moved her enough to brush his lips across hers, then moved her farther so no part of her body touched his.

"Ben?"

He leaned over and whispered in her ear, trying to keep himself from touching her as he did it. "I'm ready to throw you over my shoulder and carry you out of here, caveman-style. So unless you don't care what anyone at this table thinks of that, you gotta stop touching me."

He didn't miss the little grin she tried hard to hide, or the way her eyes drifted closed as she breathed in deeply. "I know sweetheart," he murmured.

Dottie got up on her feet and tried to pull Liv with her. "Come on girls, I wanna dance."

Oh good Lord, thought Liv, Dottie wanted to dance. Liv wanted to get out of this bar, and Ben out of his clothes. Bill and Mark were at the jukebox. Liv wasn't sure what to expect. Renie was on her feet, swaying to the music already. Her daughter loved to dance. So did she.

"Come on Paige, you're in on this too."

The heavy sounds of a guitar filled the room, something about saving a horse and riding a cowboy.

Oh God, she was going to kill Mark, if Paige didn't do it first.

Dottie, Jolene, and Mary Beth were woohooing it up, "Save a horse Livvie!" They pulled her in to dance with them, and she got into it. She'd had a damn good day, one of the best of her life. She deserved to have some fun.

They danced, and danced, and danced…Liv needed a drink, something tall and cool and wet. Ben. She'd rather have him than a drink.

"One more song Livvie," Billy Junior hollered out. "This one's a slow one."

The fiddle started to play as Zac Brown's "Free," drifted through the speakers in the bar.

"Oh, I love this song," Liv said to no one in particular, right before Billy swung his arm around her waist and proceeded to move her around the dance floor.

Ben lasted all of twenty seconds before he was on his feet, "Pardon me cowboy," he said, taking a page out of Liv's play book. "But you're dancin' with my girl."

"She was my girl before you came along…"

"Billy, you don't want to start this. You'll ruin my night." Liv kissed his cheek.

Billy stepped aside, and Ben pulled Liv in close. "This is the first time I've held you in my arms and danced with you. Do you realize that?"

"It's good, isn't it?"

"Dancing?"

"You, holding me in your arms."

He pulled back so he could see her face, and hated that he wondered how much she'd had to drink tonight.

"You think anyone would mind if you carried me out of here now? Remember that caveman thing?" She was talking so damn seductively, it was almost as though she was purring at him. He didn't care if anyone noticed, it was time for them to leave.

He danced her over near Dottie and Bill, who had his hands full himself.

"We're gonna call it a night. Thanks for everything," he said to them.

"You better ask Jolene what time Livvie's supposed to be at the barn in the mornin' there Ben. Won't be good for her to be showin' up late." Bill shook his finger at them as he said it.

"Jolene?"

Jolene was dancing with Mark, God love her, and him. Ben wasn't sure she heard him.

"Not a minute later than nine little girl. We gotta make sure you're *focused*." Jolene glared at Ben.

"She's a tough one," he said.

"She's my hero," Liv answered.

Ben put his arm around her and moved her in the direction of the door. "Are you gonna stay awake long enough to tell me where we're staying tonight?"

That seemed to jolt her awake. "Oh you don't need to worry about me stayin' awake *cowboy*."

They got to the truck and Ben didn't waste a second. His hands fisted in her hair as he backed her up against the door. His lips rubbed against hers, nibbling, teasing, followed by his warm tongue invading her mouth. Her stomach did a little flip as he first groaned then growled when her hands dug into his chest beneath his shirt. He took over, imprisoning her hips with his. She loved having the length of his body against hers.

His hands gripped her hips as he kissed her harder. He stroked the soft skin where her shirt rode up as he kissed her softer. He angled his head, changing his kiss. He was gentle, so gentle, sweet, but she wanted so much more from him.

"I can't think straight for wanting you Liv," he nuzzled her cheek, then realized his stubble probably scratched her. He reached up and softly rubbed his fingers where his face had been.

He pulled her away from the door and unlocked it. "I want you too much for it to be this way Liv."

She climbed into the passenger seat and he leaned in, laying his face against her breast, his hand squeezing the inside of her thigh. He stopped. His hand came up, and he gripped her chin. "You are so beautiful Liv," her eyes fell away from his.

"No, don't look away." Her eyes met his straight on, as if challenging him.

"You are so beautiful Liv, but, you are so much more than that. You're everything. Do you understand? You're everything to me."

He pulled away and closed the door, stopping to take a deep breath before he walked around the back of the truck. He got to his door and stopped again, and took another deep breath. God he hoped he didn't screw this up.

As soon as they were in the hotel room, Ben worked the buttons on Liv's blouse free, running his fingers along each sliver of her skin. Once it hung open, he slid it off her shoulders and let it fall to the floor.

His eyes darkened with heat as his lips followed where his tongue had been. He dropped to his knees, his tongue licked across her middle. His fingers popped the button on her jeans. He lowered the zipper and his warm mouth softly kissed along the top edge of her panties. He tugged her jeans until they were down below her knees.

"Sit on the bed Liv." She practically fell back into it. "Liv, look at me," he demanded. She was in her bra and panties. Ben was still fully clothed. He placed his hands on her knees, "Let me in."

He leaned in close enough that his jeans rubbed against her skin while his hands slid up her thighs, around her hips, up her back and around the to the clasp of her bra. It immediately fell away.

"You're too good at that," she groaned.

He palmed her breasts and she arched and let her head fall back. And then he was gone. She opened her eyes as he yanked his shirt over his head. She watched as he unhooked his belt buckle, unfastened the button, and unzipped his jeans.

"Do I need a condom Liv?"

"No, you don't."

"Is it for me Liv, only me?"

"Only you Ben, it's only you." She tried to stifle her cry. There was no one else for her. There never would be.

He swooped down and fused his mouth to hers. Kissing her hard, and rough, and eager. His lips followed the line of her jaw, up to her ear, "I need you baby."

She didn't answer with words, but arched against him. And at that moment, he went still, right before he buried himself inside her. Slowly. So slowly.

There was no better feeling in the world than her body joined together with his.

"You're mine, all mine Liv." He started to move faster, harder. "Tell me. Let me hear you say it."

"I'm yours Ben, all yours."

Later, Ben waited until her breathing became more even. He moved her hand off his hip and whispered, "Liv," to see if her eyes opened. They didn't.

"You're all I ever wanted. Since the moment I laid eyes on you. You're it baby. I love you, heart and soul, with everything I am." He rolled to his back and stared up at the ceiling. "And why is it that I can only say this to you when you're sleeping? Because I know if you heard me, you'd bolt."

Liv shifted again, her arm came across his waist, she turned part way to her side, and her body nuzzled up against his. She brought her head up and laid it on his chest. Her eyes never opened, her breathing never changed. In her sleep Liv's body sought his, she got close to him…when they made love, and when she slept.

Liv woke, Ben was next to her. Soft light filtered in through the window coverings, it was still early. She drifted back to sleep for a moment, then shook herself awake again. She wanted this time awake, while he slept.

Her eyes drifted over his face, slowly, as though they were her fingers, so slowly she let them wander. They lingered on the lines at the corner of his eye, etched there because of his smile, the one he gave so generously. They moved to the crease in the hollow above his eyes, between his eyebrows, as though as he slept stress stayed, furrowed there, not allowing his brow to be completely at rest. His mouth called her eyes to move to its pout. The corners turned down in his sleep, the same way they did when he played guitar, and got lost in it, forgetting where he was. He slept with his mouth closed. Did everyone? Had Scott? Liv didn't remember. She closed her eyes and pulled at her memory, it wouldn't bring Scott into focus. He'd faded, her mind no longer remembering how he slept, or how he looked. She opened her eyes again to continue her study of Ben's face. His eyes were open, studying her.

His hand came up, joining his eyes. His fingers feathered strokes on her cheek. His eyes added to the caress.

Liv let her eyes wander back to where they'd been, on his mouth. Then let them slowly drift over his chin that jutted strongly when he concentrated on something. As her eyes moved lower, she saw the pulse beating in his neck. He swallowed and she watched the way the muscles changed when he did. Down they continued, over his chest, at rest now, it looked softer, her fingers longed to run through the downy hair scattered over it. But this feast was for her eyes.

She let them move to his arm, shifting back to see him better, without her body laying against it. His square shoulder never rounded. Had he been a swimmer? She tilted her head to look at his forearm, and his wrist, and his hand. Masculine hands, with big, firm fingers, symmetrically calloused from their continued use on the strings of his guitar.

She looked back up to his chest, it rose and fell with a stronger rhythm, as if his heart was driving it, harder and faster.

Back to his face, his eyes were half-lidded, getting darker and hungrier as his breathing accelerated. His mouth opened slightly, but he didn't speak.

Liv's hand slowly moved the sheet that kept the rest of him hidden. Her eyes needed to take in all of him. Would he stay still and let them? He didn't move.

Her eyes lingered on his torso, watching as his body changed the longer her eyes studied him, as though they were speaking to him. Urging him on to feel their heat.

More movement. The muscles in his thighs beckoned her attention. His leg shifted, his knee bent slightly. They drifted over his calf, his ankle and to his feet. She loved his feet. Feet said a lot about a man. His were strong, and sturdy. They carried so much, his feet.

She let her hands find their way back up the slow trail her eyes had just taken, softly stroking his skin as they went. He breathed in deeply, almost a gasp. Her lips longed to finish the journey. She brought her mouth to his skin and continued the path, slowly easing back over each spot her eyes had rested on.

Ben was so still, the pace of his breathing measured against his stillness. Liv climbed up and laid her entire body against his. Body on body, skin on skin. She loved it as much as he did. Her hand took his and she gently set it against her hip, giving him permission to move, to let his body begin to take part in the exploration hers began.

His other hand came up on its own, but as slowly as the first had. At first still, they started to move along her sides. Soft fingers trailed from each hip, to the side of her breasts and then up slowly over her shoulders, hardening as they got to her neck. Grasping as they reached her face, pulling as they brought her lips to his. At the same time his mouth joined with hers, his body did too, they fit together with such ease.

Liv raised up, her hands digging into his chest, the place her eyes kept selfishly to themselves only a few minutes ago. Her eyes took their place in his, searching for the thing they needed to see. Longing, love—there it was. She kept them there as she moved, bringing them both to the place where their bodies answered the need their eyes desired.

***

When Liv got out of the shower, Ben was sitting in the chair by the window, guitar in his arms, singing.

To see you here then, it tickles me crazy.
To see you here in the midst of your fall.
I know your fear, I know your tears.
But that smile, so sweet, that longing so deep.

He stopped when he realized she stood outside the bathroom door. She smiled, leaned her shoulder up against the wall and closed her eyes.

Your eyes burn into my heart,
my love, my joy, my fall.

She wanted him to keep singing, she wanted him to finish. But she couldn't wait. Ben seemed to sense it, leaning his guitar on the floor next to the table as she stalked toward him.

He stood, and she launched herself into him.

"You're gonna be late baby…"

"Don't care."

Chapter Fifteen

"Can you stay, or do you need to get back?" Liv asked Ben as he drove her back to the rodeo grounds.

"Waitin' for you to ask me. Figured I already pulled the 'I'm here and I'm stayin'' whether you want me to or not,' card. Gotta let it be up to you sometimes."

"Can you handle giving up all that control?"

Ben threw his head back, in that way he did, and laughed. "For an hour or two, probably my limit."

"I'll be riding and working with Micah most of the day. Jolene has a horse whisperer approach she wants me to try. But it's gotta be me doing it. He only responds to me."

"Kinda like me."

Liv was lost in thought about Micah, and what they needed to work on today. He went left, every time. Right he hesitated, yet all her instincts told her to push him that way. Even that split-second hesitation carried tension into her shoulders. That's what they needed to focus on today.

She realized Ben watched her, smiling. "Where'd you go?"

Her cheeks turned the lightest shade of pink. "Turn two."

"I like you this way. All sweet and cowgirly."

"Never underestimate a cowgirl Ben, we're rarely sweet."

Liv jumped out of the Tahoe, waving her hand as she walked away. She never looked back. It was a little thing, but he started to realize she did it every time. Most people looked back. She never did.

He drove to the outskirts of town and found a shady place to sit for a while. He wanted to finish the song he started this morning.

When he went to check the time, Ben remembered he broke his phone last night. Shit. He better get to town and get a replacement, he doubted there'd be anything in Woodward, he'd have to go farther, maybe back to Hope. He needed to check in with the band, his kids, and his parents. When he left yesterday morning, he hadn't told anyone where he was going, considering he hadn't known that part himself.

***

The first call he made was to Jimmy. They wouldn't head back out on the road until Monday night or Tuesday morning, but he needed to be home sometime tomorrow to pack things up and get ready.

"Where are you again?" Jimmy asked.

"Woodward, Oklahoma."

"I don't even wanna ask."

"Yeah, there's not much here, except a rodeo. And pheasant hunters."

"Huh?"

When Ben was brushing his teeth that morning he'd noticed the sign over the sink that said, "No cleaning pheasants in sink." It stuck with him, might be a song in there somewhere.

"Whatever, never mind that. When are you coming back?"

"Sunday night, but I was wondering if you guys could handle packing up for next week." Ben wanted to stay through the end of the rodeo on Sunday night to watch Liv wrap up her first showing. He'd drive back Monday, and meet up with them.

"Yeah, I guess."

Ben heard the hesitation in Jimmy's voice. "What?"

"Nothin'. Can't say no since you never ask. What's so important in middle-a-nowhere Oklahoma anyway?"

Ben hesitated.

"Oh. No."

"What?"

"It's her, isn't it? The girl?"

"Yeah, whatever. See you Monday night." Ben ended the call.

A slew of texts started coming through on his phone, including one from Jake, who was fighting with his brother. His mom sent one saying she left a container of soup in his refrigerator, and then another asking when he'd be home.

The last texts were from Paige, most from the other night, after he broke his phone. There was one from today asking if he was still in town. Bet she hadn't asked Liv. She was a sly one that Paige.

He answered and asked where they were. He wouldn't mind hanging out with Mark today. Maybe they'd go pheasant hunting.

"How is she?" Paige asked as soon as Ben sat down in the booth with them at the diner.

"Mad as hell. At you," he teased, and smiled. He watched her face go from panicked to irritated.

"I'm not gonna let you two hang out together anymore," she said.

"How did I get involved in this?" asked Mark. Truth was Ben had never seen a guy who was more of an innocent bystander than Mark. He and Paige had been married for thirty years, so Mark had to be used to it.

"When are you going back?"

"Thinkin' Monday morning."

"Things must be goin' well then."

Mark shrugged his shoulders, then said, "If it's none of her business, you gotta say so. Until you do, she's gonna keep seeing how much information she can get you to give her."

Ben looked at Paige and straight-faced said, "Paige, it's none of your business."

"You should be thanking me," she pouted.

"Thank you Paige," he smirked.

"Can I join you?" asked Renie.

"Of course," said Paige, motioning for Ben to scoot over.

Renie sat down, turned and faced him, arm on the back of the booth. "So. You're still here."

"Renie," Ben said with a killer smile, "it's none of your business." Mark high-fived him.

***

Liv rode Micah around and around in the warm-up arena, trying to keep her thoughts on the barrels and off of Ben. She pulled a slot further down tonight, so she wouldn't be first out of the chute. That was good and bad. More time to let her mind drift.

One of the bare bronc riders had stopped by the barn today to introduce himself. She noticed him ride by, trying to stay close to her.

"Hey cowgirl, you chasin' the cans again tonight?"

"You know it cowboy," she grinned over her shoulder.

"Whoo-wee, you're pretty."

There was something about Ben being in the stands tonight that let Liv flirt a little. This time she enjoyed being safe, because it meant something else entirely. She was safe to flirt, *a little*, because at the end of the night, she knew which cowboy she'd be going home with.

Thoughts of Ben whirled around in her head, until she saw Jolene glaring at her from the fence. If Jolene had her way, Ben would be on the next bus out of town, she'd made that clear this morning when Liv showed up a half hour late.

"You think we agree to train just anybody Miss Olivia?"

Well, she was paying them, but no, that wouldn't be enough to get them to do it.

"No ma'am, I don't, and I'm very sorry I was late."

"If you aren't gonna take this seriously, there's no point in my even bein' here. I should get in the truck and head home. I got a family too."

"Please don't leave Jolene. I won't be late again. Ever."

"You see that you don't 'cause tomorrow morning, you're as much as forty-five seconds late, I'm in the truck and gone. Got it?"

"I got it." Liv walked to where Mary Beth stood holding Micah. "She doesn't mean it."

"It's better if I believe she does." Liv shook her head. "She reminds me of somebody."

"Who's that honey?"

"My father."

* * *

Liv was up next. The ground was a little softer tonight, it had rained earlier, not enough to make a big difference, but so far every rider had knocked over a barrel, resulting in a five-second penalty. Two riders remained after Liv, so if she left all three barrels standing, she had a very good chance to stay in the money.

She got the signal and Micah flew. He went left, circled around, headed right, hugged the circle in the opposite direction. There was only one barrel left in the clover pattern, he was flying fast but hugging the barrels tight. They headed for home and finished with a time of sixteen-three. She beat last night's time by five-tenths of a second.

Liv scratched and rubbed Micah's neck. He loved to roll in the dirt, and tonight she'd let him.

She led Micah to the barn, and saw a man standing with his shoulder up against the door. His cowboy hat sat low over his eyes, his jeans hung over his hips, the way they always did. His T-shirt hitched up enough that her eye caught his skin, she took her time.

The man was hot, no other way to describe him.

"God damn you're pretty," he said as she got closer. "You got any plans tonight little lady, 'cause I sure want to be the man keeping company with you."

She shook her head and smiled. "Sorry cowboy, but my dance card is already full this evenin'. Maybe another time."

"Then sugar, I'm gonna make sure you never make it to the dance." Ben took Micah's reins from her hand and pulled her in close. His thigh inched between hers and spread them apart. He bent his head to kiss her without knocking her hat off. Liv reached up and threw it off anyway. She wanted to kiss him so hard she took his breath away. And after that, she wanted to possess him. Never before had she wished somebody else could take care of Micah.

***

"Wait," she said. "Where are we going?"

"Back to the hotel."

"But what about Renie, and Paige and Mark?"

"Sorry sugar, but it's just you and me tonight."

He watched the heat rise to her cheeks.

"Liv, I need this. I need you. Different from the way it's been between us."

"What you do you mean?"

"I need to be in control tonight."

He watched as her breath caught.

"Tell me you want this Liv. Tell me with a word, that tonight you belong to me, your body, your soul."

Her eyes widened. Her breathing became uneven.

"Tell me," he said again, as his fingers encircled her wrist.

"I want this," she breathed.

When they pulled up to the hotel, Ben came around and opened her door.

"When we get in the room, I want you to take off your clothes and wait for me on the bed."

She bit her lip, hesitating for a moment, then nodded that she understood.

Ben stood and watched her do what he asked, he didn't move. His mouth watered, longing for a taste of her. His arms ached, wanting to pull her into him and comfort her insecurities.

Liv stood next to the bed, her clothes at her feet. Her body trembled as she started to pull the comforter back. He nodded for her to continue. She pulled the sheet back too, and lay down on the bed. Her hand reached for the sheet and he was on her, his hand on her wrist, stopping her.

"Watch me," he demanded as he reached behind him and pulled his shirt over his head. Her eyes moved over his body, the same way they had earlier that morning.

He stood before her, naked. He reached behind her head and put one pillow on top of the other. "Put these under your head," he said. "I want you to be able to see what I'm doing to you."

Ben's hands moved along her legs, up her thighs and her waist. He followed to her spine, until she arched instinctively.

"Ben—"

"Shh. Be still."

He wanted her to give herself over to him, even as hard as he knew it would be for her to do it. He wanted her to let him take control the same way he'd let her this morning, without her realizing he did.

Every second had been pure torture for him. He'd wanted nothing more than to grab her and throw her under him, but he hadn't. He let her eyes, and her hands, and her lips linger on his body, unhurried, at her pace. Now he needed the same thing from her.

"Put your hands at your sides Liv, and don't move them."

He needed to prove to her that he was the man to take care of her, love her enough to make it all about her, satisfy the need he saw in her eyes. He was long gone for this woman. He'd take her any way she'd let him, even if it couldn't be forever.

***

He hoped she hadn't gone to sleep, that he hadn't worn her out. "Liv?"

"Hmm?"

"Why did you leave me?"

"Oh Ben, do we need…"

"No, we don't need. I *need*. I need to know why."

"I told you then."

"Tell me again."

"I'm not enough Ben. I don't know why you think I am."

"Why do you get to decide what is enough for me?"

She didn't have an answer. Because she wouldn't be able to bear it when he realized she was right? If she left first it would hurt, but nowhere as bad as it would if she gave herself to him in life, the way he asked tonight, and then he realized she had been right along.

"Liv?"

"I guess I don't. I can only decide what's enough for me."

"Am I enough for you?"

"You're too much Ben."

She pulled away from him. He reached over and turned on the light in the dark room. He needed to see her eyes. He didn't ask, he waited.

"You need so much," she answered. "I can't give you all you need. You said it yourself. *You need*. What will happen to me if I become what you need?"

"What are you saying?"

Liv sat up and pulled the sheet over her. "Are you planning to force this Ben? Because this is what I'm talking about. It's all in, right now, or not at all."

She got up and started to put on her clothes.

"What are you doing?"

"I'm getting dressed."

"Why?"

She turned and glared at him, dropping her clothes back on the floor. "Because that is how I feel when I'm with you. That's what you do to me. You look too closely. You push too hard. You want everything, but you want it right this minute. You make me want to put my clothes back on."

She ran her hand through her hair, trying to decide what she should do. She reached out and grabbed the sheet, yanking it hard. It came off the bed and she wrapped it around her.

"You decided you wanted to know more about me, so you followed me around, asking me questions, endlessly. You wouldn't stop Ben. You forced it. Let's go back further. You came to my house. You showed up there. You didn't even call. You came. And you didn't ask. You just stayed.

"You insisted I tell you about my life, whether I was ready to or not. Then, worse, you made me, forced me, to listen to yours. I wasn't ready for that. Do you understand? I'm not ready for any of this."

Liv paced back and forth next to the bed, trying to hold the sheet up as she did, but it would slip, and she would trip on it. And every time she did, she'd glare at him, as though it was his fault.

And he, asshole that he was, thought it was the cutest, sweetest, craziest thing he'd ever seen. She tried to be mad at him, but she sucked at it. It was harder than hell for him to fight the smile trying to escape his lips. She was adorable when she tried to be mad.

Then she growled at him. He couldn't help it...he laughed. And she stopped moving. She stood next to the bed, holding the sheet up with one hand, and stared at him.

"I'm sorry," he said, but he couldn't stop laughing.

"No, you're not. You're not sorry at all. You think this is funny."

"Liv. Olivia. Olivia Fairchild. It isn't funny."

"Then why are you still laughing? You can't stop, can you?"

He couldn't. He tried to, but he couldn't. Maybe if he didn't look at her. But where else could he look? He grabbed her around the waist and pulled her on top of him.

He pulled her close. She smiled, not mad anymore. He hoped what he was about to do wouldn't make her mad again.

"Liv."

"Ben." Her eyes softened, her lips still smiling. She was being silly now. He had to do it anyway.

"I love you."

Chapter Sixteen

Ben held his breath. She didn't say anything. Her expression didn't change. Nothing. Had she heard him?

Finally, she moved. Her hand came up and her fingers stroked his cheek. Then she licked her lips. Twice. She put her hand on the back of his neck, and she pulled herself up, so her lips were closer to his.

And she kissed him. Softly at first. Lips brushing lips. Then she went deeper, her hand pulled at him, her fingers dug into his skin.

"Liv—"

"Shh." She unwrapped herself from the sheet and threw it to the side. Her hands pushed at his shoulders, forcing him to lay on his back.

"Skin on skin," she murmured as she climbed on top of him and rested her body against his.

In the night they turned, still holding each other, face to face. Ben opened his eyes. She looked peaceful, and breathtaking. He traced the curve of her jaw, once again moved by how deeply she affected him.

He glanced at the clock. A little after seven. If he woke her up now, they'd have time to have breakfast together before she had to be at the barn. It would be a normal, everyday kind of thing. It would be about her. He listened last night. He was too anxious, and he pushed too hard. She said it to him that day in Vegas. When he asked if it was too much, she answered too soon.

"Hey cowgirl, time to wake up." He kissed her eyelids, then moved down to the tip of her nose, then each soft cheek. "Wake up baby."

"Hmm, what time is it?"

"Early enough for you to have breakfast and still be on time."

"Good," she groaned, and stretched, the sheet fell away from her body. "I'm starving."

Ben needed to get out of bed now, right now, while they still had time to have breakfast. They hadn't had dinner last night, he had to make sure she ate this morning. If he got lost in her body, again, they wouldn't have time.

"Come on," he said, pulling her arm. "I'll start the shower for you."

"No, come back, we have time," she pulled him toward her.

It would be so easy to climb back in bed and take what he needed from her, but she needed nourishment more than she needed him.

He let go of her arm, bent down and put her over his shoulder. "Shower, baby, let's go."

"Nooo. What are you doing? Ben, stop!" Her fists pounded at his back.

Ben reached in and turned the shower on, ice cold water, perfect. He climbed in and set her on her feet. Liv screamed when the frigid water hit her back and started pummeling him. And laughing.

It was going to be a good day.

"Pancakes. Wait. And sausage. Or bacon. Just bring both. And eggs, scrambled. Oh, and toast. Don't forget toast."

The waitress stood with one hand on her hip, waiting for Liv to finish. "Anything else? Hash browns?"

"Oh yes, hash browns, that sounds good. Thanks." Liv turned to Ben. "What are you having?"

Before he answered, she started talking to the waitress again. "Oh, and coffee. And juice. Um, do you have tomato juice?"

"Yep, got it. Coffee and tomato juice." She continued to look at Liv, expectantly.

"That's it for me. What are you having Ben? Come on, order. We need to be quick, so I'm not late."

"I'll have what she's having," he smirked.

That got a laugh out of the waitress who seemed as amused by Liv as he was.

Liv read the program for the rodeo she picked up on their way into the diner.

"Whatcha' lookin' for?"

"Nothin'," she answered absentmindedly as she hurriedly flipped through pages. She stopped, set the booklet down, and folded her hands on top of it.

"I'm sorry. That was rude."

"It's okay, you can read if you want to."

"It's not very polite," she murmured.

"I don't mind." Ben took her hands in his. "Relax. I can be with you without having your undivided attention."

She raised her eyebrow. "Can you?"

"I can do whatever it takes baby."

"Whatever." She grinned and rolled her eyes at him. Then went back to reading her program.

"There you are." Renie plopped down on the bench seat beside her mother. "Check your phone much?"

"Huh? What are you talking about?"

"Where is your phone Mom?"

Liv reached into her back pocket and pulled out her phone. "Sorry, I must've turned it off."

"No kidding. I've been trying to get in touch with you since last night."

Liv squinted at Ben in accusation.

"What?"

"Did you turn my phone off last night?"

"No idea what you're talking about baby."

"What if something had happened to Micah?" Her tone turned serious.

"Everyone knows where you're staying Liv. They would've come and knocked on the door."

"My daughter tried to reach me. What about that?"

Renie answered. "If it had been an emergency I would have done what Ben said. Don't be upset."

The waitress, plus a helper from the kitchen, started setting plates of food down on the table.

"Who else is having breakfast with you two?"

"You are." Liv answered, her mouth terse as she spoke.

Yep, he screwed up.

***

Liv was distracted the rest of the morning. She knew it and so did Jolene.

"Get him out of here. Send him home."

"What are you talking about?"

"Ben. Send him home."

"I can't do that Jolene. It's one more race."

"I don't like having him here. You aren't focused."

"That isn't fair."

"It's a simple rule Liv, and one that'll make you win more often."

What was Jolene talking about? Was she suggesting that Liv not allow Ben to come to the rodeos she competed in? That sounded ludicrous.

"Mark my words."

"Jolene, come on, what would Larry have said if you told him he not to come and watch you."

"He never did."

"He never came and watched you? Seriously?"

"I wanted to win more than you do."

Liv still thought Jolene unreasonable, but that night, when she knocked over not one, but two barrels and rode herself out of the money, she started to think Jolene might be right.

"I don't care if you didn't place, we're going out and celebrating tonight."

"Dottie, I appreciate it, but I'm not up for it tonight."

"Buck up buttercup. Never been a day since I've known you that I haven't been proud of you. Don't make the first time it happens be tonight."

Liv felt five years old, between Ben turning her phone off last night, and Jolene telling her that she shouldn't let Ben watch her ride. Now Dottie told her she was behaving badly. Liv wanted to load Micah into her trailer and drive home. And not to the other side of Oklahoma, to Colorado.

She wanted to be alone. She craved it.

"Don't do it." Paige said.

"Oh, you scared me. I didn't see you standing there." Liv ran her hand through her hair and bit her lower lip. "Don't do what?"

"Leave."

"What the heck Paige?"

"Don't tell me that wasn't what you were thinking about."

"Doesn't mean I'd do it. Hey, where is Ben?" She realized she hadn't seen him. What did that say about her?

"He's with Mark. Thought he'd give you space."

Liv told Paige what Jolene said, about Ben not being there when she rode.

"Sounds like a load of crap to me."

Liv laughed. "Yeah, well, there's that. But also, I was distracted today. I was mad at him."

"So learn how to be mad at him and still stay focused. Practice that instead of keeping him away."

Liv had to admit, what Paige suggested made sense.

***

Ben nursed his second coke when Liv walked into the bar, her entourage in tow. Jolene walked by and glared at him.

"She doesn't like the balls," Mark snickered. "If she liked 'em better she might not be such a bitch."

"I heard that," said Dottie, tweaking Mark's cheek. "We're gettin' a table. You fellas gonna join us?"

Mark stood to follow, but Ben stayed seated. "What are you doing? Come on, we're gonna get something to eat."

"Give me a minute."

He watched as everyone else walked into the other room. Everyone but Liv, who walked toward him.

"You hidin' from me cowboy?"

"Am I in trouble?"

"Nah, you're not. But here's the thing, is this about you Ben? Or is it about me? You're not used to things being about somebody other than you. You might want to consider that."

She turned on the heel of her fancy cowboy boots and walked off in the direction of the table. When she got about two feet away from him, she turned and looked back over her shoulder. It was the first time he'd ever seen her look back. He got off the bar stool and followed her.

Before they got to the table, Ben put his hand on Liv's waist and she stopped walking.

"This is what I'm talking about. This is my time Ben, I've never had that, never let myself. Before I can give myself to anyone I have to fill myself up first. Do you understand?"

He was beginning to. And he was okay with it.

* * *

Liv almost wished she had left yesterday. She wouldn't have to say goodbye to Ben now if she had.

She had the trailer hooked up to the truck and needed to get on the road. She decided to go home for a couple days, regroup, and then get herself back out there. It was a seven hour drive, and instead of driving, she wanted to sleep. Thank goodness she'd have Renie with her to keep her awake.

Ben loaded the last of her stuff into the back of her truck. He insisted she let him do it while she said goodbye to everybody else.

"Ready?"

That wasn't what she expected. She'd expected at least a little drama from him. *Baby, I love you.* If she was learning anything, it was he was unpredictable.

He walked to her passenger door and held it open, as if he expected something from her.

"What?"

"Are you ready to go?"

"Yeah, I guess I am. Does Renie want to drive?"

"I'm gonna drive the first leg so you can rest."

"What are you talking about?"

"We're both going to Walsenburg. I'll drive for a couple hours, or I can drive the whole way if you want me to."

"Who's driving your truck?"

"Bill."

"Ben—" she sighed heavily and closed her eyes. "Oh hell with it. Never mind. Let's go. Where's Renie anyway? I guess I should at least talk to my daughter before we leave."

"She's riding with Billy. We're caravanning baby. This'll be fun."

It occurred to Liv that perhaps she had as many control issues as Ben. After all, she was furious that all of this had been decided without a single one of them asking her opinion. She wasn't crazy about her daughter being alone with Billy, but she supposed, or hoped, she considered him her "uncle."

"Hard, isn't it?"

"What?" she barked at him.

"Lettin' go."

"Shut up."

Ben put his arm around Liv's waist and swung her up into the truck. "Use the time to figure out which events you're gonna enter between now and Las Vegas."

"As if I had a prayer of making it this year. Get real."

"Gotta dream baby."

And Then You Fall

Liv hadn't gotten a penny of the purse in Woodward, not that she expected to. She'd be lucky if she'd earned enough to get her membership card before December, let alone dream about being in the top fifteen in the standings.

"What do you want to listen to on our ride baby?"

"Who's my favorite band?"

"CB Rice."

"Um, no. Isn't that weird, to listen to your own music? What do you do, sing along?"

Ben laughed. "Kidding Liv. So, who?"

"Let's listen to a country station for a bit." Ben hoped she didn't see him roll his eyes.

"I saw that."

Liv mapped out the events she'd compete in for the rest of the season. There were a couple of events in Colorado in August, and one in Idaho. In September, she'd be in Albuquerque and Salt Lake City.

"Is that it for September? You could come see me."

"Well, there's another event, in Kansas City, but it's cards only."

"You're speakin' a foreign language now."

"I'll be on what's called a permit until I win a cumulative total of $1,000. Then I'll get my membership card."

"You'll get it before Kansas City. I'm proud of you for changing your attitude."

"It's stupid," she mumbled and turned her face toward the window.

Ben put his hand on top of hers. "Scoot over here, closer to me. That's what bench seats are for."

She did, and he put his hand on her thigh. "You can do it. I believe in you. You gotta believe in yourself if you wanna fill yourself up."

"Okay, I hear you." Liv stared out the window, quiet for a few minutes. "In October I'll be in Tulsa, and then the second half of the month there are two events in Texas. One is top thirty only, in Waco. And then Rock Springs is top twelve in the Mountain State Circuit."

"There you go. See? You believe in yourself."

"What's your schedule?"

Ben's eyes got wide and he stared at her with his mouth open. "What? You haven't been on our Facebook page? You haven't memorized our schedule?"

Wow, she hadn't been. She couldn't remember the last time she had.

"Pull it up on your phone."

Ben would be on the east coast until the middle of September, and he didn't have more than one day off at a time between now and then. The second half of September he had three days off, before they went to Texas and back to Denver. After that, he left right away for the west coast, where they'd be until the end of October. They didn't have any tour dates scheduled in November, and they wouldn't until after Christmas at the earliest.

"I guess I'll see you in November then."

Was she kidding? "Come meet me on the tour."

She looked out the window again.

"Where are you?"

"Let's not try to figure this out right now."

Okay, what was this all about? He took a couple of deep breaths, trying not to let her see him do it. He needed to learn to let go, he didn't need to know right this minute when the next time he'd see Liv would be.

"I think I will try to sleep for a little while, if you don't mind."

"No, go ahead." He wanted time to think anyway.

***

They'd been lovers, off and on, for almost five months. And when it was on, it was so intense, it threatened to rob him of his sanity. Ben wondered if his lust for her hadn't cooled because they'd been off more than on. It hadn't diminished at all. Not even close. Today it seemed worse than ever.

Every time Ben thought he had a handle on wanting to pull the truck over and bend her over the tailgate, she'd make a soft sexy noise. Or she'd turn, trying to get more comfortable, and the buttons on her shirt would strain enough that he got a glimpse of her skin. He got to the point where he thought he'd be better off if he didn't look at her. It was only an hour into the drive. Five more until they hit Walsenburg where he'd get in his truck and drive west, and she'd head north.

This morning was the last time he'd be with her for…he didn't know how long. Skin on skin, that's what he thought about now. He needed her again.

Ben's hands gripped the steering wheel tighter. He took off his hat and started fiddling with the air conditioner. Man it had gotten hot in here all of a sudden.

"Ben?" The way she said his name, the perfect little lilt in her voice, made him crazy.

"Need a break baby? Let's stop at the next exit."

"Okay." There it was again, that melodic voice that made his jeans more and more uncomfortable with every word she spoke. How in the hell would he be able to say goodbye to her in a couple of hours? He needed her underneath him. He wondered what she'd say if he said so.

"What're you thinkin' about Ben?"

Oh God, his mouth went dry. Bone dry. "When you say my name that way…it burns me up baby."

Liv knew what Ben meant. She hadn't slept, but instead imagined him stopping the truck and taking her up against her pickup—fast, hard and dirty. Oh God, what was she doing?

The expression on his face was…dangerous.

"Tell me what you want baby."

"I can't wait." Her body was on fire.

"Lick your lips, the way you did when I told you I loved you."

Her tongue ran over her top lip, twice, as she had then.

"Do it again."

She did.

The sound that came from deep in his throat made her eyes close.

"Stay in the truck." Ben had pulled into a service station. Bill drove Ben's Tahoe behind them. Paige and Mark drove behind him in their car.

Wait. What? Where was he going?

"I have to talk to Bill."

"Why? Ben, what are you doing?"

Liv tried to see where he went, but the trailer blocked her view. She started to jump out, and remembered he told her to stay in the truck. And right this minute, she would do whatever Ben told her to do. That was how badly she wanted him. If he came back and told her to take off her clothes in broad daylight, she doubted she'd be able to deny him.

Ben got back in the truck and slammed his door closed.

"What's going on?"

"They're goin' on ahead."

"Ben—"

"Not now Liv. Listen to me. Please. And I'm begging you, please don't fight me on this."

She nodded.

"We'll meet them back at your place. I told them I wasn't sure when we'd be there."

Liv hadn't seen Ben this way. His eyes were fiery, no sign of his sweet smile. In its place, he was almost scowling. She wouldn't dream of arguing with him. She couldn't want him any more than she did.

She launched herself at him, throwing herself across his lap. Her mouth crushed down on his as her hands fisted in his shirt.

"Want you right now. Now Liv."

She didn't answer him. She hoped he had a plan. Her need for him bordered primal. She wanted to be taken by this man—in every way he wanted to take her. She was ready to jump out of her skin.

"God, I can't even think."

Liv pointed across the road, to a chain hotel.

"You make me crazy Liv. Only you. What I want to do to you."

"Anything you want Ben…hurry."

"Wait here."

Ben walked up to the desk and tossed his credit card on the counter. "Need a room."

"Sure. Only one night for you?"

"Yep, that works."

"Would you prefer a king-size bed or two queens?" What was that? What was she doing with her eyes? Oh no, was she flirting with him? No, he didn't have time for this.

"Whichever one would be ready first."

"Either one." Ben saw it again, the eye thing. He recognized it, but it was the last thing he wanted to see right now. He just wanted the damn key card for the room.

"I'll take the king. Listen, I'm in a hurry here."

The girl all but jammed his credit card through the machine. Yep, he recognized that look too. He didn't care how pissed off she got, as long as she hurried.

"Around the back, number one-twelve."

The door had almost closed behind him before he remembered to say thanks.

He opened the door and let her go in before him. Once inside, he plastered his body to hers. One of his hands slipped into her hair, threading his fingers through it and pulling her head to one side, so he had full access to her throat. His lips followed the curve of it up to her ear. "Driving me crazy. All day."

He stepped back, grabbed her hand and led her with him to the bed.

Liv fisted her hands in his shirt, ripped it open and ran her hands over his chest. He shuddered and crushed his mouth into hers.

"I can't stop Liv. I can't even slow down."

"Don't. God, don't slow down."

"Remember you said that."

His hands pulled off her shirt. Then her bra. Jeans and panties, and then he was on her. "Need you."

In an instant, she was underneath him with him inside her. His lips moved to her neck and lit it on fire. The calloused fingers of his strong hands clamped down on her wrists and pinned them against the bed.

He went still, his eyes boring into hers. His look so intense her eyes closed. "Don't. Open them."

She did, and they filled with tears.

"Oh girl, what you do to me. Every time, it's so damn good."

"Oh Ben, please," she arched against him, trying to get him to move.

"Tell me, tell me what I mean to you."

A tear slid down her cheek, her heart beat so hard it was all she heard. She shook her head back and forth, hoping he'd relent. "Ben, I'm begging you. Please."

"Tell me Liv."

His fingers dug into her wrists. His powerful legs on top of hers kept her from going anywhere. She cried out and tried to move out from under him.

"Tell me," he said again.

"I can't."

"You can. Tell me. Tell me now Liv."

He moved lower, kissing across her shoulders. His hands dug into her wrists.

"Don't let me go Ben. Don't ever let me go. I need you so much."

He started moving. Fast and hard, taking her with him as he exploded into her.

"I love you so much," he said and rolled onto his back, taking her with him. He wanted her stretched out on top of him, every bit of her touching him. "Your skin, Liv, on mine. Where it's meant to be."

* * *

"How long will it take us to get home from here?"

How could he answer? He wanted to ask her which home she meant. But that would've ruined this perfect memory. It would carry him through the next days or weeks, or months, without her. The memory of today, when the need for each other overtook them to the point where they had no choice but to give in to it.

"Five or six hours."

"Can you make it all the way there without stopping?" She smirked at him.

"Doubt it," he said as he kissed her neck. "Can you?"

"Nope."

Yeah, they wouldn't be leaving this room for a while yet.

* * *

Ben's Tahoe was in her driveway when they got home.

"When do you have to leave?" Liv asked, beginning to hate the question.

"I'm not leaving until tomorrow morning. I'm trying to get in touch with my dad. I'm hoping he can fly over and get me. I can get the truck when we're back for the show in Denver. If you don't mind me leaving it here."

"I don't mind. You can park your car in my garage anytime you want to."

"You've been spending too much time with Mark. And, by the way, you don't have a garage baby."

"Minor detail. By the way, if you're hungry, I don't have much food in the house."

Liv had enough food in her freezer to feed every one of the hands who worked the Patterson Ranch. He'd never seen so much food in one person's house. "Oh I think we'll be able to find something."

She unlocked the back of the trailer, and chattered to Micah all the while. "You must be so tired of being on the road, boy. Mama got a little distracted on the way home. I'm sorry for that. I mean, I'm sorry for you, not so much for me."

Was she not the purest thing that ever lived? Ben would miss her so much. Laughing with her. Talking with her. Sitting in silence with her. Touching her. It hadn't been six hours since he touched her, all of her, and he craved her all over again.

"Hey, are you sure you aren't gonna need your truck Ben? I mean, it's sweet and all of you to stay with me tonight, but you won't be back here until when? Six weeks from now?"

"I'll be on tour baby, no need for the Tahoe." Tour. God. How would he get through it without her with him?

Chapter Seventeen

Liv dropped Ben off at the airport in Centennial, but stayed in the car. They'd stayed up all night, talking, having sex, talking more. She was so tired, but she wouldn't have traded the time with him for anything in the world. When she got tired, she got very weepy. And she was weepy anyway, saying goodbye to Ben.

"This is one of the hardest things I've ever done," he said to her before he got out of the car. "Every bit of me wants to take you with me."

"I'm not full yet Ben."

"I get it."

Part of what they talked about last night was this dream of Liv's and how important it was to her. For the first time in her life, she was doing something for herself, and she had to do it. If she didn't, she wasn't sure what would become of her.

That seemed to resonate with Ben. He'd been there, more than once, when he knew that if he didn't do something, he'd be lost. True with his music, and his sobriety, once he'd decided to own it.

It was the way he felt the week showed up at her place unannounced. And again when he threw a bag in his truck and drove to Oklahoma, not understanding why, but knowing he had to do it anyway.

"Olivia Fairchild, I'm gonna miss you like crazy."

"Me too."

"I like knowing you will. Anything else you need to say to me before I go get on a plane and fly west?"

"I don't want to let go of this Ben."

***

Liv cried the entire way home. She pulled off the highway in Castle Rock because she was sobbing. But it was good crying. It wasn't *end of the world* sobbing, it was *I'll miss him so much*.

Jolene was due to arrive at her place in the morning. The next two events were in Colorado, then she'd head up to Idaho. She'd do these events on her own, and that's the way she wanted it.

When she pulled into the driveway and saw Ben's truck, she thought she might start crying again, but she didn't. To see it there soothed her.

She went in the house, climbed up onto the bed and fell asleep, clothes and all.

When Liv went to change the next morning, she found another shirt of Ben's hanging on the handle of her closet door. She loved that he did that. She wondered what he took of hers this time.

She went out to get Micah ready and take care of the rest of the horses when Jolene pulled in the long drive. She parked next to Ben's truck and pointed at it. "He's here?"

Oh for crying out loud. "No. He's not. His truck is here. Okay?"

Jolene grumbled. "Good," was the only word Liv could understand.

Jolene stayed for two days and then told Liv she was ready. They'd see what her times were at the next three events. Jolene would review the videos she arranged to have taken of Liv's rides. Then they'd get together to work out whatever kinks crept up.

Liv had never felt more excited—or free.

The first event was at the Douglas County Fairgrounds, in Castle Rock. It was only about forty-five minutes from the ranch, an easy trip. And she didn't have to get a stall for Micah overnight.

She did well all three nights, ended up in the top two, and won $757.77. If she got in the top three in one more event, she'd have her card for Kansas City.

In Pueblo, she placed second at the State Fair rodeo, which meant she had enough winnings to get her full membership in the Women's Professional Rodeo Association.

Next up, Idaho.

***

The tour bus pulled out of Chicago, headed for the show in Cleveland the next night.

"Go to sleep," Jimmy said to Ben, "and try not to be quite as much of an asshole tomorrow."

Ben wanted to tell Jimmy to go fuck himself, but his friend was right. He was an asshole. They'd been on the road nine days, and every part of his body ached for Liv. After Cleveland, they had one night off and then played four nights in a row, ending in Philadelphia. He had two days between then and the next show, in New York. He planned to see Liv no matter what. And his kids, he needed to see them too. He missed them so much, all three of them, his heart hurt.

As much as Ben hated being away from Liv, and his boys, he loved touring, loved the audiences every night. These were by far the biggest venues and biggest crowds CB Rice had ever seen. On stage, he was fine. The rest of the time he was miserable.

It was Sunday night, which meant she'd be finishing up at the Magic Valley Stampede in Filer, Idaho. It would be her first event as a full member rider. And she'd been worried about making enough to qualify in two months. She did it in two events. He was so proud of her he thought his heart would burst. He wanted to know how she did tonight. He checked his phone for the hundredth time. Nothing. He'd keep it right next to him in case he drifted off before she called.

Something woke him up. He checked his phone, almost two. No call from Liv, but one from Renie. It had come in before midnight. And then a text from her asking him to call her as soon as he got the message, no matter what time it was. *Fuck.*

"Ben?"

"Yeah Renie—"

"There's been an accident."

Every muscle in Ben's body seized. All the air left his lungs. He was about to have a heart attack. "Tell me."

"She's in a coma."

Ben's cry woke everyone on the bus.

Jimmy slept in the bunk closest to Ben. "What's going on?"

"Oh no, oh dear God. What're they saying?" Pause. "Okay, I'm on my way. I'll get there as fast as I can."

"What is it? Come on Ben, tell me what it is, so I can help you."

"It's Liv. An accident."

"On it."

"Call my dad."

They were still three hours outside of Cleveland, by the time the bus got there, Ben's dad would be waiting with the plane. From Cleveland, it would take another six hours to get Ben to Twin Falls, Idaho.

Ben talked to Renie again, then to Paige. Jimmy got on the phone with Frank, the band's manager, working on canceling the Cleveland show.

At one in the afternoon, Ben walked into St. Luke's Hospital in Idaho's Magic Valley. Mark waited for him inside the front entrance.

His eyes bloodshot, and his hands in his pockets.

No, no, no. Ben went dizzy and brushed against his father. "Tell me," he managed to say.

"She's critical."

Liv was in the intensive care unit, Renie was with her. There were tubes everywhere, machines hooked up to her. Ben put his head in his hands and started to cry.

"Stop that," Paige barked at him, then softened her tone. "She's going to get through this."

Ben's arms ached with the need to go and hold her. Renie's head came up when she saw him, and she came out.

"Go ahead," she murmured. "I'll tell you more after you've seen her."

And Then You Fall

Ben put one foot in front of the other, he saw himself moving forward, but the walk to her bedside was the longest of his life.

She had a metal device on her head, with screws going into her skull. Her face had marks on the side of it, scrapes and cuts. A machine did her breathing for her. Ben kissed her forehead, sat down and started to talk.

He talked, and talked, and talked. He told her every detail about the show the night before, in Chicago.

He told her which songs had been crowd favorites and which ones he'd chosen to do for encores. He asked her about her race, and about what happened. He had the same conversation he would've if they had talked last night. Except she couldn't answer him.

Ben told her he wanted to play "And Then You Fall," last night. He decided though, the first time he played her song, he wanted her in the audience. So he didn't. He broke down.

Paige came in and put her arms around his shoulder. "Come with me Ben." And she ushered him out of the room. Mark stepped forward, put his hand on Ben's arm, and walked with him, away from the ICU.

Ben sat, head in his hands and cried. He found her, his reason for living. What if he lost her now? Would he lose himself too?

"She's gonna be okay." That simple statement from Mark brought him back. Ben turned to him.

"No one else is letting go of Liv. If you are, then you shouldn't be here."

"What do you mean?"

"When you are with her, you need to tell her you believe she's going to be okay. She lived. She's gonna be okay."

Mark was right. He'd only been thinking of himself. Liv herself would say, "this is about me, not about you."

"Paige can tell you what the doctors said, if you're ready."

Paige told Ben the doctors had two treatment options. Liv could stay in traction for twelve weeks, to see if her neck injury healed on its own. Or, they could try surgery. With surgery, the risk was significant, with a chance Liv wouldn't survive it.

They wouldn't do anything, however, until they determined the reason for her coma. Nothing on the MRI indicated why she wasn't conscious.

"They want us to keep talking to her. She may be able to hear us. Before you go back in, I want to talk to you about the tour," said Paige.

"What about it?"

"You need to get back to it."

"What? No. You've gotta be kidding."

"If there is a change in her condition, we'll get in touch with you. But Ben, you've got sold out shows, a band and a crew depending on you."

No. He wouldn't even consider leaving. If the doctors didn't know why she wasn't conscious, that meant that she might wake up any time. He would be here when she did.

Bud found them a place to stay for the night, not far from the hospital, and rented a car. He came upstairs around five to get Ben to eat. He was sure his son hadn't eaten since yesterday. Mark came out and found him in the waiting room.

"How is she?"

"No change."

And Then You Fall

"How's my boy?"

"In bad shape. Paige plans to talk to him about going back to the tour. How many concerts have they canceled so far?"

"Tonight's. They didn't have a show scheduled tomorrow night."

"Something happened at the arena, right after Liv's accident. A close family friend was there. He happened to be competing in another event, and saw what happened. He waited with Liv while the medical team called for an ambulance. Liv was conscious."

"And?"

"She told Billy, the friend, not to let Ben know what happened. And then she asked him not to let him come if he tried."

"Why not?"

"No idea. Has something happened between them in the last couple of weeks?"

"Ben hasn't said."

"Paige is convinced Liv can hear us, that's why it's so important we keep talking to her, but not say anything that might upset her."

"So she wants Ben to leave?"

"Yes. She does."

Billy Patterson came off the elevator with Dottie and his dad.

"Where's our girl?" Dottie said to Mark.

"I'll take you to her. Give me just a minute. Bud, will you be okay out here?"

"No, no, don't worry about me. I'll wait here." Bud went to the window, talking in hushed tones to Mark. "Do you want me to talk to Ben?"

"Paige will. But she wants your help to try to convince him. We'll keep in contact with him and let him know if there's any change at all."

"I know my son. It won't be easy to get him to leave."

"I'm not sure it would be a good idea to tell him she didn't want him here."

Bud had no idea. He'd call Ginny.

Paige and Renie came out. Dottie and Bill went back in their place.

Ben came out a few minutes later.

"Hey Dad."

"Hello Ben," Bud answered.

"What the hell is *he* doing here? She doesn't want him here."

"Billy!" Paige put her hand on his arm. "Please take Renie downstairs and get her something to eat. And please bring me back a cup of coffee."

"You be gone when I get back," he pointed at Ben. Mark stepped in front of him and turned him in the direction of the elevator. "Not now," Mark said to him.

Ben turned to Paige. "What the fuck was that about?"

"Ben, son, please sit. Paige needs to talk to you."

Ben did as his dad asked, as though he was an auto-pilot. Paige sat on the other side of him, leaned forward and put her hands on his.

"You need to go back out on tour."

"I already told you I wouldn't leave."

"Son, there's something Paige needs to tell you." Bud looked at her. "Go ahead Paige."

"Liv wouldn't want you to miss this opportunity Ben. This is your tour. Your shot. Your year. We will be here with her, and so will Renie, although we're hoping she'll go back to school. We'll contact you the minute there's a change."

"No, Paige. I'm not leaving. The tour doesn't matter. Nothing matters but Liv."

"Tell him the truth Paige," said Ben's father.

Bud talked Ben into going to the hotel for a little while. Liv had more visitors than the ICU staff permitted. The staff insisted they leave, and come back in the morning. Bud convinced Ben not to sit in the waiting room for hours. If there was a change in her condition, the hospital would notify him.

"Before you say anything, I'm not going back on tour Dad. Don't try to talk me into it."

"It's your decision."

"But you think I should?"

"I didn't say that."

"What would you do, if it was mom?"

"Knowing what she wanted, I might. I *always* do what your mother wants." Bud laughed and so did Ben, almost.

"I can't leave her."

"What can you do to help her?"

He wanted to be there when she woke up. Until she did, he would hold her hand and talk to her, and sing to her. Anything to help her.

"And what if she knows you're here?"

"Then it'll be one more reason for her to wake up."

Jimmy called and told him they'd posted on Facebook and Twitter that the concert in Cleveland had been canceled due to a family emergency. And once they had, the response from the fans had been incredible. Posts of support came from everywhere.

"Support for what?"

"For Liv."

"How does anyone know about her?"

"You live in a fishbowl Ben. We're on a national tour, and it's sold out. The fan response to the new album has been phenomenal."

Jimmy was right. At the beginning of the tour, they were booking small clubs, the usual ones they'd played in year after year. They sold out in minutes. The tour promoters pushed for bigger venues, and they sold out too. Ben had a hard time wrapping his head around it. All the years they'd dreamed of success and suddenly, inexplicably, it was happening. A few months ago they'd played the Paramount in Denver, and now they sold out Red Rocks—where they'd been an opening band a year ago. And where he first met Liv.

There was a knock on the door. His dad answered it. Ben told Jimmy he'd call him back when he saw Paige.

"What would she want?"

"Let up Paige."

"What would she want?"

He wouldn't answer her.

"What would you want, if it was you? Would you want her to give up her dream? Would you tell her to sit by your side, and let her dream dissolve into nothing?"

No, he wouldn't. Ben got up from the bed and walked to the window. A few minutes later, the hotel room door closed. When he turned around again, his dad was sitting in the chair, his fingers steepled in front of his mouth and nose.

"Come to any decisions?" he asked.

"Yeah," he said with reservation. "I'll fly into Hartford tomorrow night. I'd like to use the plane Dad. If there's a change in her condition, I want to be able to get back as fast as possible."

"We'll go together Ben. I'll stay with you on tour for the time being."

Ben knew his father's biggest concern, and he was glad he didn't say it. Yeah, he wanted a drink more than anything. And not one, he wanted a whole bottle.

The next morning Ben visited the hospital, and told Liv he was going back on tour. He was doing it for her, because he loved her. He hoped Paige was right, and Liv heard him.

***

Renie made the decision to move her mother to Denver to continue her treatment. Liv's new doctors agreed with those in Idaho. The surgery was too risky given that they couldn't determine why she hadn't come out of the coma. They'd keep her in traction for the time being, and when her condition stabilized, or she was conscious, they'd revisit the surgery.

Paige talked Renie into going back to school to make arrangements with her professors to continue her classes.

Since Denver was less than an hour from Paige and Mark's place in Monument, they assured Renie that one of them would be with her mother every day.

Chapter Eighteen

Ben walked out on stage the following night in Hartford, Connecticut and was met by chants. "Liv, Liv, Liv," the audience shouted.

He pulled a stool to the front of the stage, sat down, and did what came natural to him. He told them about her. Ten thousand people went silent, and listened.

"I told her that I wouldn't play this song until she was here with me, to hear it live for the first time, but I feel her here, through you."

Ben started to play, just him, the rest of the band stayed silent along with the audience.

Sweet beauty on steps, waiting, like me
Sun masked by clouds, so free
Beautiful, if only you were able to move,
To go, to ride, to smile, to fly, to kiss, to fall.
I know how deep your smile, if only you could fall

I know how wild your passion, if only you would fall
I know how deep your longing, if only you could fall.
I know your fear, I know your tears
But that smile, so sweet, that longing so deep
Your eyes burn into my heart, my love, my joy, my fall.

You know my longing deep, you know my love, so hard
You know my longing deep, you know my passion, so wild
You know my fall.
To see you here then, in the midst of your fall
To know your joy, so deep, to know your passion, complete
To know your longing, my all, and then, my sweet, you fall.

When Ben woke up the next morning, Jimmy told him a fan had posted "And Then You Fall," on YouTube. It had three million views. Overnight.

* * *

"Don't ask me to do this."

"I don't want him here."

"I made a promise Liv. I can't keep lying to him."

"Then leave. And don't come back. I won't ever forgive you if you tell him."

"Liv…"

"I don't want him here."

Liv spent hours replaying the accident over in her head. Micah hesitated, a split second, then went right. They were tight to the barrel, and they were going to knock it over. Then Micah went down, her head was too close to the ground, she was going to hit head first. She heard the snap when she did. And now, she had no feeling in her legs.

Billy assured her that Micah had been checked out and suffered no injury in the accident. He promised her he'd make sure her horse was exercised daily, and ready to get back at it as soon as she was.

Renie, Paige, Mark, and Billy were the only people she permitted to visit. She came out of her coma two days ago—four days after they'd moved her to Denver. Paige told her that Ben had come to Idaho the day after her accident, and that she had convinced him to go back on tour.

"Now I regret my decision Liv. I promised him I would tell him if your condition changed. I promised."

"I don't care Paige. You either abide by what I want or leave. And don't come back."

If Paige told Ben she had come out of the coma, and couldn't walk, she'd never let her set foot in this room again. Or any other room she was in, for the rest of her life.

Renie had begged her to let them call Ben. Liv refused. Mark didn't even mention Ben's name. Smart man.

***

Philadelphia, Toronto, Saratoga Springs, Virginia Beach and now Raleigh. Every night, the same thing happened. The crowd chanted Liv's name and Ben opened the show by telling a story about her. He didn't plan what he'd say ahead of time. Sometimes he told a new story, sometimes it was one he'd already told. Then he'd play "And Then You Fall."

There was so much demand for the song, the band recorded a live version and put it on iTunes. Not only had the song moved into the number one spot in a few days, their new album was currently number seven, and the song wasn't even on it. The band had been gaining mass market popularity before Liv's accident, and since, fan support had grown exponentially.

The worst pain he'd ever known fueled the success of his life's dream. The irony ate him alive.

He called Paige at least once every day. Nothing to report, she'd tell him.

***

Liv was moving to a rehab facility outside of Colorado Springs. She still didn't have any feeling below the waist. The doctors were recommending the surgery, and Liv was in favor of it. The risk was high. She could end up as a quadriplegic, or it might kill her. They wanted to wait three more weeks before they did it. Three more weeks.

"Let me tell him something, anything."

"No Paige."

"I have to tell him you're being moved."

"No Paige."

"He's capable of calling the hospital Liv. They may not tell him your condition, but they'll sure as hell tell him you're no longer there. You know him, he'll be here as fast as that little plane will fly him."

"Tell him they're moving me. But that's all."

"What will happen when the tour ends?"

"I have six weeks before I need to worry about that."

One sentence told Paige everything she needed to know. Liv was paying attention to Ben's life and his career. The CB Rice tour had originally been slated to end October 30, four weeks from now. They'd added two weeks and ten more cities to the tour, and Paige was certain no one had told Liv. Why would they? That meant Liv was checking. And if she was checking, she still wanted him in her life.

***

CB Rice was bigger than they ever dreamed possible. The record label wanted them to start the European leg of their tour in January. Ben agreed to it, tentatively.

They'd be off from the middle of November until the end of December. Once he saw his boys, he'd spend the time off with Liv. He'd spend every minute of it with her, until she woke. And then he'd spend every minute after she did with her too. He'd bring his boys over from Crested Butte to stay with him.

He'd have to wait and see about going to Europe in January.

***

She checked the Twitter feed for the second time this morning, and saw they'd posted photos from the concert last night. And then she went on YouTube to watch and listen to the story he told about her, as she had every morning for the last five weeks. Then she checked iTunes. Their album was up to number two.

Tomorrow was her surgery, it had been delayed two additional weeks, they were moving her back to the hospital in Denver in a couple of hours.

During the seven-hour operation, surgeons took one of the discs from Liv's back and fused the bones. Then they mended the broken bone with surgical cement and used titanium screws and plates to fix her neck.

Renie and Paige held hands and Mark stood behind them, his hands on their shoulders when the doctors came out to tell them how the surgery went.

"Everything went well. Now we have to wait and see. We won't know anything until she wakes. She'll be under sedation for a couple more hours. You should be able to see her then."

* * *

Jimmy saw it first, and prayed Ben would stay distracted until he could confirm its truth, or just a cruel attempt by the press to make a buck.

The post read, "CB Rice Cashes In Big with Fake Coma Story." It went on to say that CB Rice's recent meteoric rise to fame was due in large part to the fans' near hysteria over Ben Rice's girlfriend's accident and subsequent coma. According to reports, the woman in question had been out of her coma for weeks. She'd come out of it not long after the first concert Ben told his naive fans the tragic story of the alleged love of his life.

Jimmy looked at Ben's face. He'd seen it.

"What the fuck is this?"

Ben, Bud, and Jimmy were trying to reach Paige, Renie, Mark, or the hospital. None were answering, and the hospital wouldn't even confirm that they had a patient by the name of Olivia Fairchild.

* * *

Paige and Renie were talking with Liv when Mark saw the story on CNN.

"You better turn on the news," he said when he walked in the room.

"Oh my God." Liv's head fell back on the pillow.

Paige looked at her phone. "Shit. Seven missed calls. All from Ben." She raised her eyebrows at Liv. "What now?"

***

"Get me on a goddamn plane."

They were in LA. It would take two hours to fly to Denver. Ben was taking a commercial flight. It would get him there faster.

***

Ben stormed into the hospital…and Mark waited for him. Again.

"Tell me," Ben managed to say. "No, wait. I'd rather hear this from Liv herself. Since she's awake." The bitterness dripped off his tongue like poison sludge.

Mark took him up to Liv's room. Renie and Paige were with her.

"Well hello Liv," Ben sneered at her. "Ladies, please leave. I need to talk to Liv alone."

Renie stopped in front of him, tears in her eyes. "I'm sorry," she said. "It wasn't ever about you Ben. My mom needed to come first."

Ben didn't think anything could get him to take his eyes off Liv, but that had. He closed his eyes. That's the way it was, wasn't it? It wasn't about him, or what an absolute fucking idiot he was. It wasn't about him unintentionally duping millions of people who now thought he was the scum of the earth for lying to them.

It wasn't about the pain he carried in his heart, his head, throughout his body for the last two months. Or him thinking he wouldn't have the chance to tell the incredible, beautiful woman in front of him, how much he wanted to spend the rest of his life with her.

No, this wasn't ever about him.

He didn't move. Paige and Renie were gone. Liv was right in front of him, her eyes were open, something he'd been dreaming about, thinking about, praying for, but he couldn't move.

"Why?" he asked. "And don't say this wasn't about me. Don't."

"It was all about you," she answered.

"All about me? I guess you didn't think about the other people in my life who would be affected by this. Do you have any idea what this will do to the band? Forget about me, think about the band. And the crew, all the people we employ. We're done Liv. People think we've been conning them. So you wanna tell me how this was all about me?"

He was angry, hurt, and confused, but at that moment, it all went away, none of it mattered. Liv was conscious, and talking to him. He'd dreamt about this every day, even when he wasn't sleeping. The need to touch her overwhelmed him.

He stalked toward the bed and leaned down close to her. "I don't want to do anything to physically hurt you, but I'm going to kiss you, and I'm going to kiss you hard. So if I can't touch a part of you, tell me right now."

Ben's lips met hers and pushed her head back up against the pillow. His mouth devoured hers and dared hers to respond. His hand came up and stroked her face, gently, as if knowing only his mouth could cause her pain. The rest of his body had to protect her at all costs.

He tasted the saltiness of her tears as they ran down her face and into their mouths. He heard her cries, but he chose to ignore them. He needed to take this from her and everything else be damned. She pulled at him, trying to bring his body closer to hers.

"Don't make me hurt you Liv," he said as he pulled back from her. "It isn't your body I want to hurt, just your heart." His eyes were dark, not from hunger, but from rage. "Are you even going to try to explain?"

"I never meant to hurt you. I wanted to protect you."

He backed away from her. "Protect me? Protect me? Is that what you said? You wanted to protect me? From what? Peace? Sanity? Do you have any idea how these last few weeks have been for me?"

He stood up and walked toward the window. "Every day I called. Every. Single. Fucking. Day. And I'd ask how you were. And every single day, Paige lied to me."

"It wasn't her fault. I made her do it, *to protect you*."

"Look at me. Can you see me? I'm not a man who has been protected. I'm a man who has had his insides chewed up every day for the last two months. My body has been racked with pain. Every single fucking day." His eyes welled with tears. "I would've crawled into that body, taken the coma on myself and set you free. I didn't care about me, only you."

Her leg moved, a reflex, and it startled her. It had been so long since she felt anything below her waist. She gasped.

"What?" Ben asked.

"My leg moved."

Since Ben hadn't known she'd come out of the coma, he also hadn't known she was paralyzed. He didn't know that she had surgery, and that they'd been waiting to see whether it was successful.

The nurse came in to check her vitals. "Any sensation yet?"

Liv looked at Ben, then at the nurse. "My legs."

The nurse's eyes opened wide, and she pulled the sheet back. She started tapping different areas. "Can you feel this? What about this?" Liv kept nodding. She felt it all.

"Oh Liv, this is wonderful! Let me call the doctor. I'll be right back."

Ben watched the scene play out in front of him. He didn't know what it meant, but he started to put it together. He didn't speak. He stood and stared at her.

She looked uncomfortable, yet elated at the same time. She stared back at him.

The nurse came back. "I paged him and he's on his way. Oh honey, I am so happy for you. This soon after the surgery." She turned to Ben. "It's wonderful news, isn't it?"

"It is wonderful," he answered.

The nurse continued to check Liv's extremities, marveling, making notes.

"It's been a long, hard road for our girl here, but what a miracle. Liv, by tomorrow, you may be walking. Short distances and with a walker, but walking."

The doctor came in before the nurse finished. He appeared as excited by Liv's ability to move her legs as the nurse had been.

"We'll take it slow. Don't get any ideas about getting up for a drink of water in the middle of the night. Tomorrow morning we'll see if we can get you on your feet. Do not, I repeat, do not try to do it tonight."

The doctor turned to Ben. "No one more stubborn than our girl here. Don't let her try to get out of bed."

He turned back to Liv. "As long as this young man agrees to keep his eye on you, we won't restrain you," he joked.

She smiled, but hadn't said anything since the nurse asked her if she had any sensation. Not a single word.

The doctor leaned down and kissed the top of Liv's head, then stood back. "I've become fond of many of my patients through the years Olivia, but I can tell you, few have come to mean as much to me as you do. If there was anyone, anyone at all, I would've wished this for, it's you."

The doctor said good night, and left. The nurse said she'd be back in a while to check on her again, but to ring if she needed anything. She asked Liv if she wanted something to eat, but she nodded she didn't.

"What will you do?" she asked him once they were alone again.

"Tell the truth."

"Well," she said, as if she expected him to leave.

He didn't think she was as fragile as he did when he first got here. Not after watching the doctor and nurse exam her.

"Scoot over," he said. He kicked off his shoes and lay down next to her, putting his arm around her waist. "You have a lot to tell me. Start at the beginning. Tell me about the accident."

It felt good to have him next to her, but nothing had changed, and she needed to make Ben see it as clearly as she did. If anything, she had more reasons to. "Ben, we can't do this."

"We can, and we're gonna. You kept me away for weeks. I'm not going anywhere tonight."

"I need to rest, and so do you. We can talk tomorrow. If..."

"Oh I'll still be here if that's what you're wondering. If you need to rest, go to sleep. I'll be right here when you wake."

She did need to sleep. Her eyes would not stay open another minute. She didn't have the strength to argue with him. She let herself drift off, snuggled into him.

There was a never-ending war of emotions taking place in Ben's head, and in his heart. He tried to decide what topped the list. On the flight from LA, anger had been number one, followed closely by hurt. Confusion, while not an emotion, was way up there. As of right now, love had risen to the top, but hurt still nipped at its heels.

Why had Liv done this? None of it made sense to him. Why would she let him go on believing she was in a coma? If it was because she thought he'd leave the tour, she would've been partially right. He would've come to see her. But knowing she was awake would've fueled his desire to make music. He would've rejoiced.

It was clear that up until tonight, Liv hadn't had feeling in her legs. Which meant she was paralyzed. And tried to protect him from it. It was like a bad remake of a movie that had been done ten times too many.

Ben wondered if he would ever get through to her. She mattered. Not what she did or achieved. Just her. She was enough.

That was the point, wasn't it? He'd never get through to her. In the last year, he'd begged her to let him be a part of her life, and she either told him or showed him she didn't want that. He'd been telling himself that she did. But what if he was wrong? Was it that simple? Liv meant more to him than he did to her. She told him so many times. Even ten minutes ago she said it again, "Ben, we can't do this."

He wanted to touch her, for a little while longer. Maybe his arms would memorize how it felt to have her wrapped in them. And his chest would remember how it felt to have her head resting softly on it. Maybe his heart would remember how to rejoice in the fact that she walked this earth, rather than mourn that he couldn't watch her as she did.

Hard as it was, he had to force himself to do it. He eased her head down on the pillow, got up, and walked out of her life.

Chapter Nineteen

The fallout with CB Rice's fans had been less than anyone initially expected. Since they had a full week of shows still booked, Ben did what he did best. He came out at the start of every show and told the truth.

He told people he never meant to deceive anyone, and until the story broke in the press, he believed Liv was still in a coma. He told them about her paralysis, and that Liv was so strong, so independent, so brave, that she wanted to protect him from it. He went on to say she'd had a successful surgery, and everyone believed she would be up, walking, and back to her old self in no time. Each night the crowd roared when he said it. He didn't tell them that he and Liv were no longer *together*. But then they never truly had been anyway.

***

For the first time in over three months, Liv would soon be home. She wasn't sure what to expect when she got there. Renie planned to restart the semester she'd taken off to be at her mother's bedside, in January. It proved too difficult for her to juggle her course load and commute from the hospital. In the meantime, she'd be home with her mom, helping with her continued recovery.

Liv hated not having her independence. While her recovery went faster than anyone anticipated, not being back on her routine made her wretched to be around. She'd be the first to admit it. Renie took it in stride.

When they pulled into the driveway, the first thing Liv noticed was the absence of Ben's Tahoe. Someone must have come and taken it home. As she had been doing for days, even weeks, Liv buried her feelings about Ben. She didn't want to talk to anyone about him, today or any other day.

"Would you like to ride today?"

"No, it's too soon," she murmured.

Liv wasn't sure she had the courage to walk into the barn. She needed to see Micah, but the thought terrified her. She missed her boy, but she worried about how he would react to her.

"I'll walk to the barn, that'll be enough for today."

She didn't see Micah when she walked in, but by the time she got to the stall, his nose peeked out. She stood and let him nuzzle her. His hind leg bent, and his breathing evened out, he almost purred.

Liv stood and loved him until one of her legs gave out. She grabbed the top of the stall's half-door. Renie ran over to her, with a stool for her to sit on.

She saw tears in Renie's eyes, and how hard she fought not to break down. Liv understood.

"Will you be okay for a few minutes Mom?"

"Sure honey, go ahead. I'll catch up with my boy."

Liv managed to hold her sobs in until she heard the back door of the house close.

"Oh Micah, what have I done?" She sobbed into her beloved horse's mane.

***

When she woke up in the hospital and Ben was gone, she thought maybe she dreamt everything from the night before.

She moved one of her legs to be sure that part wasn't a dream. It hadn't been.

The nurse came in with breakfast. She told her she'd be going to rehab in two hours. And then she was gone, leaving Liv alone. The ache of what that meant spread through her chest.

He didn't stay, even though he said he would. She had to face the fact that he wouldn't ever come back. She'd spent the last few months pushing him away. And now, he was gone for good.

Liv spent the next two weeks trying to get her legs to work properly, and doing her best to kick everyone close to her out of her life. Even Paige reached the point where she'd had enough.

"I'll be your friend until the end of time, and I love you, but I won't be your punching bag. You know where to find me when you want to," she said before she stormed out.

Mark still came to visit every day. He didn't talk much, he rarely even said hello. He arrived when she began rehab, and left when she finished. And in between, he helped.

Renie came in the afternoon, every day. They spent so many afternoons in silence, that Renie started bringing a book with her. She'd watch her mother, as she stared out the window, lost in thoughts she had no desire to discuss.

"Depression is normal," the doctor told Renie. "Her body has been through a significant series of traumas. She needs to heal. She'll come around. I've offered to prescribe something for it, but your mother refuses it."

Billy came as often as he could, with Renie. He was in the top five nationally for saddle broncs. He'd tell her about the barrel racing standings, and talk to her about the finals, which were the first couple weeks of December.

At first she thought it would bother her, but then she realized Billy talked to her as though she was on the injured list, not the retired list. He told her she'd be back.

"I'll help you. Anything you need. I'll be there for you Livvie. Soon as you're ready, we can get back out on the road together."

"I appreciate that Billy. We'll see, okay?"

***

Thanksgiving morning, eight days after she came home, Liv decided it was time to ride. Renie suggested her mom ride Pooh, but Liv was determined to ride Micah. Her leg muscles were stronger than they'd ever been. She'd never exercised before, she rode and worked. Now she had a strength-building regimen she followed every day.

The day dawned a perfect, blue-sky Colorado morning, and she wanted to ride. Renie followed on one of the boarded horses. Pooh wouldn't be able to keep up with Micah.

"Where do you want to ride today Mom?"

"I'm gonna let Micah run today sweetie."

"To the meadow?"

"Yep."

"You're sure?"

"Never more sure."

As soon as they came over the hill, the prairie stretched out in front of them, and Micah took off like a rocket. Liv hadn't felt this alive in months. There was no hesitation between her and her horse, it was as though they rode this way every day.

Billy saw Renie and Liv from the back steps of his parents' house. He loved to watch them ride. No one rode the way the Fairchild women did.

Liv and Renie were coming to the house later, to have Thanksgiving dinner with them. Something in his gut told him, one day they would be a real part of his family.

***

Ben walked out on the back porch with a cup of coffee in hand. In an hour, he'd go pick up the boys and bring them back for Thanksgiving dinner with his family.

He looked out at the valley and up at Mount Crested Butte. The sky was blue, the sun was shining, and he was spending the day with family. All should have been right with his world. Nothing could have been further from the truth.

He went to the Goat the night before, wanting a distraction. He found one. Pretty little thing, and sweet. Her name was Melinda, or Melissa…or Melanie. He couldn't remember, so he called her Mel. She was a firecracker, dancing up a storm. He had fun with her, the most fun he'd had in a long time.

"Let's get out of here," she said to him, pulling him by the hand. He grabbed his coat off the rack and followed her to the parking lot. They got around the corner, and she was on him so fast, Ben didn't see it coming.

He picked her up and held her against him. She wrapped her legs around his waist, and he pressed up against her.

"Wait," he said, unwrapping her body from his and setting her back on the ground.

"What?" she answered, breathless. "What's wrong?"

"As much as I want to get close to you tonight pretty girl, I can't do this." He was about to say it was him, not her, and he decided against it. Better to walk away. No explanation was necessary.

* * *

"Come here girl and give me a big ol' hug," said Dottie when Liv walked in the back door.

"Hey Dottie."

"God I missed seeing that color of pink in your cheeks. How're you feeling? Billy said he saw you out ridin' a bit ago. You and Renie. He said it was like watchin' a beautiful wind blow."

"I can't describe it. If felt right."

"You goin' back out then?"

"Soon as I can. Not much left this year."

"Nothing stoppin' you from training. Get yourself down to Oklahoma in January and get busy."

"Am I crazy Dottie? Do you think I should just give up?"

"I've told you before, there hasn't been a day since I've known you that I haven't been proud of you Liv. Don't make it today. You're no quitter, but what do the doctors say?"

"That I'm fit to ride, or do whatever else I want to do. My injury is healed, and that part of my spine is in better shape than the rest of me."

"Any pain?"

"Not much."

"What does that mean?"

"My pain has nothing to do with my injury Dottie."

"You wanna talk about it?"

"Not today."

Renie walked in with Billy behind her, carrying the rest of the pies. "Where are these supposed to go Miss Dottie?" Renie asked.

"Down to the bunkhouse. We've got a crew with us this year, we'll eat in the main dining hall down there."

"Hey Livvie, you comin'?" asked Billy.

Dottie watched her son escort Renie and Liv out of her kitchen. Liv was still in love with that guitar-playing man from Crested Butte, Dottie just knew it. It would be a matter of time before one or the other would give in to their stubbornness. They hadn't seen the last of Ben Rice around here.

Bill finished carving the last turkey when the door to the dining hall opened. Paige and Mark came in with their youngest daughter. Renie and Blythe hadn't seen each other in months. It had been weeks since Liv had seen Paige.

"I figured Thanksgiving was as good a day as any for us to make up," said Paige.

"There isn't any making up to do." Liv hugged her. "I'm sorry Paige, so sorry. I hope you can forgive me."

"I forgave you before I walked out that day. You needed space. I kept tabs though. If you needed me, Mark would have said so, and I would have come."

"Mark is such a good man."

"He's the best. No one else would've put up with you and me combined all these years. He seems to like us."

The dining hall soon filled with ranch hands and wranglers.

"Gotta love cowboys," said Renie.

"Yep, you do," said Billy. "How about you and Blythe sit with me today."

"You're not flirtin' with my daughter are you Billy Patterson?" Liv asked.

Paige turned around in time to catch Dottie's eye. Was this the first time Liv noticed it?

***

"Whatcha' doing Dad?" Luke asked him.

"Hey buddy. Nothin' much. What are you up to?"

"I been watchin' you."

"Oh yeah, and what have you seen?"

"You're sad."

He hugged his son to him.

"It's easy to see when someone is sad if you love 'em Daddy."

"How'd you get so smart pard'ner?"

"I don't know. But if you're sad, you should do somethin' about it." Luke looked at his feet. "That's what you'd tell me."

"What if I don't know what to do about it?"

"Oh come on Daddy, you know what to do."

"I do?"

"Sure. You gotta go see the girl."

His kids, they slayed him. He thought that a lot. They knew how to get right to his heart.

***

Thanksgiving dinner came to an end. Paige and Mark went home. Blythe and Renie went into town to meet up with friends home for the holiday. Liv sat out on the porch of the bunkhouse, looking at the stars, not ready to go home yet.

"Livvie, mind if I sit here with you for a minute?" Billy asked.

"Of course I don't mind." She scooted over, and he sat on the bench next to her.

"Did you have a nice Thanksgiving?" he asked.

"I did. How about you?"

"I did. I'm glad you and Renie were here with us this year. That's why I'm most thankful."

"You're such a good friend to me Billy, and to Renie too. What would we have done without you these last few weeks?"

***

Billy asked her and Renie to ride with him every day between Thanksgiving and the first week of December. He made them laugh so hard, and if anyone understood her desire to get back into barrel racing, he did.

"Livvie, I'm tellin' you, you ought to consider hookin' up with a bronc rider. You might like it."

If Billy Patterson wasn't so much younger, there might have been a day she would've considered it. It made her think of Ben, and how she thought he was younger too. But he wasn't.

Billy wanted her and Renie to go to Las Vegas with him. Dottie and Bill invited them to go too. Billy ranked second in the world going into National Rodeo Finals, or NFR, the highest he'd ever gotten.

Liv missed Jolene and Mary Beth, who would be there too. There wasn't a serious competitive cowgirl, or cowboy for that matter, worth her or his weight in salt who didn't try to attend the finals every year.

"I booked us rooms at Bellagio, hope that's okay."

As long as they weren't staying at Mandalay Bay, Liv didn't care where they stayed.

The NFR consisted of ten rounds on ten consecutive days. Cowboys and barrel racers earned money by placing first through sixth in any round, and picked up more money by placing first through eighth in the average (cumulative times or points earned during the ten rounds).

At the end, there would be two champions in each event. One was the average winner, who won the NFR by having the best cumulative time or score in his or her event over the ten rounds. The other was the *world* champion, the person who finished the year with the most money, including what he or she earned at the NFR. For each event, the average winner and world champion might be the same person.

Billy was riding better than he ever had, consistently placing first or second in every round. Before and after each ride, he'd find them in the crowd and wave.

He was on top of the world, he told them. There were few things sexier in life than a confident cowboy, and Billy was all that and more. She and Renie were the recipients of several dirty looks from girls in the stands whenever he raised his hat and smiled in their direction.

What would it have been like to fall in love with someone more like Billy? Someone who allowed her to be herself, who encouraged her to be all she could be.

With Ben, she lost herself completely. The same way she had with Scott. It terrified her, that all encompassing love. The kind where nothing else mattered but being with him.

Renie was nudging her. She almost missed seeing Billy ride, because she'd been lost in thought. Thank goodness her daughter had been paying attention.

Dottie watched Liv. She hadn't missed that far-off expression on Liv's face. If she were a betting woman, she'd take a bet that Liv was thinking about Ben. She wasn't over that man, not even close.

And Renie? Dottie hoped that Billy would start paying attention, and soon.

***

Ben sat in the Goat nursing a coke, a little out of it. There wasn't enough snow to ski, the boys were with Christine, and he was bored. Worn out from the tour and the emotional roller coaster with Liv, he didn't want to play, or write songs, or do much of anything.

When he looked at the big screen TV on the other side of the bar, the last thing he expected to see was Liv, but there she was, bigger than life, with Billy Patterson. The news ticker across the bottom of the screen read, "Billy Patterson, NFR's Saddle Bronc Champion." And based on the smile on Billy's face, it was Liv he planned to celebrate with.

Ben felt as though someone sucker punched him. Hard.

Chapter Twenty

It snowed Christmas morning, a beautiful white blanket covered the ground. Liv and Renie were joining the Pattersons later. Billy promised to take them out on a sleigh ride after Christmas dinner.

"Let's go skiing tomorrow Mom," said Renie after they opened presents.

"Oh, that sounds heavenly…" But where? Liv knew where Renie would say she wanted to go, but Liv would not consider setting foot in Crested Butte.

"Do you want to call and can get a reservation for tomorrow night? How many nights do you want to stay?"

"First we need to decide where we're going. Maybe Breck."

"Oh for God's sake Mom. We love to ski Crested Butte, more than anywhere else. You don't plan to ski there again, do you?" Renie sounded angry.

"It isn't a big deal to go somewhere else. It doesn't mean I'll never go back, it means I don't want to go back tomorrow."

"Never mind. I don't want to go anymore."

Liv hated hearing the disappointment in Renie's voice, but not enough to change her mind. If they did go to Crested Butte, she'd be so uncomfortable the entire time, she wouldn't enjoy herself at all.

She felt the same way she had before she and Paige went to Las Vegas. Going to Ben's hometown, at Christmas, was asking to bump into him. And was that fair? It was his home.

And Then You Fall

She hadn't heard a word from him since the night in the hospital. For a couple weeks, she continued to check Twitter and Facebook, but it didn't sound as though he wrote the posts himself. And the pain of seeing photos of him, became too much for her.

She saw photos of his boys that he posted right after Thanksgiving, an outing the three of them took together. They were beautiful boys. She wished she'd met them, but it was better she hadn't. They didn't know her, and she didn't know them. It would've complicated things if they had. Then she might miss them as much as she missed Ben.

Liv closed her eyes, and imagined how their Christmas morning would be. In her daydream, Ben's boys were with him, at his parents' house. Will and Matt, and their wives, would be there too. She wondered if they had any kids, she hadn't spent enough time with them to ask.

She saw him in her mind so clearly, as though she was with him. She didn't want to open her eyes and have him go away. He crept closer, so close she felt his breath, his arms, his kiss. The ache for him spread throughout her body.

The rest of the day, Liv's thoughts wandered to Ben, and each time, she closed her eyes and let them. The ache got worse, so much worse that she tried to shake it away. She needed to stop this, she needed an off-switch. If she kept it up, it would destroy her.

***

"Come in here and talk to me for a minute," Ginny said to Ben.

"Yeah Mama?" Ben smiled and gathered his mother into him for a hug. Thank goodness he had his family around him today. They distracted him enough that morning that he only thought about Liv two or three hundred times.

"I'm worried about you Ben. Is there anything you can do?"

"About?"

"Don't. You know what I mean. Let's not waste time playing games."

"It's over. There isn't anything to do about it. If you work that hard and it still doesn't come together, it's time to give up and move on in another direction."

"She's the one for you."

"Thanks Mom. It makes me so happy to hear you say that." Ben walked away from her.

"Do something about it Ben. *Do something.*"

"*What? What the hell am I supposed to do? Jesus—*"

"What's going on in here?" Bud asked, coming in through the kitchen archway. "You're raising your voice to your mother on Christmas Ben?"

"I'm sorry Mama," he pulled her into another hug. He never raised his voice to his mother.

"Sorry Dad."

"It's okay Bud. I started it," said his mother. "I'm pushing him to contact Liv, which means I'm pushing his buttons."

Bud shook his head and walked back out of the kitchen.

"We're both so worried about you," his mom continued.

"She's with somebody else."

"How do you know that?"

"I saw them together."

"Oh."

And even if she wasn't, Ben wasn't sure he had the balls to try again with her. She hurt him. Bad. He couldn't imagine opening himself up to her again.

She knew where to find him. If she wanted him, she could make the first move this time. Which, obviously, she hadn't. Again, he had his answer. He needed to keep reminding himself, she meant more to him than he did to her.

***

They drove to Patterson Ranch when it was time for them to go, since it was below zero. Liv doubted they'd take the sleigh ride with it that cold.

"Mom, wait," Renie said, before Liv turned off the truck.

"What honey?"

"I do want to go skiing tomorrow."

"Okay honey, I do too. We can make this happen."

"Do you think you can? Ski, I mean."

"We'll find out. I'll take the first couple of runs easy, but honestly, I'm stronger than I've ever been. I never worked out before the accident. I worked, but I didn't work out."

The doctors told her she could do anything she wanted. Her body would let her know when it was too much; she needed to listen when it did.

"I want to go to Crested Butte Mom."

"Oh Renie, not this again."

"We ski there every year. Every single year. We love it there, it's a second home to me. If I had a bad breakup with a guy who lived there, would you let me get away with what you're doing?"

"This is different."

"How so? You and Ben dated for a few months. Granted he was in love with you, but it didn't work out. If you start dating someone else and it doesn't work out, will you hide from them too?"

"I'm not hiding."

"Then what do you call it? 'Cause it sure looks like hiding to me."

"All right, we'll go. If, and it's a big if, I can get a hotel room booked for tomorrow night. They got as much snow last night as we did, if not more. They'll be packed tomorrow. All the ski areas will be."

"Already did it."

"Did what?"

"We're staying at the Grand for six nights."

"Six nights, are you crazy? What if I can't ski?"

"Then we'll cancel. But if you can ski, we can stay."

Liv thought about it for a minute. "No, Renie, I can't spend New Year's Eve in Crested Butte. It's too much."

"Then we'll come home. But if we want to stay, I want us to be able to. We don't have to ski all six days, we can take day trips and do other things."

Liv supposed if they ate in the hotel every night rather than going downtown, they'd have less of a chance of running into Ben. Who knew if he was even home?

She'd check Twitter and see if he'd posted anything. But she'd do it later. They were late as it was.

"We're leaving in the morning," Liv heard Renie say to Dottie later that night, after dinner. She and Billy were sitting in the family room, in front of a roaring fire.

"Who's leaving in the morning?" Billy asked.

"We are. We're going skiing. Billy, do you ski? Why don't I know that about you?"

"Not my thing."

"Have you ever tried it?"

"Can't say as I have."

"Why don't you come up with us? You can give it a try, and if you don't like it, there are plenty of other things to do there."

"Where are you headed?"

"Crested Butte."

Billy tensed up. "That's where Ben lives."

"Yes, he is from there, but Renie and I have been skiing there for years. It's our favorite place to ski. I won't avoid it because an old boyfriend happens to live there."

It sounded more like Renie talking, than herself. But if she kept repeating it, maybe she'd convince herself it would be okay.

Liv got up and went into the kitchen. Dottie followed her. "I'll be back in a minute."

"Hey sweet girl, whatcha need?"

"Nothing. I needed to stretch my legs."

"Renie told me you're headed to Crested Butte."

"I don't know Dottie. It's wrong. It's his home."

"You gotta take the chance. The same way you have to get back on Micah and race again. You gotta live sweetheart."

***

He saw Renie before Liv. He was next in line for the lift and was focused on Jake and Luke, making sure they had their boards lined up and were paying attention. He looked up and there she was, flying down the hill. She looked behind her, who was she looking for? Was Liv with her?

And there she was, the woman who held his heart. Liv was skiing, what a beautiful sight. She was laughing, talking to her daughter, skiing toward the racks. They must be taking a break.

"Daddy!" Luke yelled. Ben hadn't been paying attention, and they hadn't moved forward to get the next chair.

"Oh sorry."

They moved up and took the lift. He'd look for her when they got back down the mountain. He hoped he'd be able to find her. If not, he'd camp out by the ski racks until they came back. Even if it wasn't until tomorrow morning. They'd have to get their skis sometime.

She was here. In Crested Butte. That had to mean something. She had to know there was a chance she'd run into him. He wondered when she had gotten here. Surely they would've spent Christmas at home.

And where was Cowboy Patterson? Was he here with them? Just because he'd only seen Renie and Liv didn't mean he wasn't a minute or two behind them.

**

"So, how did it feel?" Renie asked Liv after they'd gotten their hot chocolate.

"Amazing. I love to ski. I was so wrapped up in not being able to ride again it didn't occur to me that I might not be able to ski. I'm so thankful I can."

"You look happy."

"I'm having such a good time with you Renie. Thank you for doing this, getting me to go."

And Then You Fall

"My pleasure, I'm glad you agreed. We are going to have a great week."

"We are that."

"I'm gonna hit the ladies room. You ready to get back out there yet?"

"You bet. I'll meet you down by the skis."

Liv paid the bill, refastened her boots, and put on her helmet and gloves. She walked toward the door, looking down to make sure she didn't trip on anything with her clunky ski boots, and bumped into someone.

"I'm sorry, I didn't..." Liv tilted her head up and looked at the man she bumped into. Ben Rice.

"Oh my God," she gasped and started to fall backwards. Ben caught her and righted her on her boots. "I'm so sorry."

She tried to flee, but he still had his hand on her arm.

"Slow down for a minute. Take it easy."

Liv stared up at him. Here he was. She longed for this and dreaded it at the same time. Now what?

"Liv," he said softly, "there's a couple of people I want you to meet."

His boys, she'd recognize them anywhere. They were such beautiful boys, like their father.

"Olivia Fairchild, I'd like you to meet Jacob and Lucas Rice." Liv extended her hand and both boys shook it. They were polite too, again, just like their dad.

"It's very nice to meet you both," said Liv.

"You too, ma'am," they said in unison.

"Ready Mom?" Renie said adjusting her helmet and goggles. "*Oh!* Hi Ben."

"Hi Renie, it's nice to see you," Ben answered. "These are my boys, Jake and Luke. Boys this is Liv's daughter, Renie.

Renie took her helmet back off and tossed her head around to fix her hair. "Helmet head," she said, and both boys laughed. "Bet you're in here for hot cocoa. Am I right?"

They nodded. Ben realized at that moment what a beautiful girl Liv's daughter was. His boys would likely follow her to the ends of the earth, the same way he'd follow her mother there.

Renie motioned for them to follow her.

"Wait," said Ben, trying to hand Renie money.

"Don't worry, I got it."

He watched them walk away, and took a deep breath before he turned toward Liv.

"Hi," he said.

"Hi."

"I'm always bumpin' into you."

"I never watch where I'm going."

Ben touched the side of her face. "It's so good to see you." Someone else bumped into Liv, and he realized they were standing in the doorway.

"Come with me," he said. "Let's get out of the way."

"I shouldn't—"

"Please Liv, come with me," he said again, in that stern voice he used that made her melt a little.

She took her helmet and gloves off and followed him. He motioned for her to take a seat on the sofa next to the fireplace. Liv sat down near the end, and Ben sat next to her.

"Good to see you're back out on the slopes."

"It's great to be back. It's wonderful to ski again. I just told Renie, I hadn't thought about whether I'd be able to ski. Not until Christmas morning, when she suggested we go."

"Did you have a nice Christmas?"

Jesus, she thought, were they making small talk? "Yes, how about you?"

"Not the best, but Christmas is always fun with the boys."

"So they were with you then?"

"After about mid-morning. They're used to waking up with their mom then coming to my place a couple hours later."

What would they talk about next? Oh God, she couldn't do this. It was so awkward between them.

"How long are you in town?"

"Quite a while. Renie reserved a room for us through the first."

Ben reached out and touched her face again. Her eyes closed and she leaned her cheek into his fingers. She hadn't meant to do it, her body reacted to him instinctively.

"Is there anyone else with you?"

"What? Um, no. We're alone. Why?"

"I wondered if you brought a new boyfriend along with you."

"Nope, no new boyfriend. What about you?" Oh no, what made her ask him that? If he had someone in his life, she absolutely did not want to know.

"Nope, no new boyfriends for me either."

"Very funny."

"Ask."

"No."

"Why not?"

"I don't want to know."

"Why not?"

"Ben, stop it," she moved her face farther away from his fingers.

Ben reached out, cupped her neck with his hand and pulled her closer to him. "There's nobody. *Nobody.* Only you." His eyes were dark, dangerous, angry when his lips covered hers. His kiss was just as angry, just as dangerous.

Her cry was stifled by his mouth on hers.

He licked her lips with his tongue, bit her bottom lip, and crushed his mouth back into hers for more. There was nothing like kissing her. Nothing.

Whoever else was sitting near them, the rest of the people in the restaurant, all disappeared. He couldn't hear anything other than her soft, sweet murmurs.

Liv pulled back from him. "Your boys," she said.

His boys. He'd forgotten about his boys. Not that he minded them seeing him with Liv, but she was right, he was out of his head with wanting her. That wouldn't be good for his boys to experience today.

Ben stared into her eyes. Nothing was any different. The hurt, longing, anger, pain—none of it mattered. He loved every single thing about this woman, the good, the bad, all of it.

Renie returned with Ben's boys in tow. "They're ready to go back out. Do you want me to take them? I'm on skis, they're on boards, but they should be able to keep up." Renie turned and smiled at the boys who were about to protest her dig.

"I can head out too," Liv said. "Ben, how about you? You ready to get back out on the hill?"

No, he wasn't. He wasn't ready to do anything but get Liv alone and out of her clothes.

The five of them spent the afternoon together. Liv and Renie skied, Ben and the boys snowboarded. When they announced the lifts would be closing in fifteen minutes, Renie offered to take Jake and Luke up one more time if Ben and Liv wanted to relax for a few minutes.

"That was the best afternoon I've had in a very long time," Ben said. "I'm sure my boys would agree."

"Me too." Liv didn't remember the last time she was this relaxed…and happy. She took off her helmet and gloves and started to unfasten her boots.

"Here, let me help you with that," Ben offered. He knelt down and ran his hand up the inside of her leg.

"Uh, my boots are in the other direction mister," Liv teased.

Ben leaned forward, his mouth next to her ear. "I cannot wait to be alone with you Liv. Am I wrong about this? Please tell me you want this as much as I do."

"I do Ben, but we should talk first." Who was she? He was the one who wanted to talk about everything, not her.

"Wow, you want to talk. I can't tell you how much that turns me on baby." He nipped at her neck playfully.

"I know. Who am I?"

"Will you and Renie have dinner with us tonight?"

"I'll have to ask her, but I'm sure we'd love to."

"She's good with my boys. They love her. You'll be a distant second I'm afraid. They're already smitten."

"I will not begrudge my daughter your boys' affection. I'm generous that way."

There were so many ways she was generous. She had no idea. He hadn't been exaggerating, today was one of the best he'd had in as long as he remembered. The last time he remembered being this happy was day they drove back from Woodward, Oklahoma, before her accident.

This was something new for them, Liv would be spending time with his boys. He had no idea what to expect. She interacted with them on the hill, but they were so taken with Renie and getting her attention, they didn't pay much attention to their father's girlfriend.

Renie came in with the boys.

"No, I want pizza," he heard Luke say. Luke always wanted pizza, that didn't surprise him.

"I'm sick of pizza," said Jake, trying to look more mature. "We should go to Uncle Matt's restaurant."

"What's there?" asked Renie.

"Sushi."

"Oh, a man after my heart. I love sushi."

Ben watched as her response took his son completely over the top. Renie Fairchild may very well be Jake Rice's first love. This would make family get-togethers interesting.

He shook his head. Family, with Liv. It was what he wanted, and he intended to get it. He wanted forever with her, it was what he'd always wanted. This time he wouldn't let go of it.

"Sushi then?" Ben asked Liv.

"It's good by me."

"Luke, you like sushi. Plus Uncle Matt will make you anything you want."

"Pizza? Will he make me pizza? 'Cause that's what I want Dad."

Ben ruffled Luke's hair. This was what happiness felt like. He loved it.

When they walked into LoBar, Matt stood near the end of the bar. When he spotted Liv, Ben thought his brother might have strained his neck, his head spun around so quickly. Matt walked toward them.

"Well hello. This is? Remind me your name again."

Ben almost choked. As if Matt didn't remember her name, what a crock.

"Liv…Olivia. And this is my daughter. Renie, this is Matt, Ben's brother."

Renie stepped up to shake his hand. "Pleasure," she said.

"A table tonight Ben? Something away from the noise of the sushi bar?"

"That sounds great," answered Ben, not bothering to look in Matt's direction. His eyes were focused on Liv's smile, and he intended to keep them there.

Matt led them to a table near the back, hidden away from the rest of the place. "You'll get fewer interruptions back here," he said as he placed menus in front of Liv and Renie.

"Daddy said you'd make me pizza," said Luke.

"You want pizza, you'll get pizza…how about squid pizza, or octopus, or tuna pizza, how's that sound?" Luke started giggling and fell sideways, right into Liv. She reached around and hugged him closer to him, laughing with him.

Suddenly Luke realized where he was. And there it was, Ben knew that look, Luke had fallen in love with Liv too.

Luke monopolized the conversation with Liv for the rest of the night. It was okay with Ben, he enjoyed sitting back and listening to the two of them. Luke was a huge rodeo fan, and Liv told him about going to the finals only a few weeks ago. She talked about the cowboys and the bull fighters and the barrel racers.

"Do you really race around barrels?" Luke asked her.

"I do, but I'll tell you a little secret, if you promise not to let anyone else know, unless they're a real rodeo insider."

Luke nodded his head in agreement.

"We call it chasing the cans," Liv whispered in his ear.

"O-o-h...cool," said Luke, as though he'd learned the secret of the universe.

Ben reached his arm around her and pulled her back closer to him. He leaned down so his mouth was close to her ear. "I love you so much Olivia Fairchild."

She turned to him, and smiled before she brushed her lips across his. A shudder of pleasure ran through his body.

Chapter Twenty-One

After dinner, they walked down Elk Avenue. The boys wanted frozen yogurt and Renie made fun of them for wanting something cold when they were already freezing.

"She's very playful," Liv commented to Ben as they walked behind them. "It's too bad she never had any brothers or sisters."

"I'm sure Renie would say her childhood was perfect."

"I doubt that," laughed Liv. "No father in her life, no siblings. There are definitely times I regret my choices and what they meant for her."

"Your daughter is one of the most gracious, seemingly well-adjusted people I've ever had the pleasure to meet. You did a great job as her mother Liv."

"Thank you. I appreciate you saying so."

"You have no idea. It takes me a while to remember."

"What do you mean?"

"You have no idea how great you are."

"I'm a sure thing cowboy, you don't have to pile on the charm."

Ben thought he might lose it right there on the sidewalk in the middle of his hometown. Had he heard her right? Yesterday he would've predicted he'd never see her again. Now it felt as though no time had passed since they were together happily. The hard times forgotten, for now, for tonight. Unless that was why she wanted to talk. He almost dreaded it. He didn't want to talk about anything, he wanted to hold her close. Skin on skin.

"Will you stay at the house tonight?" he asked.

"I don't think you want to stay in the hotel room with Renie and me, do you?"

"Uh, no," he laughed.

"Well then, I guess I better stay at your house." She said it softly, demurely, seductively. Very, very soon Ben would have a difficult time walking.

"How about a horror movie marathon?" he heard Renie say to the boys.

"Yeah," said Jake.

"Nooo," said Luke. "Liv, I don't want to watch horror movies. Can we watch somethin' else?"

Oh no, Luke wasn't horning in on his time with Liv tonight. No way. There'd be plenty of time later for movie marathons with his boys. Tonight she was all his.

"Well," said Renie, "tonight we should watch what Luke wants to watch, and tomorrow night it'll be Jake's turn to pick. Does that sound fair?"

"Boys, a gentleman would let the lady choose."

"Um, okay. Renie, you can pick, but please don't pick horror," said Luke.

"I want to watch *Caddyshack*," she said.

"*Caddyshack?* What's that?" asked both his boys.

"You haven't seen *Caddyshack?* You're kidding. It's the funniest movie ever. Don't tell me you haven't seen *Airplane* either.

"Oh this will be a very fun week. Renie's ride through the funniest movies ever made, before you both were born. We'll have a blast."

Both boys were excited. "Are you gonna stay at my dad's house?" asked Jake.

Liv nodded yes.

"Yay!" said Luke, jumping up and down.

"Do you remember how to get there?" asked Ben.

"I can probably find it," answered Liv. "Are you sure about this?"

"Never more sure of anything," he answered. "Tell you what, we'll follow you to your hotel. You can check out, we'll help load your stuff into your car and then you can follow us to the ranch."

"Wait. Check out? I'm not sure about that."

"Liv, please," he whispered. "Come and stay with me. Please. There's plenty of room."

"I have to talk to Renie about it first, make sure she's okay with it." Although, she hadn't seen any sign of protest from her daughter about staying there tonight.

"It's okay with me Mom, if it's what you want to do."

"Please," Ben said again. "We are not letting go of this, not ever again. I'm not, and you're not."

***

It was dark, so Renie wouldn't be able to appreciate the ranch for what it was until tomorrow. The boys fought over who got to carry the bags inside, and once they did, they had no idea where to put them.

"Where are you sleeping?" Jake asked Renie.

"I don't know, let's ask your dad. This is a very nice house, by the way."

"My mom used to live here too, but now she lives in a different house, and she has a different husband," added Luke.

He was a wealth of uncomfortable information, thought Ben. "Okay pard'ner, let's get Renie settled in the guest room downstairs, and we'll let Liv stay in the one upstairs."

"Liv isn't gonna sleep in your room Daddy?"

Luke again. Where did his kid get this stuff? "We'll see about that later. Now how about that movie? If you don't start watching it in…thirty seconds, you won't be able to watch it tonight because it'll end later than your bedtime. Follow me Renie, I'll show you where you can set up your movie marathon."

Liv stood in the family room, looking out the windows she never thought she'd be looking out again. She was here, with Ben. And Renie was with her. They'd spent the day and evening with his boys. If anyone had told her last week that this would be happening she would've bet a million dollars they were wrong. Yet here she was.

"Come on," Ben said, taking her hand. "They're settled in, and Renie promised she'd make sure she'd find whatever they needed on her own."

They went upstairs to his bedroom, and Ben closed the door behind her. And then somehow, suddenly, she was in his arms. She pressed herself into him, so she felt his heart beating and heard his ragged breathing. The warmth of his body seeped through the clothes she longed to rip off him.

"You're shaking," he whispered. "It's okay Liv, this is where you're meant to be. Kiss me Liv, give it all to me, every bit of you."

Her eyes drooped, and her breathing became labored, she was so close to turning herself over to him in that way he loved.

"Ben, we have to talk."

"No Liv, we don't. Not now. Now I want you naked, under me. Then later, over me. And then all around me. I love you so damn much I can't think about anything else."

"But—"

"Liv, I'll get down on my hands and knees and beg if I have to. Please, take off your clothes. Please, I can't stand it another second."

"Okay," she said, as if the battle was lost and she had no fight left in her. "But you first."

Ben's clothes were off as fast as he could tear them away from his body, and he was helping Liv get rid of hers.

"Baby, need you, God, I need you so much."

"Ben..." There it was, the way she said his name, as if he hadn't been on fire already. "Ben, stop."

Something in the way she said it resonated with him, and he stopped.

"Tell me," he said, his breathing lumbered.

"I'm not on birth control anymore."

"Liv, I—" What? What could he say? That he didn't care? They would be spending the rest of their lives together, and if she had his baby it would make him the happiest man on earth? She'd run out of the house naked to get away from him if he said any of that.

"Don't worry sweet girl," he said instead, kissing down her neck. "I'll take care of you, you know that." His mouth worked its way lower, across her breasts, down to her stomach. He put his arms around her and pulled her close, laying his cheek against her, imagining how it would be to know she carried his child inside her.

He stood and lifted her on to the bed. "I need you baby, all of you." He rolled onto his back, so she was on top of him. "Be still, this way, your skin on mine.

"Look at me." He put his hands on each side of her face, and sang to her.

Having had your joy, having had your desire, and then, baby, you fall.

"I dreamt of this," she said. "Fantasized about it would be a better way to put it."

"Oh yeah? When?"

"Only all the time."

"Tell me."

"Better to show you." Liv opened the drawer on the nightstand. Ben held up his hand and showed her he already had what she was looking for.

"Put it on for me," he said.

Liv's cheeks turned pink, but she took the small package from his hand.

"We could go without, if you wanted to," he ventured.

"Ben—I don't..."

Why had he opened his mouth? Now wasn't the time to have this conversation. "I'm sorry. Forget I said that. Keep doin' what you were doin' baby. Don't stop."

She rolled it on, then straddled him until he was buried deep inside her. She leaned back, but her hands drifted to hold on to his chest. Ben held her still, then started to move beneath her. He leaned up, moving her closer, to get more of her against him as he drove himself into her. Her hands dug into the skin on his back as his moved down hers, to cup her bottom and bring them closer.

"Liv, can't wait. Waited so long for this. Oh baby, God, I love you."

His mouth moved over her lips, his teeth scraped hers and he bit her swollen bottom lip.

He rolled her beneath him, the way he saw her in his fantasies, writhing under him. "Here," he said, "right here Liv." He drove into her, relentlessly, pushing her, pushing himself, until they both came together.

Liv put her face against his sweaty neck and licked up to beneath his ear. She breathed in deeply, as though she wanted to say something. Ben stilled, waiting. But nothing. Her lips kissed from his ear to his jaw until her mouth found his. She kissed him hard, putting her arms around his shoulders to hold herself closer.

"Tell me," he said, easing her back down on to the pillow.

"Ben."

"Don't just say my name. Tell me. You know what I want to hear. Please, tell me."

She closed her eyes and turned her head on the pillow, away from him. Here he went again, pushing her too hard. What was wrong with him? She was back in his arms, they were joined, two as one, but he still pushed her.

"Liv, open your eyes." He waited until she did. "I'm sorry, I won't push. I need you so much baby, but I'll only take what you'll give. I won't keep asking for more."

She nodded and reached up again to put her lips on his. "Ben...will you catch me if I fall?"

"You know I will baby. I'll catch you."

He eased off of her, and went into the other room to get rid of the condom. He looked in the mirror and shook his head. Why was he so impatient with her? What was it he had to know right now? That she loved him? She did, but something stopped her from saying the words.

Ben got back in bed and pulled her closer to him, so her back was to his front.

"What did you want to talk about?"

"We should wait until tomorrow."

God, she was killing him. He wanted everything, her body, her love, and now her thoughts. This woman made him crazy with desire to get inside her in every way possible. He could never be close enough to her and yet, the harder he tried to hold her close, the more she inched away.

"Okay, I'll talk." He felt her body tense. "I was so afraid I'd lost you forever. I never would've allowed myself to think about you being here, as you are right now."

"I know."

"The universe is telling us something. We keep coming back to each other. Maybe we should try harder to stay together."

"It won't be easy to do Ben."

"Why not?"

"I want to race again. Give it all I've got. It will take hard work and training. And travel."

"We can do this, as long as we're both committed."

"And what about you? You'll obviously continue to tour."

"I will? Have you been on Facebook darlin'? You watchin' my tour schedule?"

"I'm a stalker, remember?"

"We need to get you setup with your own fan page, so I can watch you. See you in those tight jeans and cowgirl shirts. The way your body bends and moves when you're racin'. Jesus that gets me hot." What had it been? Five minutes? And he wanted her again. He planned to wear her out tonight. She might not have enough strength left to ski tomorrow.

Oh, now there was a good idea. Renie and the boys could go, while he and Liv stayed here at the house. They were all kinds of places he imagined her naked, beneath him.

"What are you thinking about back there cowboy?"

"You. Naked. All over my house." She shuddered. Evidently she liked that idea as much as he did.

***

Luke woke them the next morning. He climbed up on the bed and situated himself between his dad and Liv.

"What's up there pard'ner?" Ben groaned, his voice still thick with sleep.

"What're we doin' today Daddy?"

"What do you want to do?"

"Let's go snowmobiling around the ranch."

That wasn't a bad idea. They had several, he wondered if Renie would be interested in doing that. He could show her and Liv all the best places on their land, the best views.

"How's that sound Liv?"

"Good to me. I don't know about you little guy, but I'm starving. What do you say we get up and make a giant ranch breakfast?"

"You know how to make a ranch breakfast?"

"I do. I live on a ranch myself. Guess you didn't know that."

"You do?" Luke's voice caught. "Does Renie's daddy take care of it for you?"

"No, Renie's dad died many years ago. He was a pilot in the Air Force."

"Oh." Luke's voice shook a little. "Does that make you and Renie sad?"

"It used to, but we know he keeps us safe."

"So who takes care of your ranch for you?"

"I do. And we have hands. Do you have ranch hands that help your daddy and your grandparents?"

"We do," he answered and then proceeded to tell her about the more colorful hands that worked their ranch.

Ben slipped out of bed to let the two of them talk. He threw on sweats and a T-shirt, and went to the kitchen to start the coffee. Renie stood by the window.

"It's breathtaking," she said, hearing him behind her.

"It isn't bad."

"How do you ever leave it?"

"I could say the same thing about your spread."

"It's my mom's spread, but you're right, it's awesome too." Renie walked to where he was in the kitchen.

"Somethin' on your mind young lady?"

"Hoping you two figure it out this time," she sighed.

"Me too," he said, laughing and pulling her closer to hug her.

"I like you Ben, and you're good for her."

"What about the Patterson guy? What happened there?"

"Billy?" Renie blushed, then laughed. "They're friends, that's all they've ever been."

"Are you sure?"

"Um, yeah," she laughed. "I'm positive."
He wondered what Renie's reaction meant.

"I want bacon," Luke said, pulling Liv behind him by the hand. It occurred to him that he abandoned her under the blankets without any clothes, but here she was, wearing a big shirt of his and her long underwear from yesterday.

Ben raised his eyebrows as she walked into his arms for a hug.

"It wasn't easy. Thank goodness little boys have to go potty."

Ben threw his head back and laughed. "I wondered."

Liv started rummaging around Ben's cabinets.
"Whatcha' lookin' for baby?"
"Finding my way around your kitchen."
"Make yourself at home," he winked. There was nothing he'd like more.

They spent the day exploring the ranch. Ben took them by his parents' place mid-afternoon.

"Well, well, am I happy to see you." Bud came off the porch and swept Liv into a big hug. "I prayed for you little lady."

Liv buried her face into his shoulder to hide her tears. A few simple words, coupled with his unmasked joy, made her cry.

Ginny came out of the door and gasped when she saw Liv, standing next to Ben, his arm around her shoulder.

"Aren't you a sight for these old eyes? Come here girl and let me look at you."

Liv was touched by the warmth and love these two people, who barely knew her, expressed so openly. The same way Ben did. She envied the way they loved without hesitation. For the second time in a few minutes, Liv was moved to tears when Ginny put her arms around her.

"When did you get here?" Ginny asked.

"We got into town the day after Christmas."

Ginny raised her eyebrows at Ben, who laughed. He pulled Liv back closer to him. His body craved hers. Riding on the snowmobile, with her arms around his waist, her body pressed against his back, was heaven to him. Whenever she moved away, he wanted her back, closer, so his hands were on her, somewhere, anywhere.

He leaned down and whispered. "My mama gave me a little lecture on Christmas. Somethin' about getting off my butt and going after you. I bet she's givin' herself credit for you being here today."

"Ah," was Liv's only response. She turned back to Ginny and saw the happiness etched on her face.

How easy it would be to fall into this family. They would embrace her and her daughter without hesitation or question. And life would be good. But would it be enough?

She still had to find out whether she could live her dream or not. It wasn't something she was willing to give up, no matter how comfortable and inviting it was here.

"Let's have a big dinner here tonight. We'll get your brothers and their wives to come."

"I'd like to help," Liv offered.

"Me too," added Renie.

"Why don't we take the snowmobiles back to the house boys?" Ben turned to Liv again, pulling her close. "I can't keep my hands off you. And you in the kitchen…that'll make me hot for you again."

Liv laughed. "There isn't much of anything that doesn't make you hot for me."

"You in another man's arms didn't do it. I can tell you that." There he went, opening his mouth again. He needed to work on filtering.

"What are you talking about?"

"The rodeo finals, I was watchin' them and there you were, with Patterson. Bigger than life on the screen in front of me."

"We were there, but it wasn't that way Ben. I wasn't with him."

"Not somethin' I can let myself think about Liv. I'm sorry I brought it up."

Other people, they needed to talk about other people. Had Ben been with another woman while he was on tour, or since he'd been home? He asked about her. He wanted to know what she was thinking, yet he didn't offer the same information about himself.

"I can't let myself think about you with anyone else either."

"Nobody Liv. I told you that. There isn't anybody else for me. I would have become…what did you call it? A redo-virgin if you hadn't come back to me."

Liv laughed. "Me too."

"What about you and Patterson."

"No, it wasn't ever that way."

Ben exhaled, loudly. "Thank you for telling me. God, the thought of you in someone else's bed. Ugh. I can't think about it."

"Come on Daddy," Luke tugged on his coat sleeve. "Let's go ride again."

Ben looked at Jake, who hadn't said more than two words this morning. He was so wrapped up in Liv he hadn't noticed. "Sure thing buddy, in a minute. Why don't you see if your grandma has any cookies you can snack on?" Ben pushed Luke in the direction of the house. "And don't forget to wash your hands. Oh, and bring me some."

Ben motioned with his head in Jake's direction. Liv nodded that she understood.

"Come on Renie, let's go help Ben's mom."

Ben sat down on the porch steps waiting to see what Jake would do now that they were alone. He turned and faced the mountains, his back to Ben.

"What's on your mind Jake?"

"Nothin'."

"You've been awful quiet. Not that you're talkative to begin with, but this seems quieter than normal."

"It's nothin' Dad. I'm fine."

"Okay. Well if you decide it's somethin', let me know."

"It's..."

"Yeah, I'm listening."

"It seems as though you really like her."

"I do."

Jake kicked at the snow with his boot.

"What's worrying you man?"

Still nothing out of Jake. He waited for a while, but all Jake looked was uncomfortable.

"Okay, well let's get your brother, take the sleds back to the house and get the truck. We can talk later if you want to."

Jake got on one of the snowmobiles and started it up, without answering his dad.

Bud came out on the porch. "I'll ride one back with you. That way if you want to go out again this week, they'll be up at your place."

"Thanks Dad. Hey, somethin's bothering Jake. Any idea what it might be?"

"Nope. But I'll try to get him to talk to me about it later."

"Where's Luke?"

"He's stayin' here. You won't be able to get him away from those two pretty girls. Not sure which one he's more taken with, Liv or her daughter. Although Liv is winning out."

"She's easy to get taken with." Ben knew that first hand. "She okay? I mean, should I go in and see if she needs anything before we leave?"

Bud put his hand on Ben's shoulder. "She's fine, you can be out of touching range for another five minutes or so, don't ya think?"

"No. But I'll leave her be anyway. Her and mom getting along?"

"As though they've known each other for years. You know, she reminds me of your mama. She's got that way about her."

Chapter Twenty-Two

Ben went into the kitchen in search of Liv only to find her seated at the center island, deep in conversation with Allison and Maeve. Whatever they were talking seemed serious. He wondered if he should try to back out of the room before they noticed him.

"Heya Ben," said Maeve, stretching her hand in his direction.

"Am I interrupting?"

"No, Liv was telling us about the fall she took. Serious stuff. I cannot believe she's skiing and riding the ranch on the back of a snowmobile, four months later. Isn't it unbelievable?" Allison, Matt's wife, asked.

"Unbelievable," answered Ben. He still felt it, the pain, the worry, the hurt. He tried to push the hurt down deeper. She was here now, he didn't want to think it. He closed his eyes, and tried to shake the ghosts away. When he opened them again, Liv studied him. She'd been right yesterday. They did need to talk.

"Everything is cleaned up in here. Liv, you ready to head back to the house?"

"Sure." She hesitated before she stood up, then stretched a little.

"Are you going skiing again tomorrow?" asked Maeve.

"Liv, is that what you want to do?" Why was he so uncomfortable? There was more going on in this kitchen than was on the surface.

"We should. That's why we're here."

And why did that hurt? It was the truth. She and Renie came up to ski. And he bumped into her. She didn't come to see him, he already knew that.

"Ready?" Liv asked.

He realized he had been lost in thought. What the hell was going on with him? He was having trouble breathing.

"Yep, let's go. Night ladies."

Ben carried Luke to the car, he'd passed out sitting next to Renie on the couch. Jake sat on the other side of the room, sullen.

Bud and Ginny lingered on the porch saying good night. Ben came back up after he got Luke in the truck.

"Any luck with Jake?"

"Nope," answered Bud. "He was closed up tight. Not interested in talking about anything, not even baseball."

It seemed that Jake wasn't the only one suddenly in a funk. Ben was too. The euphoria was wearing thin. They were coming down from the heady rush of being together again, and the reality of their recent past was raising its ugly head. But it didn't explain what was going on with Jake.

"We should see if we can get our room back," Liv murmured when Ben got in the truck.

"What? No. Why? Why would you say that?"

"Something has changed."

"No, everything's good. We're all tired."

"You're sure?"

"Positive. We aren't gonna get anywhere being apart, we have to work through this Liv. We have to learn to be together even when it's not all pretty."

"So something did shift."

"It isn't anything that's a secret. You said it yourself, we need to talk."

"Yes," she sighed. "We do."

Jake was sitting in the way back. Ben turned up the radio a little and motioned for Liv to lean closer to him.

"Something is going on with Jake. He gets more withdrawn with each passing minute."

Liv had noticed. Luke had become her shadow, but Jake kept his distance. Even Renie was unable to jostle him out of his funk. She had no business trying, or even offering, but she was willing to see if he'd talk to her. She asked Ben if he'd mind.

"I don't think you'll get anywhere, but I'm not going stop you from trying."

Ben carried Luke in and put him in bed. Liv told Renie she wanted a minute with Jake, so she went downstairs too. Jake was ready to follow when Liv stopped him. "Got a minute?"

She watched his internal struggle. If it had been anyone else asking, he would have shrugged them off and continued up the stairs. But he'd been raised to be polite. He didn't know Liv well enough to refuse her request, so he turned around and walked back down the steps.

"Yeah?"

"Can you come sit down with me a minute?"

"I guess."

Liv walked to the chair next to the fireplace and motioned for Jake to sit across from her.

"I can tell you have a lot on your mind," she said softly.

"I guess."

"Does it have something to do with my being here? Would you rather I wasn't?" She kept her voice low and soft, hoping he was less threatened by her.

"No!" Jake was immediately embarrassed by his response.

"It sounds as though you might be more worried about my leaving."

Jake looked away from her and into the fire.

"Jake, I care about your dad." He flinched.

His eyes met hers. "He told us about you."

She nodded, hoping he'd continue if she didn't speak.

"He wanted us to meet you. It was after he visited you. While we were in Arizona with our mom and Joe."

Liv leaned forward, to hear him better. He turned back toward the fireplace, so she bent her head. "Keep talking."

"Luke and I were excited to meet you, 'cause my dad told us you meant a lot to him."

This must've been when she was here, and then turned around and left. "I'm sorry I didn't get a chance to meet you that visit."

"My dad…he was so sad. He tried to cover it up, but he didn't fool us. He didn't want to talk that much, and my dad loves to talk." That got a little smile out of him. Liv smiled too.

"He does. Sometimes too much."

That made Jake laugh.

"Go on," she said, softly again.

"Then you had your accident, and my dad was on tour. And then all that stuff happened when he thought you were in a coma, but you weren't."

"You're looking out for him."

"He was so sad." Tears well up in his eyes. Jake tried to turn his head away from her, so she wouldn't see.

"Your dad tried to hide it from you, didn't he?"

"Yeah, but I knew anyway."

"Your dad tried to hide his sadness from you to protect you from it. He was hurting, and he didn't want you to hurt too."

"Is that why you lied to him?"

Ouch. Now that he was talking, he got right to it, didn't he? "Yes Jake, that is why I lied to him. I didn't want him to worry about me. I wanted him to enjoy the tour, and be successful, and have all the things he's been working so hard to attain all these years."

"But it didn't work."

"You're right, it didn't. What I did jeopardized it all. He hadn't lied to anyone, but people thought he did."

"My dad did his talking thing though, and people didn't stay mad at him. I don't think they did anyway."

"Your father is a very good man, and as soon as people get to know him, even a little, they see it. Even if it's only seeing him on stage. They know he wouldn't lie."

Jake nodded.

"You're afraid I'll hurt him again."

He nodded again. "You kinda do it a lot."

Ow, another one. He sure got right to the heart of it. "I'm sorry for that, and I'm sorry for how it's affected you. I care about your dad very much."

Jake turned toward her, to see if she was lying.

"I don't want to ever hurt him again."

"That would be good, if you didn't."

Liv marveled at the depth of caring Ben's son possessed. He was so much like his father.

"Do you ride Jake?"

"Horses? Yeah."

"I was hoping you and I could ride while I'm here. And someday soon, I'd like it if your dad brought you and Luke to my place. I board horses at my ranch. Did you know that?"

"No. I didn't."

"Think you might like to take a ride with me."

"Yeah, it'd be okay."

"And come and visit?"

"Sure. I'd like that."

"How about coming to see me race? Would you like to do that too?"

Jake sat up straighter. A smile started to form.

"That'd be cool I guess."

"Cool you guess? Sugar there ain't nothin' cooler than a barrel-racin' cowgirl. The sooner you figure that out the better."

There it was, he smiled. He had his dad's smile, it lit up his whole face.

"Okay. It's cool."

"You got that right. And Jake?" She tilted her head again, hoping he would look her in the eye. "Thanks for talking to me."

"Sure. Anytime."

She said good night, and he went upstairs. Liv leaned her head back against the chair and closed her eyes.

Ben stood around the corner from Liv and Jake and heard the whole conversation. She might as well have been talking to him. All of Jake's concerns were his too. When would she decide she needed to leave again? And when she did, would he have any idea when he might see her next? And, how much a part of her life did she want him to be?

She'd answered all those questions while she talked to Jake. She made plans with his son. Plans for them to come and see her ranch, and plans for them to come and see her race. Those were significant plans. Coming to see her ranch meant she was willing to let his boys in, to get to know her better. He knew Liv well enough to know that she wouldn't take his sons' feelings lightly. She wouldn't lie to them, and she wouldn't let them think they mattered if they didn't.

Ben was happy. Happier than he'd been in a long time. If he'd had the same conversation with her, he wouldn't have let her talk as much. And before she extended an invitation to come and visit, he would've pushed for one. He also would've pushed to come and see her race. It was amazing how much more she was willing to give when she was afforded the time to come up with the offer on her own.

Ben came around the corner. Liv was sitting in the chair. He wondered if she was asleep. "Hey," he said softly.

"Hmm? Hi. Come sit with me." Liv stood and moved to the couch, holding out her hand for him to join her.

"How'd it go?"

"It went well. He cares about you. He wants to make sure I do too."

"And?"

"You know I do."

"I overheard your conversation with him."

"I know."

That made him smile.

Liv leaned into him, rested her head on his shoulder and put her arm around his waist. "You're too used to being in control of everything to have let that go."

"You think that was about control?"

"Of course it was. I was talking to your son. The one you're worried about. If things had started to go badly, you would've stepped in to make sure he was okay."

"I guess I would've."

"We have a lot to work on, you and I."

"If you're willing, so am I."

Liv stood and held her hand out to him. "Come on, take me to bed cowboy."

***

The next day they went back to the ski area. A long-time snowboarder, Jake wanted to ski instead, so Ben rented him ski equipment.

"He's got the best snowboarding stuff made, and today he wants to ski. What's that all about?"

Liv raised her eyebrows at him. "You should consider this a good thing. At least he's talking."

She was right. If Jake wanted to be closer to Liv, or Renie, all day it was better to have him want to be a part of things than off sulking in a corner, or refusing to go along with them.

Renie decided at the last minute to try snowboarding. Ben's groan was audible.

"Great. Now he'll want to go back to slidin' down the hill. I know the guys in the rental place, I'm sure they'll give me my money back."

But Ben was wrong, Jake wanted to spend the day with Liv. The two of them went on several runs on their own and showed up twenty minutes late for their designated lunch hook-up.

Ben put his arm around his oldest son, "Tryin' to steal my girl, are ya?" He messed up his son's already mop-top hair.

"She enjoys my company," answered Jake, standing up taller and throwing his shoulders back.

Liv and Jake went out on their own all afternoon too, and Liv got to know Ben's oldest son.

"We're making dinner tonight," they announced when the group met back at the lodge at the end of the day.

"Who is?" asked Ben.

"Jake and I are."

"What are you making?"

"You'll see."

"Are you makin' pizza?" asked Luke.

Jake started to answer his little brother and Liv stopped him by putting her finger in front of her lips. "Shh," she said.

Ben knew that if heaven existed, today was a slice of it.

"Stop at the market on the way back to the house, Jake and I will run in and get what we need."

"But—"

"Ben, please, let us do this. Let go a little, it's only dinner."

God she knew how to call him out on his control issues. He'd always have those issues, he knew control meant sobriety, that part he couldn't let go.

To let go with other people, that took trust. And with Liv, that part was even harder. He had visible tread-marks lingering on his heart when it came to her. If he was honest about it, every morning when they woke up, he wondered if that day was the day she'd leave him again. He wasn't sure how he'd be able to move on from it.

***

Jake and Liv made a Spanish dinner for everyone, complete with paella. Liv also made an individual pizza for Luke. The kitchen was spotless because Liv insisted she and Jake clean as they go, which was the exact opposite of Ben's approach. Throughout dinner, Jake extolled the virtues of Liv's style of food preparation at the expense of his father's.

All Ben could think was how he much he wanted this to be their lives, all the time. He wanted to spend every day with Liv, and Renie too, for at matter, and his boys. If this was his world, he would give up everything else in order to have it.

But it wasn't the reality of any of their worlds. The boys would soon go back to their mom's, at least for a few days. In January, Ben would be halfway across the world on tour. Renie would be back at school, finishing up her last semester before she moved onto her graduate program. And Liv would be out doing the thing that almost killed her only a couple of months ago.

Control? *Shit.* He had none over that. All he wanted to do was wrap her up and take her with him. But that would be exactly what he'd be doing, taking her with him. She'd be a thing, not a person, and that was her greatest fear, losing herself for him, or anyone else. Somehow he needed to figure out how to respect that about her, but not go insane with worry at the same time.

"Fret, fret, fret," she whispered in his ear.

"You caught me."

"Why the scowl?"

He didn't realize he'd been scowling, but he supposed it was indicative of his train of thought. "I don't want this to end."

"None of us do. But that's what makes it so special. Otherwise, diminishing returns, and nobody likes that."

"What?"

"The more you have something, the less joy it brings you."

"Oh no, I don't agree with that at all. I would be very happy to have your skin on mine all day every day, for the rest of our lives. And I would never, I repeat *never*, experience less joy from it. My joy will only continue to grow.

"On the subject of skin on skin, what do you want to do for New Year's Eve?"

"I bet I know what you want to do."

Ben's eyes roamed over the scene in front of him. "It may be what I want to do, but whether I get to or not, that's another story."

"Blythe is flying in to Gunnison tomorrow. Oh, I meant to talk to you about that. I'm glad you reminded me. Blythe is Paige and Mark's daughter, she and Renie have been best friends since kindergarten. Anyway, she's flying in to ski and hang out for a couple of days. Since we don't have the room at the Grand any longer—"

"Yes."

"But you don't know what I'm asking yet."

"I don't? You aren't asking me if she can stay here?"

"No, as a matter of fact I wasn't. I was going to ask you if you had any connections in town to help me get a room somewhere. I've called everyone, but they're all full."

"Okay. Again, she can stay here. There's room."

"I don't want to impose Ben."

He wasn't sure why, but that made him angry. Something twisted inside of him. "Liv, for God's sake. What are you, a guest here? Is that how you see yourself?"

She got up and headed toward the stairs.

"What are you doing now? Leaving?"

She turned back. Her eyes met his, and he watched them fill with tears. She kept her hand on the stair rail as she slowly turned and sat down on one of the steps.

Ben ran his hand over his head and walked back and forth in the kitchen, then hit the counter with his hand. "Shit, I'm sorry. I don't know why I said that."

He sat down next to her.

"You said it because we're pretending. We're pretending that we know each other. We're pretending that this is fun, and perfect, and everything we want it to be, but the truth is, we're all walking on eggshells. Even Luke."

She was right. The first thing Luke did every morning was come and crawl in bed with them. It wasn't like him. It was as though he was checking to make sure Liv was still there.

"The only person who has expressed and dealt with it, is Jake. And I'm including myself in this Ben. I haven't done it either."

Ben so wanted things to be okay between them, better than okay, he wanted them to be happy, and have fun. Every so often the hurt would make its way to the surface, and he forced it back down.

Ben put his head in his hands. "You hurt me Liv."

"I know I did."

"Did I hurt you?"

"No, you didn't. You only scared me. You still scare me."

"I scare you. As in you're afraid of me?"

"I'm afraid of this more than I'm afraid of you. I don't know how to do this. It's so much easier for me to tell myself that I don't need anyone else, that I can rely on only myself. I know it's not true, but it's what I'm used to."

"You rely on Paige, and you rely on Mark. And Dottie and Bill." He didn't say Billy, he hoped she didn't rely on him. "And Renie."

"With the exception of my daughter, I keep very strict boundaries with everyone you mentioned, even Paige. Do you know the last time I talked to her?"

"No."

"Neither do I. It was sometime before Christmas. But see, that's the thing. It doesn't matter. We'll talk when we want to, but we don't have to."

"Are you suggesting that's how you want it to be with us?"

"No. I'm not. And once Renie goes back to school, I won't necessarily know when I'll see her or talk to her again either. What I know is that when I need to, or she needs to, we will.

"So you see Ben, it's the way I am. You need more."

"No, please tell me we're not going back to that again."

"But it's true. You need more from me than I know how to give."

"So we're back at the place we always get to. I love you. I want you in my life. But according to you, I need you too much. Before you say it, I know you're right. I do need you, all the time. I want you all the time too." Ben tilted her chin. "Is that so bad?"

"Did you hear what I said? Ben, listen to me. *You need more than I know how to give.* It's not that I can't, or don't want to, I don't know how to."

"What does that mean?"

"It means that I'm trying to learn."

Chapter Twenty-Three

Bud and Ginny offered to have the boys spend New Year's Eve with them; Renie and Blythe planned a night out and finagled a room at the Grand for the night. Ben and Liv were alone.

After their talk, things weren't as strained, but they were still tiptoeing around each other. He felt her anxiety building as their time together came closer to an end. Or maybe it was his own anxiety. It was impossible to tell the difference.

He'd be leaving January 10 for Europe, and they'd be on tour there for six weeks. New US tour dates were being announced in the next couple of weeks, so even after he got back, he would still be on the road for who knew how long.

Liv was going back to Oklahoma to train with Jolene, and hoped she'd be ready to compete by March. All he knew was that she wanted to get back on that horse and race.

"We have the night, and the house to ourselves Liv. What should we do about it?" He winked and elbowed her.

"I'm thinkin' we should talk," she winked back.

Ben pouted a little. "Okay, I told you before how much it turns me on when you say that, so go ahead, you've been teasin' me about it all week. I wanna see this…Liv Fairchild is gonna talk."

"I can't talk until you stop cowboy."

Ben made a motion that he was zipping his lips and held his hands out for her to continue.

"I have a plan."

This he had to hear.

Liv told him that she was going to go to Oklahoma to start training again, but she wasn't leaving until he left on tour. If he wanted her to, she'd even stay here with him until then. She admitted she worried about Renie driving home alone, but Blythe could ride with her, and then Liv could catch a flight out of Gunnison when Ben left.

"You're flying out of Denver, right?"

He nodded.

"I'll fly to Denver with you, that way I'll be with you as long as possible before you leave for Europe."

Liv kept her body next to his the whole time she talked. She could feel him start to speak, he'd inhale, his muscles would tense up, but then he'd stop himself and not interrupt. They were both getting out of their comfort zones. She was as proud of him as she figured he was of her.

She went on, "while you're on tour, I'll be training. I've already said that part. But, here's the thing, if I don't believe it's working, I'll quit."

There he went again, tensing up, Liv put her fingers on his lips to stop him from saying anything.

"I'll know Ben. I have to try. But if something isn't right, I'll know. If it is right, and I believe Micah and I can compete, I'll do that too. I'll know by the time you get back in March."

She stopped talking and turned to him, indicating he could speak now.

"Now? I can talk now?"

"Mmm hmm."

He let out a huge sigh. "Wow. That was hard."

"I bet. Imagine how hard it was for me? I actually had to make plans from now until March," she laughed. Ben laughed too.

"What about going to Monument, and leaving from there?"

"Wouldn't that create a hardship for you?"

If he did, he wouldn't see his boys again before he left. That wasn't such a good idea. "The boys."

"That's what I was thinking."

Liv had been here a week, but she was offering to stay another ten days. She was trying. And she was thinking about him.

"You're sure—"

"Shh." Liv put her fingers on his lips again. "Let yourself go with it. Do you mind if I start the laundry? If I'm staying, I need to wash a few clothes."

"No, not at all, go ahead." Ben answered, as though he was in a *Twilight Zone* episode and couldn't figure out who the alien was who had descended into his kitchen.

When she left the room, he sat forward on the sofa a little, put his elbows on his knees and his head in his hands. It seemed as though the new year would be all about crazy-ass-shit happening when he least expected it.

Liv came back in and sat down next to him. She tucked her legs under her and leaned into him. "Ben?"

"Yeah?" He kept his elbows on his knees.

"I've never done this. I barely remember the few months I lived with Scott, it all went by so fast. I was a kid, a nineteen-year-old kid. Renie is two years older than I was when Scott was killed. Work with me, okay?"

He leaned back, put his arm around her and pulled her closer to him. "I'm sure I'm guilty of the same thing. I was either on the road, drunk, or overwhelmed the whole time I was married to Christine. I didn't know what I was doing then any more than I do now."

He kissed her forehead. "So what do you want to do now?"

"Let's go to your parents' house and spend time with them and the boys."

"Really?"

"Mmm hmm, as long as we're back here by eleven or so. I have a few ideas about what I want to be doing at midnight cowboy."

**

"These have been the best two weeks of my life."

"Mine too."

"Is Paige picking you up?"

"Her or Mark, I should head out and see if they're here."

"Not yet."

Ben got a text from Jimmy letting him know he needed to get through customs or he would miss their flight.

"I gotta go baby. I'm gonna miss you so much." Ben pulled Liv in close. He was getting tired of saying goodbye to her.

"Liv," he put his hands on either side of her face. "Thank you for coming back to me, thank you for giving us a chance. I love you so much."

Liv reached up and pulled him closer, her lips brushed across his and she kissed her way across his cheek, to the spot below his ear. "I love you too Ben. So much," she whispered.

He leaned his head back, the same way he did when he laughed, or when he played guitar, but this time he only closed his eyes and pulled her closer to him.

***

"He did it to you," said Paige on the ride home.

"He came to visit. This is different."

Paige shrugged her shoulders. "Not that different. By the time you get back from Oklahoma and put everything in motion, he'll be on his way home. Just do it Liv."

"Okay. I'll talk to Billy tomorrow."

***

"You can do this," said Jolene, in a comforting tone Liv hadn't realized the woman possessed.

Liv and Micah had been working hard for three weeks—riding hard, riding fast, but the one thing Liv couldn't bring herself to do was take him around the barrels.

"Start slow. Ride around the barrel, don't try to hug it. Ride around it."

In took three more days before Liv completed the entire cloverleaf pattern, and even then it was barely at a trot.

A few days later, Liv was starting to pick up speed. She knew Micah was itching to do it right, but each time she pulled him back.

"Let him go this time, all out," Jolene yelled from the fence.

"How's she doin'?" asked Mary Beth, standing near her.

Jolene showed her Liv's last time. Thirty-four seconds.

"This ain't a race timer, but it's close enough. She's ready, but she's sure not gonna be happy with these times."

"Does she know you're timin' her yet?"

"Nope."

"Keep at her."

"Yep."

"You should get mean."

"What're you talkin' about?"

"She likes it when you're mean, you remind her of her father."

"I am *never* mean."

"Jolene, I love you dearly, but you are *always* mean. You're coddling her. Stop it. Push her, make her do it. You've eased her in enough. I've been watchin' Micah. He's fine, he's ready, he's waitin' for her."

"I don't know."

"Do it Jolene. She'll be okay. Stop protecting her."

"That's it for today," Jolene shouted to Liv, who waved and rode Micah in the direction of the barn.

Jolene walked away in the opposite direction, but Mary Beth knew she'd been listening. She couldn't wait to see what was going to happen tomorrow.

She made a couple of calls on her cell phone on her way home that night. "Yep, you might wanna try to get down here tomorrow morning," she told each person she called.

"We're running the timer today," Jolene said when Liv walked into the barn.

"Good morning to you too, and what?"

"You heard me. I've had enough sittin' around watchin' you stroll around the barrels. We're either gonna start runnin' times or you might as well go back to Monument."

"But—"

"Those are the only two options I'm willin' to put out there Olivia. Which is it gonna be?"

Liv turned and stomped out of the barn. Uh oh, that hadn't been the option Jolene thought she'd pick. Now what would she do? Was Liv leaving? She'd have to think about this.

A few minutes later Liv stomped back into the barn. "Are we gonna do this or not?"

"Sure, um, you wanna get Micah saddled up?"

"Yep." She stomped to Micah's stall and led him out.

"Liv, can I ask you a question?"

"Sure."

"Where'd you go?"

"To change my shirt." If she and Micah were doing this today she wanted Ben wrapped around her, so she went and put on one of the shirts he left on the door handle of her closet. But there wasn't any way in hell she would tell Jolene that.

Over and over and over Jolene made her do it. Her first times were in the high twenties.

"Again. Focus. Get the lead out girl."

Fourth time out, she came in at twenty seconds.

"What're you doin' out there? Is that Micah or Pooh you're ridin'?"

Mary Beth was sitting on the fence at the opposite end of the arena and wasn't certain, but she swore Liv flipped Jolene off.

She turned around and waved at Renie, Paige and Mark, who were sitting in a truck taping the whole thing. Mark gave her a thumbs up. Yep, he'd seen it too, and got it. Liv had been so focused all day, Mary Beth didn't think she'd even noticed the truck sitting there, let alone the people in it.

The next day when she came in just above seventeen seconds, Liv jumped off Micah, threw her arms around Jolene, and kissed her. Mary Beth hoped Mark had a zoom lens strong enough to pick up the tears on Jolene's cheeks.

Mark uploaded the video, and hit send on the email.

"Ready?" Renie said, and the three of them got out of the truck.

Liv heard yelling and turned to see her daughter and her two best friends jumping up and down, waving their hands and running toward her.

"What the—"

"Mary Beth," said Jolene. "They've been here since yesterday." Jolene doubted Liv even heard her, she was halfway to them already.

"Did you see me?" Liv kept repeating.

"We did," answered Paige. "Mark even recorded it."

"How was it Mom?"

"So amazing…even better than skiing," she laughed.

***

Ben had been sitting by the computer waiting for the email. The last couple weeks, he'd only gotten what Jolene sent him, which were bits and pieces of Liv's day. She was getting better, but it wasn't until he saw Mark's video from the day before, that he thought she would be able to do it.

He hit the play button and watched her fly around the barrels, as if she'd been born to do it. Mark panned over to the timer Renie held in her hand. Seventeen-three. Ben was alone in his hotel room, but he jumped up and down and danced around anyway. One more week, he'd be home, and they'd celebrate together.

***

Ben was in the stands in the second week of December, when Olivia Rice came in fourth place in Barrel Racing at the National Rodeo Finals. He knew next year his wife would win, he felt it in his bones.

The CB Rice concert, taking place later that night at the Mandalay Bay complex, was sold out, as every other show on their tour had been.

They met backstage right before he went on, "I can't wait to get you home baby."

"We're not getting out of bed until Christmas," Liv answered.

"The only thing is…"

"What? What could there possibly be Ben?"

"I miss your old kitchen."

"Then we'll remodel ours."

"I doubt Billy Patterson appreciates what he got when he bought your place. Do you think he even knows how to cook?"

"Doubt it, but I'm sure he'll find a pretty little cowgirl to do it for him."

About This Book

The Author

My books are filled with things that bring me joy: music, wine, skiing, families, artists and cowboys. Not always in that order.

I'm an author, speaker, editor, teacher, blogger, and in my spare time—became certified as an executive sommelier.

I bring years of experience in the publishing world to all I do. I've edited and designed more than two hundred books, including fiction, non-fiction, children's books, coffee table, and cookbooks. And then one day, I decided to write my own.

I'm an east coast girl, who spent half her life on the west coast. But now my husband, our two boys, and I happily call Colorado home.

Also available in the Crested Butte Cowboy Series: book two, *And Then You Dance*, book three, *And Then You Kiss*, and book four, *And Then You Fly*. Coming soon, book five, *And Then You Dare*.

You can find me here:
Website: http://www.heatherabuchman.com
Twitter: http://twitter.com/heatherabuchman
Facebook:http://www.facebook.com/Heather-A-Buchman

The Music

The character of Ben Rice and the band, CB Rice, are fictional—figments of my imagination. However, certain songs and lyrics used in this book are not. GB Leighton has graciously given permission for their use. For more information, or to download the songs featured in this book, please visit gbleighton.com.

More from author Heather A. Buchman

CRESTED BUTTE COWBOY SERIES
And Then You Dance
And Then You Kiss
And Then You Fly

COMING SOON
And Then You Dare

EAST AURORA LINGER SERIES
Linger - Book One
Linger - Book Two: Leave